DEATH AT DOVECOTE HATCH

DEATH AT
DOVECOTE HATCH

Dorothy Cannell

This first world edition published 2015
in Great Britain and the USA by
SEVERN HOUSE PUBLISHERS LTD of
19 Cedar Road, Sutton, Surrey, England, SM2 5DA.
Trade paperback edition first published 2015
in Great Britain and the USA by
SEVERN HOUSE PUBLISHERS LTD.

British Library Cataloguing in Publication Data

Cannell, Dorothy author.
  Death at Dovecote Hatch. – (A Florence Norris mystery)
  1. Murder–Investigation–Fiction. 2. Family secrets–
  Fiction. 3. Great Britain–History–George V, 1910-1936–
  Fiction. 4. Detective and mystery stories.
  I. Title II. Series
  813.5'4-dc23

ISBN-13: 978-0-7278-8480-0 (cased)
ISBN-13: 978-1-84751-592-6 (trade paper)
ISBN-13: 978-1-78010-642-7 (e-book)

All Severn House titles are printed on acid-free paper.

Severn House Publishers support the Forest Stewardship Council™ [FSC™],
the leading international forest certification organisation. All our titles that
are printed on FSC certified paper carry the FSC logo.

Typeset by Palimpsest Book Production Ltd.,
Falkirk, Stirlingshire, Scotland.
Printed and bound in Great Britain by
TJ International, Padstow, Cornwall.

ONE

Tradition was the linchpin of Dovecote Hatch. A nineteenth-century vicar of St Peter's, the parish church, had once soliloquized from the pulpit that tradition was the present reaching out to hold hands with the worthy past. For most of the residents it wasn't that uplifting, merely a matter of liking things the way they'd always been. Life at its best for the well-to-do and those living far more humbly was as comfortingly habitual as a pair of slippers molded to the feet.

This is not to say there was resistance in Dovecote Hatch to change as part of the natural order – births, marriages, deaths and all that mingles in between are the lifeblood of any close-knit community – but any marked alteration of the centuries' old way of life was unwelcome. The advent of the motor car, let alone shortened skirts for women, had not gone down well initially. It was therefore understandable that in May of 1932 the murder at Mullings, ancestral home of the Stodmarsh family, had shaken the village to its core.

For weeks afterwards, Dovecote Hatch had been besieged by newspaper hounds in full cry; besides which, the story had been trumpeted all over the wireless to the point that residents hesitated to turn it on. 'Murder!' The word curdled on the tongue. A most unpleasant experience for the Stodmarshes. Sympathy poured out to young Lord Stodmarsh, who was very fondly regarded, but that did not alter the general sense of ill-usage at the unwelcome notoriety. That was what rankled most – being thrust infamously upon the national scene. The strong-minded faced it by reminding themselves and others that the village had weathered unpleasantness in the past.

There had been Eliza Spellbinder in sixteen hundred and something who'd been hanged on Cold Wind Common for being a witch. Her undoing lay in providing a mother of eight with a potion that should have prevented number nine putting in an appearance, instead of which the woman had given birth to triplets. 'Had to be witchcraft,' the father had asserted wrathfully at the trial. He'd never been one of them pestering husbands. Once a night, not thrice, had always been good enough for him.

And what of Highwayman Harry, who'd turned out, when his mask was stripped away, to be the weak-chinned curate, shot dead when attempting to hold up the stage coach on the road to Small Middlington? Both Eliza and Harry still had descendants living in Dovecote Hatch, and none of them ashamed to acknowledge these blots on their heritage. Ah, but time is an artist; it can repaint the bygone and put it in a gilded frame. The present cannot so easily fool the eye or lull the ear into misconstruing a dirge for a lullaby.

Dovecote Hatch, therefore, gained little comfort from trying to convince itself that the murder at Mullings fitted in with a thrilling tradition of dark events and so would before long make for delightful discussions over the bridge table or down at the allotments. As old Mrs Weedy of Laurel Cottage remembered it, the nineteenth-century vicar's hope when lauding tradition had been to persuade the financially well-disposed to follow the example of their antecedents by giving generously to the church roof repair fund. She'd been only a girly in his day, but was quite sure he would never have evoked the memory of Eliza Spellbinder except as a dire warning to ungodly women. In regard to the curate turned highwayman, it was Mrs Weedy's view that he would not have been mentioned at all, only thought of as an instructive reminder to the vicar when feeling overworked that it was as well St Peter's could no longer afford to provide him with an assistant.

Even when national interest in the murder at Mullings died down, a majority of otherwise sensible people in Dovecote Hatch continued to declare volubly that life would never be the same. Inevitably, however, in the months that followed, the strong hand of the known and familiar reasserted its benign hold. A factor in this rebounding was pride in the knowledge that Florence Norris, the housekeeper at Mullings, had been largely responsible for discovering the identity of the killer, while the police inspector brought in from outside had barked up the wrong tree.

Florence Norris might not be a native, but close as made no difference to those ready to stretch a point in special circumstances. Not only had she come to Mullings as a kitchen maid at the tender age of fourteen, she was the widow of Robert Norris, whose family had worked Farn Deane, the Stodmarshes' home farm, for time out of mind. Versions of her role in the case had leaked out from several sources, the correct one being confirmed by the postman Alf Thatcher, whose word was not to be doubted. He was never one to embroider the truth; besides which, he and his wife Doris were close friends and therefore in the confidence of George Bird, proprietor of the Dog and Whistle pub, whose godson had been wrongfully suspected until the truth was revealed. If this had not been sufficient cause for George to rejoice, there had been another – that he and Florence had come to realize they had each loved the other for the past several years and now felt free to anticipate a future together.

The only person whose nose was put out of joint by Florence Norris's invaluable contribution in bringing the killer to justice was Constable Len Trout's wife, Elsie, and she had the sense to keep this resentment to herself, not even hinting at it to her husband. The constable was a buttoned-up sort in or out of uniform. His remonstrance would have been the one he voiced on duty when sighting someone littering or committing some other infraction. 'Now, now! None of that! This is England, not foreign parts!' Mrs Trout had nothing against Florence in the general way, a nice woman who'd bought two jars of her blackcurrant jam at that year's summer fête and told her later she'd never tasted any close to as good. But naturally enough, Mrs Trout would have preferred her husband to be the one heaped with gratitude for solving the case.

She was, therefore, the rare exception in thinking she wouldn't mind too terribly if lightning did strike twice in the same place and another person got bumped off in Dovecote Hatch. Not anybody tragically young or the sort that'd be sadly missed, she decided virtuously. The good thing about the Mullings' murder was that the victim had deserved to come to a sticky end. What if next time the body of, say, a blackmailer, a swindler or some other nasty piece, got found on Cold Wind Common or in Widgecombe Marsh? She imagined her Len knowing right off, when the higher-ups didn't, that it was toadstool poisoning, not the knife sticking out of the back, which had done the job!

Such were Mrs Trout's ruminations as she went about her daily round in apron and hairnet. She was a pleasant-faced, comfortably built woman. There was nothing to be ashamed of in thinking what might be, she reasoned. Wasn't like wishes was horses, was it? 'Course, she knew that willing anyone dead wouldn't be right coming from a regular churchgoer, though some might think it earned a wink and a nod from above in Dovecote Hatch. Miss Milligan, who bred boxer dogs and was very much a local personality, had been heard to say the Almighty himself could've been excused for inventing a headache on a Sunday morning to avoid sitting through one of Reverend Pimcrisp's interminable sermons.

Life was filled with random misfortunes. That's what Mrs Trout told herself later that year when the sneaking hope stirred in her wifely bosom that there might have been a second case of foul play in Dovecote Hatch. This resulted from the death of Mr Tenneson of Bogmire, a sizeable Victorian house as grim-looking as it sounded. He was a nice enough gentleman, no doubt, but from all accounts a bit of a nonentity, unlikely to be wept over long and hard by any save his nearest and dearest.

As for those, thought Mrs Trout as she hovered in the background during the graveside service, neither of his two spinster sisters looked close to heartbroken. They were both his senior in age, but with him being over fifty it couldn't be lamented that he'd been snatched up in his youth. Still, there was no need for the short one to look like she was taking forty winks on her feet, or for the taller to be chatting her head off to Mr Sprague, the church organist. Horribly embarrassed, he'd looked. The only one that'd sniveled some was the housekeeper, who'd found Mr Tenneson dead from a fractured skull at the bottom of the staircase at Bogmire. Perhaps she was fretting about being given her walking papers now the master was gone. Maybe the sisters wouldn't want to be the ones coughing up her earnings now. The Misses Tenneson (according to old Mrs Weedy) were so tight-fisted it was a wonder they could get their gloves on. As for the deceased's ward, a girl of seventeen, she actually smiled right through the bit about ashes to ashes, dust to dust. Could have been nerves, though Mrs Trout hadn't thought so. It was a dreamy, pleased sort of smile.

Not that, she was forced to admit, the behavior of anyone present could reasonably be considered significant. The inquest which had preceded the funeral had brought in a verdict of accidental death. Only stubbornness allowed her to prolong the fantasy of Willful Murder by Person or Persons unknown. A few days before the fatal incident, Kenneth Tenneson had mentioned to the doctor that he was having dizzy turns. In summing up, the coroner stated it would appear that on the evening of 30 October Mr Tenneson had experienced such an episode whilst on his stairs and, as a result, taken a hard tumble down them. Possibly his health had been affected by his mother's death several months previously. By all accounts, he had been a devoted son. 'Very sad! Very sad, indeed!'

Mrs Trout agreed. Still, it was a pity.

TWO

On a cold Monday in late November, under a sky seemingly uncertain whether to cheer up or start weeping, only three people stood on the platform at Large Middlington, awaiting the arrival of the one thirty-seven train to London. A man and woman exchanged smiles and nods as they conversed. A small tan suitcase was set down to their left. Further down the platform to their right stood a solitary female figure. Had either of the other two looked her way they'd have thought she'd positioned herself closer to the rails than they would have found comfortable. And neither were of nervous dispositions or unsteady on their feet.

The woman talking with the man was tall, although her companion towered above her. She looked to be in her forties and wore a dark green coat. A grosgrain band of the same green circled the brown velour hat that concealed most of her hair except for the coil at the back of her neck. It was the third year for both hat and coat, but that didn't announce itself. These, along with the rest of her outer apparel – gloves, handbag and sensibly heeled court shoes – had held up well, as clothes bought to last tend to do. An observer might have taken her for a school teacher or the local bank manager's wife, or even an unpretentious member of the upper crust. Nothing, including her voice, indicated she had started her working life as a kitchen maid.

'I think I'll take Hattie to lunch at Selfridges or D.H. Evans,' she was saying to her companion, 'and perhaps the pictures one evening.'

'There's no shortage of ways to enjoy yourselves, the two of you getting on so famously,' replied the man, sounding comfortably working class. 'It'll be a holiday if all you do is talk your heads off over cups of tea.'

'A lot of shared past and present to be stirred in with the milk and sugar.' The woman had a very pleasant smile.

The look that met hers were deeply fond. 'It's heartwarming to have that sort of relationship with a cousin. There's lots of people has no family feeling, even to the point of wishing they'd been born orphans.'

'And justified too in some cases.'

The man nodded. 'It didn't take me long after moving out this way to learn you can't live in a village without getting wind of what goes on indoors as well as out. Can't avoid it, even if you go out of your way to avoid gossip – or, as I once heard it called, verbal littering. Take for instance that Mr Tenneson as just passed away. Dropped as a babe into a nest of vultures from the sound of it. The stork sometimes has a lot to answer for.'

His companion eyed him thoughtfully. 'According to old Mrs Weedy, who knows all and then some, it was peck, peck, jab, jab, day in, day out at Mr Tenneson by those he shared the nest with for his entire fifty-some years.'

'A nest has some coziness, but that awful tomb of a house . . .' The man shook his head and appeared about to say more, but didn't.

'Hattie's two-up two-down would fit into Bogmire twenty times over. To more agreeable thoughts!' Another of those pleasant smiles. 'She's indeed a treasure. So good and kind.'

The man nodded, his eyes tender. 'And none could be a better judge of those qualities than you, dear. Be sure to give Hattie my best.' He was several years the older, in his early to mid-fifties, and wore a dark blue mackintosh along with a flat cap. 'I'm more'n glad you decided on giving yourself this treat of a week away after the year this has been.'

'There were dark days for you too.' She placed a hand on his arm.

'You won't hear me complain, love, seeing as they brought us together and none we're fond of is left suffering.'

'Yes, so much for which to be grateful.'

Their smiles had the effect of combining them in an embrace. Entirely focused on each other, they remained oblivious of the woman further down the platform towards the end where the train would pull in. Had they looked they'd have seen a shabbily dressed figure with a scarf tied over her head, stepping even closer to the rails.

The couple went on talking. What had sounded a possibility (there had been several snarls of thunder) became the unmistakable approach of the one thirty-seven. A guard appeared, flag in hand. Around a bend of track panted the train, hoot-hooting and billowing steam. The man bent to pick up the suitcase. He had hold of the handle when he felt a convulsive clutch at his arm. On straightening his back he wasted no time asking what was wrong. His gaze followed his companion's to fix on the woman in the headscarf, but he saw nothing beyond her taking a couple of steps backwards. It was a common enough sight – the retreat by someone who'd shifted nearer the edge of the platform to confirm that the train coming in was long enough to be the right one. There was nothing to explain the look on the face under the brown hat. The release of held breath. The sudden pallor.

'What is it, love?' he asked anxiously, his arm going around her.

'Silly of me . . .'

'Come over faint?' The train had pulled in and was dislodging passengers. 'In too much of a rush to eat a proper meal before setting off?'

'An omelet with chips and peas at noon. Even jelly and custard for pudding. I'm fine, dear. Truly.' She started forward.

He didn't look near convinced.

'Just silliness, like I said.' She lowered her voice. 'I got it into my head that woman in the headscarf was going to jump. The one getting into that carriage now. An instantaneous impression and obviously wrong.'

'What was it made you think so?'

They were threading their way down the platform in the direction she had indicated with a nod, peering into carriage windows. 'She was already rather too close to the edge . . . a change in her stance . . . a sudden rigidity. As though she were bracing herself the way runners do at the start of a race, readying for the precise moment to leap forward. Oh, you shouldn't have to put up with my nonsense! And now I'm going to make it worse by saying it'll spoil my time with Hattie if I don't at least attempt to reassure myself by getting another look at a complete stranger, to try and size up if she looks despondent.'

'I've never heard you talk nonsense and I'd trust your instincts anywhere, any time.'

'This one!'

It had started to rain, but the woman in the headscarf was blurrily visible through the carriage window on account of being seated right next to it.

'You've got some of your color back, dear. That's a relief. What you need is a strong cup of tea with lots of sugar, but that not being at the ready, eat a sweet if you've one with you.'

'I do. Some boiled ones in my handbag.'

He had the door open and would have followed her in with the suitcase, but a male voice from within said to set it down and he'd get it on to the rack for the lady. The guard trotted up, ushered the man impatiently aside and blew his whistle as if it were something he lived for morning, noon and night. The man waved his hand in farewell, even though it was doubtful he could be seen from within. The train churned out of the station.

The carriage was unusually full for that time of day. This had made it necessary for the woman in the green coat to take the one remaining space at the far end from the woman in the headscarf. However, given that they were seated on opposite sides, she was provided with a sideways view of the right profile. Her intentionally casual glance took in the shabby coat, the down-at-heel shoes, the lack of a handbag; a face (what could be seen of it) stripped of life.

The woman in the green coat wished the very stout man cramming her into the corner would shift sufficiently to allow her breathing room so that she could concentrate on formulating any further impressions that might suggest a disturbed state of mind. Meanwhile, her eyes automatically took note of the other passengers.

Seated on the stout man's right was a female in a no-nonsense hat with a pince-nez perched on her nose, who seemed by her pained expression to feel under an obligation to make up for his excess bulk by shrinking a couple of sizes. Next to her was another man with a weather-roughened complexion suggesting the land worker, puffing away on a gnarled pipe he might have carved himself after chopping down an apple tree. Beyond him were perched three children, all under the age of ten. The man who had brought her to the station would not have been surprised by this mental note-taking; her walk of life had schooled her in observation.

In addition to the woman in the headscarf, the seating across the way was partially taken up by four more youngsters. Positioned between them was the man who had kindly stowed the tan suitcase in the luggage rack. A clerical collar showed at the open neck of his coat. The woman in the green coat wondered if all the children, four boys and three girls, were his own or ones from his parish he was taking on an outing. Their outer clothing indicated the latter – very much of the make-do-and-mend sort. Socks bunched down around ankles for lack of garters; haircuts that suggested blunt scissors hurriedly wielded while the stew threatened to either burn or boil over; the girls were hatless and the caps worn by some of the boys were not school uniform ones, but the sort Tiny Tim might have worn when hobbling outdoors for a breath of air.

The woman in the green coat couldn't imagine Reverend Pimcrisp, the vicar of her parish church, doing anything as noble as spending time with a group of such children beyond shoving the vicarage door closed on them. He had an equal fear of lice and common accents. Producing a thin smile for a child would be the performance of an act of extreme penance for indulging in dreadful sin, such as that of gluttony by eating two chocolate biscuits. And in preference he would likely have chosen to put his feet in the fire. She knew she was filling her mind to block out the fright she'd had. But she was fond of children, and glad to see the smiles on the faces of these ones as they chatted cheerfully, without being noisy, amongst themselves. Like little sparrows, those most ordinary of birds, but stout-hearted – willing to brave the English winter days when their more finely feathered cousins lacked the stamina.

Her companion at the station would not have been surprised at her ability to find interest in her surroundings, even whilst the woman in the headscarf still tugged at her mind. A reprieve for her physical discomfort was at hand.

'Will you not out of Christian charity put your knees together?' said the woman with the pince-nez to the stout man. His face turned puce, but before he could expire in the futile attempt, the train pulled into the next station. Heaving himself up with what dignity he could muster, he maneuvered himself out onto the platform. When they were away again, his insulter shifted down the seat. 'More comfortable?' she asked the woman in the green coat. On being reassured, she leaned towards the clergyman. 'I'm sorry, Nigel, but it had to be said. You could have driven this train through his splayed legs.'

'Possibly. But I hope he wasn't headed all the way to London. And please, my dear Mary, don't say it wouldn't hurt him to bike it.'

'There's a lesson here for these children, whose minds we have chosen to steer heavenward, that selfishness should never reap reward.' A couple of the youngest ones giggled.

So it was a vicar and his wife or sister, or simply a worthy female, escorting the boys and girls on an outing. More appropriate than a man on his own doing so if they weren't his flesh and blood, thought the woman in the green coat. She sat still for several minutes, allowing herself to be lulled by the rhythmic chug-chug, chuff-chuff and occasional rocking motion of the train. Memory returned of her one train ride as a child and how she had thought the corded mesh luggage racks were hammocks for sleeping babies. As a girl she'd had a particularly vivid imagination, which had sometimes led to embroidering the ordinary into the fantastical out of very thin thread. It was a trait she'd striven to control on reaching adulthood so as not to allow her judgment to be compromised, but that did not mean she never read more into a situation than was warranted.

Had this been the case with her alarm for the woman in the headscarf? The woman in the green coat turned her head to the right for what must appear another casual glance. A snub-nosed, red-haired boy by the far window on the same side as herself was leaning forward and staring fixedly at the woman, but in response to a look from the clergyman shifted back in his seat. His expression was thoughtful. The woman in the green coat wished for the opportunity of a full-face view of her object. Profiles can be deceiving. She'd been unable to see the left one on boarding because it had been pressed against the window, eliminating any attempt to fit the two together in her mind. Now, endeavoring to give the impression of staring into space, she let her eyes linger briefly before leaning back and closing them. Something stirred behind her lids, like a fish slipping into the shallows, then disappearing back into the deep before it could be caught.

The headscarf had slipped sufficiently back from the forehead to show dark hair threaded with silver. Its wearer could be any age from thirty-five to fifty. Her bone structure suggested there might once have been something arresting, even beautiful, in a vaguely foreign way, about her. Before defeat took hold and squeezed her dry.

That's what the woman in the green coat saw – the withering that can come with grinding poverty along with a multitude of other troubles. But such was the tragic fate of many. Some might be driven to think about taking their own lives, but the majority would decide against doing so. If the woman in the headscarf had worked herself up to the point of nearly throwing herself in front of the train, she'd had second thoughts and might even now be thinking of ways to better her situation. The train drew into another station, the pipe-smoking man got out, and away they chuffed again. The clergyman's associate directed her pince-nez at the woman in the green coat.

'I don't know about you, but I've never thought tobacco has any place in close quarters. A number of these children,' she added severely, 'are chesty. All we need is to have them coughing throughout the performance.'

A child's voice piped up. ''Ansel an' Gretel on ice. That's what we's goin' to see.'

'How lovely,' enthused the woman in the green coat.

The clergyman's associate mellowed sufficiently to take a confidential tone. 'Some might think the cost of tickets would be better spent on vests and liberty bodices. St Clement's has always been a very poor parish, made worse by the closing of the shoe factory. However, my brother,' a nod across the way, 'believes that raising the spirits lifts the soul. And,' as if anticipating disagreement, '*Hansel and Gretel* could be termed a morality play.'

'Most definitely,' agreed the woman in the green coat without a hint of amusement. 'The death of the witch representing the destruction of evil . . .' There the conversation ended; the train was pulling into Waterloo Station.

The clergyman became a whirl of activity. He took down her suitcase and those of his flock. The children jostled each other in eagerness to be first on the platform, after allowing the woman in the headscarf to get out ahead of them. By the time the woman in the green coat descended there was no sight of her. But what could have been done had it been possible to catch up with her? An attempt to engage her in conversation would surely have been rebuffed. Even so, there remained the wish that fate had been more cooperative.

Having handed in her ticket and passed through the barrier, the woman in the green coat was glancing around in hope of spotting her cousin amongst the milling crowd, when a burly man in a seaman's jacket cut past her at a rapid rate. Characteristically, her eyes followed him, taking in the tightly curled salt-and-pepper hair, lowered eyebrows and pugnacious set of a square jaw. Through a fortuitous gap in the throng, she saw him moments later barge up against the children who had been in the railway carriage with her. The clergyman's sister responded with a jab of her umbrella, resulting in a sideways jerk on the part of the offender, and the boy with red hair jumped up and down, pointing after him as he raced on his way. On the face of it the man's behavior had been boorish. But that condemnation discounted the possibility that he'd discovered his pocket had been picked and was darting after the thief, or that he had remembered he'd left the gas fire on, or had been seized by regret at walking out on his wife in the middle of an argument.

The woman in the green coat stood thinking how unreliable it was to make assumptions, sympathetic or negative, when only seeing the tip of the iceberg. She was about to continue further down this road of thought when she was hailed by a dearly familiar voice and saw her cousin, Hattie Fly, coming towards her, her face wreathed in a welcoming smile. All other considerations were pushed firmly aside. Nothing must spoil this meeting after not having seen each other for nearly a year.

They exchanged greetings, each said how well the other looked and headed for the underground to catch a train to King's Cross, from which Miss Fly lived a short walk away in a narrow terraced house. At the corner of her road was a telephone box. From it the woman in the green coat put through a call to the man who driven her to the station at Large Middlington to let him know she had arrived and was now with Hattie.

The two women spent the rest of the afternoon and evening catching up on each other's lives and discussing other mutual interests. In particular, Miss Fly took pleasure in hearing about her cousin's gentleman friend, George Bird – such a lovely man from the sound of him. Never having known romance herself, she delighted when the scent of it drifted her way. Living alone, apart from a lodger presently away on business, Miss Fly enjoyed listening to the wireless, but did not turn it on that night until shortly before they went to bed.

'Just for the news, if you don't mind, Florie?'

'Of course not, dear.'

Hattie was one of very few who still called Florence Norris by the abbreviated form of her Christian name. The rest of her family had stopped using it as a dig at her for having gone up in the world. Those feelings had smoothed over with time; she was no longer made to feel she walked around with her nose in the air, but neither had she ever regained the place in their hearts that was 'our Florie.'

The male voice from the wireless informed his listeners that a bank robbery had been foiled in Exeter, a backbencher in the House of Commons had engaged in a fiery exchange with the Foreign Secretary regarding the Gold Coast, and at three thirty that afternoon a woman had been pronounced dead at the scene after walking in front of a bus. He then provided the name of the street . . .

'What's the matter, Florie?' asked Hattie, looking anxiously at her cousin's blanched face.

'I'll tell you in a minute. Did he say Fletcher Street?'

'Yes.'

'Is it anywhere near Waterloo Station?'

Hattie was a Londoner, born and bred. 'A five-minute walk away.'

'The train we were on arrived at three twenty.'

'We?'

'I'm making a huge leap in making a connection, but . . .'

Florence told Hattie about the woman in the headscarf.

THREE

That afternoon had seen Mrs Trout busily making shepherd's pie for the constable's tea in the kitchen of the cottage that also served as the police station. The population of Dovecote Hatch wasn't considered large enough for a proper one, the closest of these being located twelve miles away at Large Middlington. Mrs Trout was proud of her home, of having done it up nice with the floral wallpaper, new net curtains and antimacassars in the front room. Then there was the garden looking lovely now next door had cut down the near-dead tree overhanging the fence. Her thoughts returned to the question of Mr Tenneson. All in all, perhaps it was for the best if he had died accidentally. If it had been murder and her husband was to get promoted for going above and beyond his job solving the case, he'd be moved on from Dovecote Hatch to somewhere bigger, such as Large Middlington, or even further afield, say Kingsbury Knox. And that wouldn't have gone down well with him or their eleven-year-old son, Rupert.

Earlier on, Mrs Trout had sometimes regretted that she and Len had stopped with the one and only, but not this last six months or so. She'd come to think you'd need to grow a second pair of eyes for every additional child. And even then you'd still be caught napping. Rupert was an angelic-looking boy with fair curls and forget-me-not blue eyes. His looks were not scarily deceiving in that he was a diabolical child. But neither could it be said butter wouldn't melt in his mouth. He was at the stage of boyhood where his friends made up his entire world; whatever they got up to by way of mischief, he'd be right in there with them. Miss French, their teacher at the village school, had year after year been a marvel of patience. But recently she'd been having trouble with her back and felt pushed to the limit by spit balls, stink bombs and white mice let out of satchels. Fair or not, it was Rupert's innocent face that riled her more than the smirks and giggles; she had him pegged as the ringleader, and so she told Mrs Trout on meeting her in the street. He was presently up in his bedroom, supposedly doing his homework. Miss French had said he could do a lot better in school if he tried.

As it happened, Rupert liked Miss French, not that he'd be sissy enough to show it. He was also fond of his parents, though at some point during the past year he had consigned them in the manner of a couple of faded photographs to the back of a shelf. Mrs Trout, now peeling carrots, could not delude herself that prising him away from Dovecote Hatch was a pretty prospect. Occasional misbehavior would become the pattern should he feel really hard-done-by. As it was, he made enough stink about not getting the pocket money his friends did, or being allowed off on camping trips with no grown-ups in charge.

Checking on the syrup tart baking in the cooker, Mrs Trout wondered if bringing up a girl would've been easier. There'd been that business a few weeks gone of Rupert coming home more than an hour later than promised after setting off after school with his best pals Timmy, Bert and Eric. That'd been the evening of Tuesday, 1 November. The day Mr Tenneson died, putting Len – having come in to find her in a panic – in no mood to dwell on whether the man's fall down the stairs had been accidental or not.

Despite vowing herself to wring his neck if he turned up safe, it'd been one of the times she'd thought Len a mite too strict with Rupert. The boys had been out collecting money for next Saturday's Guy Fawkes' night and, as she'd told Len, 'You must remember what it was like when you were a child. Skipping through the streets, taking turns with your friends pushing an old pram with an effigy of Guy Fawkes inside. Rattling the money tin and shouting out: "Penny for the Guy!"' It was easy to lose track of time when you were eager to rake in enough coins for lots of fireworks. She could see that now she wasn't panicked. Not that she'd've let Rupert off scot-free. She'd have done the same as Len in sending the boy to bed without his tea, but wouldn't have told him there'd be no bonfire night for him that year.

As it happened, the other boys came down with bad colds, so the fun got cancelled anyway – the fireworks didn't get bought and the Guy ended up tossed in a dustbin. Len had thought she was the one in the wrong on the big night for being soft on the boy, saying he could look out of his bedroom window at other people's fireworks. She'd ended up agreeing that Len had been in the right on that. Rupert had scorned her offer and instead sat hunched at the top of the stairs, singing at full pitch: 'Remember, remember the fifth of November, the gunpowder treason and plot. Remember, remember the fifth of November, should never be forgot,' until his dad threatened to clout him one. Not that he'd ever laid a hand on Rupert, but it did the trick.

His brow like a thundercloud, Len had dragged up the original offence, along with going on at her about other times Rupert had been late home. Times when there'd been sound reason to worry. Take the day he'd decided to take a dip in the river and got caught up in the current down near the bridge where it turned tricky. Mrs Trout hadn't needed reminding he'd likely have drowned if Mr Sprague, the church organist at St Peter's, hadn't been taking a walk along the bank and gone in after him, without wasting time taking off his jacket with hymn music in the pocket. And there was no forgetting the time Rupert and three of his pals decided to explore an abandoned farmhouse and his leg had gone through a rotted floorboard. He hadn't been badly hurt – just scrapes and bruising – but the others had wasted an age trying to prise him loose before Timmy had made it back to let her know what had happened. Eliza Spellbinder had lived in that house and they'd wanted to see her ghost. 'I'll give him ghosts up the backside,' Len had roared. And no wonder when thinking how much worse it could've been. Timmy had owned up to his mum later that all four boys had taken turns swinging from the rafters minutes before Rupert got himself in trouble.

If getting him away from his friends would gain him some sense, that would be one thing, thought Mrs Trout as she got the syrup tart out of the cooker and put in the shepherd's pie, but all moving from Dovecote Hatch would do is make him act up worse 'cos of being hopping mad. And, truth be told,

she wasn't keen on uprooting either. That settled, she told
herself resolutely that she was done with her imaginings that
Mr Tenneson had been murdered. It was a lot of rubbish
wishing her Len was the ambitious sort. Ungrateful. Most
women would thank their lucky stars for a man that did his
job the best he could, but when all was said and done put his
home life first and foremost.

She stood thinking about the first time she'd seen Len in
his uniform. They'd been married three weeks when he got
the job of constable and she'd turned all giddy from the thrill
that had gone through her. He wasn't much to look at in the
ordinary way – stout build and ruddy face – but he'd put a
ring on her finger. That had counted for a lot, seeing as so
many women had gone unwed as a result of the war. But now
done up so smart! All that navy blue and silver buttons! She'd
gazed at him, wondering if this heart-flutterer could possibly
be her safe and steady Len. That night she'd gone to bed
without her curlers. Made Len irritable, it had, getting one in
the eye at the wrong moment. The mistake had been suggesting
he might wear his helmet in bed. The memory of his 'Now,
now, none of that, Elsie, my girl!' still made her flush. He
hadn't added, 'This is England . . .' but she could hear it all
the same. She'd thought he might like her being a little flirty.
Instead he'd made her feel like an immoral woman. These
days there wasn't much of what her mother had referred to
as 'that business', not with Rupert in the bedroom next door
already at the age of knowing something of what was what.

Mrs Trout shook her head in an effort to clear her mind.
What had got her going over any of this? A reason by way of
a name popped surprisingly to mind: Florence Norris. There'd
been talk of her going up to London that day. Was it possible
that she, Elsie Trout, was jealous of a woman who'd lost her
husband years ago and, though living very nicely no doubt as
housekeeper at Mullings, didn't have a home of her own? Was
that where the resentment came from about it being Florence,
not Len, that'd solved the murder? Mrs Trout sat smack down
on a chair. She wasn't usually a woman to dig inside herself,
but now she'd started she plunged deeper. Since the murder,
Florence had started going out again with George Bird of the

Dog and Whistle. They'd done the same a few years back and no one had any idea why it had ended. Now Mrs Hewett of the general shop-cum-post office had put it about that the two were definitely courting. What could be lovelier than that for a couple of their age – Florence in her forties and George his fifties? Not many got the chance of true love a second time round!

Mrs Trout had agreed when Mrs Hewett rhapsodized to her that it was all very romantic. But maybe deep down there'd been a stirring of envy, the sense of having been short-changed with Len. Not the bedroom part, which he got down to when necessary as if it was something the doctor had ordered to ward off colds, but he wasn't the sort for an ordinary kiss and a cuddle. A peck on the cheek or pat on the arm was it. Now she wondered if that could be as much her fault as his. Maybe in taking umbrage all those years ago she'd gone too far – not showing enough wifely affection. It didn't have to be about you-know-what, did it? Or could this silliness, this being small-minded, come from having too much time on her hands? It wasn't as if she doubted Len was fond of her. Never a word of criticism about her cooking or how she kept the house. Maybe what she needed to keep her head on straight was a little job. It would leave less time for wool-gathering.

When Len came into the kitchen a few moments afterwards she was wondering if he'd agree to her asking Mrs Hewett if she knew of anyone needing a woman to do a few hours' cleaning a week. As a result she didn't notice he was frowning and consider the possibility there'd been more to his day than dealing with lost property.

Also her eyes were on the kettle. 'There you are,' she chimed cheerily, 'ready for a cuppa?' It was the same greeting as always, but she'd switched to a clean pinny of a shade of blue that he had said, when they first started walking out, matched her eyes. Or had that been his mother's?

'Where's our Rupert?' His rumbled outrage got her in the back.

'In his bedroom. Why?'

'If I've told him once I've told him a hundred times to put

his bike in the shed, but oh, no, he has to leave it thrown on the ground! Blast me if I didn't nearly trip over it just now.'

'Oh, dear!' She turned to face him, teapot in hand. 'Betty Jones says her Timmy's just as thoughtless and six months ago he was as good as gold. Still, no wonder you're cross. But leastways it isn't raining; that'd have you on the rampage.'

'Like I'm always telling you, Elsie,' the frown had deepened to a scowl, 'if it'd bin me at eleven pulling some of Rupert's stunts my mum would've clouted me into the middle of next week. It's too bad when a man comes home from a trying day . . .'

The rest was reduced to a series of grunts as Len removed his jacket, followed by his helmet, and went to hang them on the hall tree. He must have caught sight of Rupert on the stairs before the boy could nip back up. They returned to the kitchen together. Mrs Trout saw her son was ready with a mouthful of cheek, his usual reaction these days when knowing he was in the wrong. She shut him down with a glare. This was followed by the order to get his bike back in the shed where it belonged. Accurately reading his twitching lips as mimicking Len's frequent pronouncement that 'bikes don't grow on trees', she added that if he wanted to spend the night out there with it that'd suit her and his dad just fine.

'Think I won't?' Rupert stalked out the back door.

The reason Mrs Trout let that go was Len's mention of 'a trying day.' It probably wouldn't amount to much, but she was eager to find out if, just possibly, something was stirring in the village – something questionable with undertones and overlays worthy of being picked through by a man too long under-appreciated. She wasn't back to wishing Mr Tenneson had been murdered. A burglary would do nicely. Len settled himself in his chair by the domestic boiler and swallowed down his tea – brewed strong, with a dash of milk and three sugars – before getting down to brass tacks.

'So what's on your mind, Len, besides our Rupert?'

'Don't ask me to rehash, Elsie.' He shifted irritably in his chair, but before the disappointment could settle in her throat (a bit of chat was nice, even if it was only about helping old Mrs Weedy put her washing line back up) he hunched a shoulder. 'Oh, well, why not? Ivy Waters collared me this afternoon as I was passing her gate. Still that same old palaver about Doris Thatcher not giving back her dog after taking it in when hurt. And of course there was a mouthful about it being our Rupert that ran over it with his bike. Now don't get that look on your face, Else, I'm not blaming him for that. Nothing to be done when an animal runs out under your wheels.'

Her expression had become quite fierce. 'I hope you told that brass-faced witch we don't just have his word, or Doris Thatcher's, for that matter. Several other neighbors saw it happen and told me it was a wonder Rupert didn't take a hard fall and end up in hospital. And what happened when he ran to her house while Doris stayed with the dog? She said she wasn't coming out and didn't want it brought inside. Too squeamish. I'll give her squeamish! Hard as nails.'

'All right, Else!' The constable rubbed the side of his nose, a sure sign his crankiness was on the rise. 'No need to go on and on. I've still got Ivy Waters's voice going round inside my head like a blasted record with a scratchy needle. Haven't even told you the worst yet. She's now talking about taking the matter to court.'

'What? Suing Rupert . . . us?'

'Now, now!' growled the voice from the chair. 'I do wish you'd listen closer, Else. I just said the ranting was about Doris Thatcher refusing to give the dog back now it's well again. Stealing, she called it. Yes, Else,' he heaved a sigh, 'I did remind her who done the nursing and paid the vet bill for what some would say was naught but a mongrel, for all her claims he's almost a proper wire-haired fox terrier she paid good money for. Got him off the market, so Mrs Jenkins from next door told me. And if she paid more than a half crown I'd say she was had.'

'Doesn't matter what it is or where it came from, it's still one of God's creatures.' Elsie, like Rupert, was fond of animals; it was Len who wouldn't let him have a dog, saying he wasn't responsible enough to take care of one. 'And I don't for a minute believe Ivy Waters wants Scamp, or whatever its name is, back. More a case of trying to get money out of Doris and

Alf Thatcher by putting the wind up them. You say "court" to some people and they immediately see themselves behind bars. What's she hoping for out of you?'

'Says it's bin six weeks since the accident and the only reason I've done bally all on her behalf is because it was Rupert on the bike. Threatened to write to the chief constable about me. I wouldn't have thought she'd of known there was such a person.'

'Detective stories.' Elsie refilled his cup and handed it back to him. 'In them someone always decides it's time to bring in the chief constable instead of having the sense to have a good old natter with the local bobby that knows his beat inside out.' There was a meaningful pause. 'But cheer up! If Doris Thatcher is murdered you'll know to point the finger at Ivy Waters. And if no one else gives you a medal, I will.'

Hope was absent beneath Elsie's bright voice that he would ever get his due elsewhere. Murder had made its one visit to Dovecote Hatch. No judge or jury would convict Doris Thatcher of dog theft. Ivy Waters would direct her spite back to regularly reporting elderly Mr Sargent for playing his wireless too loud. There would continue to be the rounds of small upsets that would never amount to anything more than village unpleasantness. What must end was her wishing for more than a reasonable woman had the right to expect. Hadn't Ivy Waters's husband left her because nothing he ever did was good enough?

Uncharacteristically, Elsie kissed the top of her Len's head, then patted down his hair. It hadn't registered with either of them that Rupert had sidled back in and sat down at the table.

'Why would Mrs Waters murder Mrs Thatcher?'

'She wouldn't,' answered his father, taking his seat. 'Nor would nobody else.'

'You can't be sure of that.' Rupert was talking to be argumentative; being ticked off for leaving his bike lying on the ground still rankled. 'Just because Mrs Thatcher's the postman's wife and not someone exciting doesn't mean,' he was warming to his theme, 'that she isn't a menace to someone with . . . with a deep, dark secret to protect, or . . . maybe she isn't who everybody thinks she is?'

His mother stared at him as she placed the shepherd's pie

between a dish of carrots and turnip, and another of cabbage. Suddenly it was him she could see years down the road being honored for his brilliant police work, Inspector Rupert Trout of Scotland Yard, standing on a raised platform giving a speech, saying how he owed his success to the example set him by his constable dad and then a nice long bit about the encouragement given him by his devoted mum.

Usually it annoyed her when husband and son smothered their helpings of shepherd's pie with tomato sauce, as though it would be tasteless without it. But now she fetched the bottle from the pantry, set it in front of Len's plate and told him to pass it to Rupert when he was done. She'd just sat back down when the doorbell rang.

'You sit,' she ordered Len as he heaved himself upright. 'If someone's cat's up a tree it can stay there till you've finished your tea. The advantage people take! Rupert, you go and see who's on the step, and best hope it's not one of your friends or he'll get an earful from me about consideration next time I see him!'

'Blimey!' Rupert muttered under his breath, but the bell rang again and he lost no time in getting to the front door. He was sure it would be one of his friends, probably Timmy, who'd come round, and he'd feel so stupid telling him he had to buzz off because they were in the middle of tea. Other parents didn't have all these rules; although he wasn't used to Mum snapping at him like she'd just done. Back at the kitchen table, Elsie was thinking about getting her son a book of detective stories for Christmas. Perhaps he would mention it one day when speaking publicly in the dimly glowing future. She looked up to see Rupert in the doorway.

'Was it about a cat up a tree?'

'No, a man. Said he was missing a pencil from when he was last round this way and wondered if someone had turned it in.'

'A pencil?' his parents echoed in unison.

Rupert sidled towards his chair. 'Could be a new one, I suppose, not just a stub to tuck behind the ear. Anyway, I told him to hop it 'cos we was having our tea. Said he could come back later if . . .'

His father's face turned three shades deeper red, cheeks billowing out to the point of exploding. 'And you had no inkling who he was?'

'Looked a bit of a toff,' said Rupert dismissively.

'Then it was likely someone important.' Constable Trout ground out the words. 'Peculiar sort, of course, if not actually mad if he's running around looking for a pencil, but then the upper crust sometimes seem to enjoy coming across as barmy. But we at the lower end, Rupert, don't get to give them their marching orders. We know our place and stick to it, however much your friend Timmy's dad wants to think nobody's any better than no one else. Run down the road and bring that man back!'

'Keep your hair on, Dad! I'm going!'

'But don't put him in the front room!' Elsie called after him. 'What if he's one of those newspaper men? That would go with the pencil, and there's my knickers in there on the clothes horse.'

FOUR

The Dog and Whistle stood at the top of the short high street, its profile of arched oak door and leaded window panes angled towards the village green, while a strip of cobbled lane separated its courtyard and side entrance from the wall surrounding the Mullings woods. In the wall was an iron gate which gave onto a footpath leading to the rear of the great house. Viewed thus, from all aspects, its dignified proportions had been gentled through the centuries by the respectfully guided hand of nature. The Stodmarsh family had resisted any urge towards architectural embellishment or aggrandizement. They had allowed their ancestral home to age as it chose, whether it be with a green shawl of ivy cast over the shoulder of its east wing, or by the fading of russet brick to rose pink.

In the November twilight the house was, as can be the case with trees in winter, perhaps more beautiful for being stripped to its bones, silvered by a sliver of moon. Shadows painted the evening's thoughts upon the ground. Lights glowed from rooms where curtains had yet to be drawn, opening the imagination to what might be transpiring either above or below stairs. Or so ran the thoughts of the man looking towards the house from the near end of the woodland path.

A man in his early forties, tall, lean-faced and aquiline-featured. Had his bearing not marked him as being unmistakably of the gentry, his attire would have done so. His coat was finely tailored, his shoes handmade. As for his hat, it could only have come from the sort of establishment where customers are preferred, though not strictly required, to have titles.

Taking a couple of steps beyond the rim of expansive lawn, he paused for a few moments, put a well-shod foot forward, drew it back and, turning, retraced his steps. Coming out through the iron gate at the village end of the path, he glanced at the lighted windows of the pub, looked at his watch then

sauntered down the lane to a car parked neatly against the
curb and climbed into it. The elderly Morris was not in accord
with the rest of him. A hint of self-mockery touched his mouth
as he leaned back in the front seat and closed his eyes. Young
Rupert Trout would have recognized him, having a half hour
before turned him away from the front door of the cottage
that doubled as a police station. Settled into the driver's seat,
he decided on a twenty-minute nap.

Meanwhile, at the Dog and Whistle the early rush had
subsided. The customers, most of them regulars, had shifted
into groups, some seated, others standing. Their surroundings
were typical of many an English village pub dating back to
the days of coaching inns – patina-aged plastered walls, low-
beamed ceilings and narrow latticed panes above window seats
with faded tapestry cushions. A log fire glowed and crackled
on the brick-surrounded hearth, brightening the sheen of horse
brasses and the copper utensils on the mantelpiece. To the
accompaniment of downed bitter or mild, the murmur of
various conversations drifted amidst the tobacco smoke that
coiled into shapes suggestive of spirit entities striving to mate-
rialize two hundred or more years beyond their worldly time.

George Bird stood behind the bar idly polishing glasses,
glad of the momentary respite that allowed him to gather his
thoughts and center them on Florence Norris, whom he had
seen off on the train to London that afternoon. It had been a
relief to hear her sounding cheerful when she'd phoned about
an hour and a half later to say she'd arrived and was with her
cousin, Hattie. There'd been that business of the woman on
the platform looking like she was going to jump. He hadn't
noticed anything odd himself, but what Florence said wasn't
to be taken with a pinch of salt. He was a large man, close
on six feet four and of a robust build to accompany the expansive geniality that rarely evaporated, and then only when some
unpleasantness was the cause. Florence had said that he put
her in mind of John Ridd, the gentle giant hero of R.D.
Blackmoor's *Lorna Doone*.

George had never been much of a reader until he met
Florence. And even now he preferred listening to her tell him
about the books she had read. These days he never tired of

looking into her fine hazel eyes, but it was her voice that had first drawn him to her. He remembered struggling to explain to himself after their first meeting what it was about it that so appealed; the best he'd been able to come up with was that it was *a listening* voice.

It was as a recent widower that George had moved to Dovecote Hatch five years previously. He'd had no interest in looking about him for female companionship, let alone anything of a closer nature. He and his Betty had been blessed with twenty good – very good – years; a man didn't get that lucky twice. He was as content as he'd ever be, so had gone his thoughts at the time, to live off his memories where a woman was concerned. Certainly he couldn't complain of being lonely, having been readily accepted by the regulars on taking over the Dog and Whistle, which had the spreading effect of absorbance into the village community as a whole.

Being a modest man, George Bird did not realize that in his case a concession had been made to the tradition that outsiders were to be viewed warily for decades. Sometimes it took till a headstone had stood in the churchyard long enough to develop a slouch for someone to remark, as if compelled to do so for the sake of his or her conscience: 'Not bad sorts, they weren't, Ann and Bob Smith; makes for wishing they'd been given a warmer welcome in the forty-odd years they was here, especially since their son went all out to fit in by marrying the boss-eyed Wheaton girl, who'd otherwise have sat on the shelf till she toppled.'

Alf Thatcher the postman had been the first to mention Florence Norris to George, who he'd quickly come to call Birdie. He'd done so when talking about the household at Mullings, relating how she'd arrived there in 1900, at age fourteen, to work as a kitchen maid, had left on her marriage to Robert Norris of Farn Deane (the home farm) to return a couple of years after he was killed in the war to take up the reins of housekeeper. Midway through Alf's extolling Florence as a highly capable and wonderfully kind woman, George had sensed there was some hopeful matchmaking going on behind the words. Therefore, in the weeks ahead he genially changed the subject when Alf brought up her name. Then one Sunday

morning he'd met her in the churchyard following the morning service. It had been one of those general conversations, with her asking how he liked living in Dovecote Hatch and mentioning places of interest in the locality that he might enjoy visiting.

Yes, it had been her voice at the beginning. It had warmed him through like brandy sipped on a winter's night; even so, he didn't at first realize it would thaw out the chill place in his heart that he hadn't known had been there since Betty's death. Then the discoveries began of so much held in common – the remarkably similar values and beliefs, the shared sense of humor and, perhaps most important of all, the love each held for the boy in their lives. For George this was his godson, Jim; for Florence it had been Master Ned, the orphaned grandson of Lord and Lady Stodmarsh. Her employers had encouraged her to take more than a housekeeper's interest in him, the poor health that plagued Her Ladyship preventing her taking a more motherly role in his young life.

It had been at the point that George accepted what should have been obvious before – that he loved Florence Norris – when distressing events at Mullings made her feel compelled to sever their relationship rather than let it continue on a basis of concealment. It was not until after the murder at Mullings, when all could be explained, that they had come together again.

Now all appeared to bode well for the future. At twenty-one the boy who had been Master Ned was now Lord Stodmarsh, eager to assume the responsibilities that went with wealth and title. Jim, six years older, had recently married and was becoming recognized as an impressive new artist. The question Alf Thatcher, in particular, would have liked answered was what did George and Florence have in mind for the next stage of their own lives? Did they harken to wedding bells pealing for them? Or would they prefer to carry on as they were? All Alf could get out of George was that Florence hoped that within a couple of years Molly, now head housemaid at Mullings and recently married to Grumidge the butler, would take over as housekeeper, leaving her, Florence, with the opportunity to spread her wings.

'Nice,' Alf had acknowledged, 'and no one should go clipping

them if she wants to fly to Australia, say, although why anyone would want to cut themselves off from civilization to go and live with convicts and kangaroos, I dunno.'

Alf had been in the Dog and Whistle earlier that evening in November, but only briefly. George had sensed from his glum expression the moment he walked in that he was on the outs with his wife Doris. This didn't happen often, but when it did it turned him into a visible forecast for weeks of relentless rain.

The two men were of similar age – mid-fifties – but otherwise stood in sharp contrast to each other. George's height and girth reduced Alf to gnome size. In compensation, Alf had a shock of thick, albeit gray hair, whilst George had lost most of what had topped his head.

'It's like this, Birdie,' Alf had leaned forward and lowered his voice. 'Once she makes up her mind right's on her side there's rarely, if ever, any budging her.'

'Strong-minded, you could call it,' suggested George who, along with Florence, was very fond of Doris. He waited patiently for his friend to make matters clearer; he had a habit of entering upon a topic by way of a side door.

Alf had made a dubious sounding noise. 'Now I'll not deny I was for her taking in the dog at the time . . .' he'd continued over the foaming rim of his glass. He was cut off the next moment when Tom Norris, Florence's late husband's brother, approached the bar with a request for 'same again.' By the time George had produced it, amid asking Tom how things were at Farn Deane and Tom speaking with obvious pleasure of young Lord Stodmarsh's continued interest in helping work the home farm, Alf was gone. George wasn't surprised. It didn't usually take his friend long to regret making for the pub after cross words with Doris.

Tom was now in the far corner of the window wall chatting with old Mr Sprague, one-time church organist and father of the present one. Being decidedly deaf, he was inclined to talk in a voice that could have cut across two counties. Every so often a sentence or two grabbed the room by the ears.

'It was my birthday and you don't get to be eighty-four every day of the week. If my wife had been alive there'd have been a cake that evening and no excuses. But I wish I hadn't let on I was upset. Neville's not been himself since . . .' The man went back to chewing on his thumb.

On the opposite side of the room Major Wainwright was talking with Derwent Shepherd, former headmaster of the preparatory school young Lord Stodmarsh had attended before going to boarding school, and now estate manager at Mullings. It would be more accurate to say Mr Shepherd was doing the talking. George had noted when the major came in that he didn't look up to snuff.

George gave the counter a needless wipe. He enclosed his thoughts even more tenderly around Florence. It was Eugenie Tressler, Lord Stodmarsh's maternal grandmother, who'd proposed the week's holiday, saying Florence was long overdue one. Mrs Tressler had been visiting at Mullings when the murder occurred and had stayed on afterwards at her grandson's request, taking up the reins as mistress of the house until he decided to marry. The arrangement had worked well. She had been cheerfully accepted in her new role by the servants, and for this she had thanked Florence, knowing her influence in this matter had been crucial. And right she was about that, thought George. An entrenched housekeeper could make for misery above as well as below stairs.

His attention refocused on his duties when the pub door opened and a man approached the bar. He was the one who had taken a twenty-minute nap in his Morris around the corner. Not a local man, but not a stranger either – to George Bird, who had spent some extremely tense moments with him during the police interrogation that was the immediate aftermath of the murder at Mullings. If any of the patrons recognized him they made no display of it. Their conversations continued, the drinks went down, the cigarette and pipe smoke went up. None, whether intentionally or otherwise, looked towards the bar.

'Well, Inspector LeCrane,' George looked readily into the face dominated by the aquiline nose, 'what can I do for you this evening? A pint on the house or something stronger?'

'That's very gracious of you, Mr Bird.'

'Unless, that is, you're on duty. Don't want to get in your bad books again.'

Amusement gleamed in the keen gray eyes. 'We did dog your footsteps for a few days, didn't we? But if all may be forgiven and forgot, I'll take you up on your offer. Make it a half of bitter, please.'

'Nothing to be held against you, Inspector.' George set the filled tankard in front of him. 'Quite the reverse, seeing you solved the case so quick.'

'Ah, there we both know you are being too gracious. Had it not been for your friend, Mrs Norris, we'd have continued blundering down the wrong path for a while longer. By the way, how is she?'

George beamed. 'Very well indeed. Gone up to London to spend the week with her cousin, Hattie.'

The inspector reached for his glass. 'Indeed! Then I would have wasted my time going to Mullings to see her. I was heading that way a half hour ago when I decided it might be better to ask you to give her a message for me – the sight of me being bound to rake up unpleasant memories for young Lord Stodmarsh should he happen upon me on the grounds – perhaps whilst walking his dog.'

'A message for Florence?' George allowed his puzzlement to show.

'A request.'

'Go on, sir.'

'I'd as soon not go into it now, when you have customers to tend. How would it be if I come back after closing time?'

'That'd suit.'

'Let's say ten thirty.'

'I'll let you in the side entrance.'

'Splendid.' The inspector raised his voice to a level that could be readily overheard. 'Glad to know you and Mrs Norris have come well through what had to be a very nasty experience. Didn't like to pass through on the way to visit my aunt without stopping for a word.' He set down his drained glass, cast a cursory glance around, nodded acknowledgement of those whose eyes met his and headed for the door.

The moment it closed behind him Miss Milligan strode up to the bar. She had as much of a nose for something in the wind as the boxer dogs she bred. 'So, George,' she brandished the cigar she was smoking, 'who was that fellow? And don't go all mysterious on me. Won't do, old chap. Will only make me and the rest more curious.'

'No reason to make a secret of it,' responded George as several of the other patrons gathered around her to rivet their gaze on him. 'That was Inspector LeCrane who was brought in to solve the murder at Mullings. Wanted to thank Florence Norris for the help she provided and apologize for any distress he caused me before the right person got arrested.'

'Well, I call that gentlemanly, I do,' said Mrs Bunch, the butcher's wife. 'Wouldn't have thought policemen, excepting Constable Trout, that is, had hearts. I wonder where his auntie lives?'

George shook his head. 'Didn't say.' He doubted there was an aunt, but if the inspector was spotted entering the Dog and Whistle after hours and mention was made of it, the explanation could be that he'd got lost en route and returned for directions, or to use the telephone. He hoped he wouldn't be put in the position of lying. The situation would have to merit it. During the hours up to closing, his mind returned frequently to one question. What was the request that the inspector wanted him to pass on to Florence? Could it, he wondered at one point, have anything to do with the woman in the headscarf that afternoon on the platform at Large Middlington? That did seem to be stretching possibilities, but what else could it be?

He was still deep in thought when a man he hadn't seen in the Dog and Whistle before, or around the village, came in and ordered a Guinness.

'Just passing through or recently moved here?' George enquired with his customary air of fellowship. He received a roundabout answer.

'Suppose some people like living in a backwater like this. Probably has its moments.'

'Neighborly, that's the big thing.' George was not about to mention the murder at Mullings, let alone the inquest following Kenneth Tenneson's death. Behind his smile he was sizing the fellow up: seaman's jacket, knitted hat pulled down mid-forehead – looked a bit of a rough customer, the sort to turn nasty after downing a few. But you could never tell. He slid the foam-topped glass across the bar, noting the grazed knuckles of the hand that wrapped round it.

'Neighborly. Sounds good, but often as not means gossip. Get a lot of that, do you? The spiteful sort, I mean.'

'Can't say we do.' George saw Miss Milligan's eyes glued on them. The same could likely be said of her ears. That she didn't come up to the bar to insert her nose as well was likely due to deciding it was time to get back to the boxers. Her punctiliousness to their routine took a back seat to no other consideration.

She headed out, and the stranger, while downing his Guinness, came through with the information that he was going after a job in Small Middlington the next morning. One involving manual labor? George wondered. Given the grazed knuckles and rough clothing it seemed a probability. The man did not say where he was spending the night, but there were several people in the village who took in overnight guests. He left without ordering another drink and the evening wore on towards closing time.

After calling 'time, ladies and gentlemen,' and having watched the last lingerers hustle off into the November chill, George cleared up and went to keep watch at a window in the passageway behind the taproom.

At the appointed hour a knock sounded at the side door and he opened it to admit Inspector LeCrane, who accepted the offer to divest himself of hat and coat. George hung them on the bottom banister knob of the stairs leading upwards and ushered him into a paneled room shabbily but comfortably furnished as both office and sitting area. The curtains were drawn and a gas fire provided both glow and warmth.

'Here's where I do the books or sit down of a half hour with the paper,' he explained more awkwardly than was characteristic. 'Please take a pew, Inspector, and I'll fetch you a drink. What'll it be?'

'Nothing, thank you,' replied Inspector LeCrane, settling his long, lean form into an easy chair. He smiled, his eyes narrowing into something close to a twinkle. 'Wouldn't wish to show up at my aunt's door reeking of the devil's brew. Her butler will already be disposed to disapproval by my late arrival

– no point in exacerbating the situation. He's an abstemious fellow. Ah, yes, Mr Bird, the aunt is not an invention and I intend spending the night at her house. Not the most welcome of prospects considering she has at least two dozen cats, but I endeavor to stay as close to the truth as possible. The public is not always as credulous as one would like. And who can blame them for an understandable desire to get even in return for the law poking its fingers through their affairs?'

'Don't want to go raising awkward questions about what's really brought you here?' George sat, more than filling a chair across from the other man. 'Seems to me the one most likely to dwell on the why and the wherefore is Constable Trout. I'm not saying he won't buy your story, but it won't go down well learning about your visit second hand. And when a man gets touchy . . . takes umbrage, so to speak . . . well, what I'm saying is the constable could decide something's up and—'

'Start digging?' Inspector LeCrane leaned back, arms folded, fingers interlaced. 'Yes, Mr Bird, I think that's just what he might do. And for the present I'd prefer to keep him out of this. For that reason I called in at his cottage on reaching Dovecote Hatch. My pretext for doing so was that I had mislaid a propelling pencil when I was last in the area and wondered if it might have been handed in to him. A remote chance, I explained, but one that seemed worth an enquiry as I was passing through on my way to visit my aunt, especially as the pencil, or so I told him, had been a gift from her. Constable Trout was most sympathetic. He agreed wholeheartedly that it would be upsetting for the old lady if she noticed I did not have it with me, and regretted deeply that he did not have it to return. Hardly surprising, since it never existed. As I have said, I strive not to misrepresent, but when needs must I do not allow scruples to weigh heavily on my conscience. No, Mr Bird, I don't think Constable Trout will present a problem. If he has trouble sleeping tonight it will be because his son initially turned me from the door, saying he and his parents were in the midst of dinner. I do hope that didn't land the lad in trouble. I rather took to him; he displayed a gutsy type of impudence. Up to all kind of larks, would be my guess.'

George nodded. 'That describes young Rupert right enough.

His parents are probably finding him a handful just now, but I wouldn't be surprised if he ends up doing them proud. What is it you don't want his father digging into?'

'Mind if I smoke?'

'Go right ahead, sir. Occasionally enjoy a pipe, I do, when I can find it.'

The inspector drew a slim silver cigarette case out of his inside jacket pocket, poked into an outside one for a matching lighter and lit up. 'I'm conducting an unofficial investigation into the recent death of Kenneth Tenneson. Or to call a spade a spade, I'm meddling, which is why I don't want Constable Trout up my sleeve. I wouldn't have paid any attention to the case but for my having been left with an interest in Dovecote Hatch. The verdict of accidental death brought in at the inquest didn't sit well with me. Call it a hunch, and the chief constable puts no stock in them, but I'm inclined to the possibility the man was murdered.'

'I see,' George studied him thoughtfully, 'and you'd like Florence's assistance in discovering the truth. Well,' he paused, 'I can tell you she has kept to wondering if he was pushed down those stairs.'

Inspector LeCrane flicked at the ashtray on the table by his chair. 'Her reasoning?'

'Position of the body. Face up. Injury to the back of the head.'

'Ah! Precisely what struck me. Not conclusive by any means, but it does make one think. Sufficiently intrigued, I asked to see the photographs taken at the scene and noticed another possible telling point. The button from Tenneson's right coat sleeve was missing.' A satisfied smile accompanied the words. 'But let us return to the position of the body. Had Mr Tenneson been ascending the stairs when he became dizzy, which is what the inquest concluded, it seems to me likely he would have toppled forward. Should he have then slid down to the bottom, surely he'd have been found face down? As would also seem most probable had he been descending.'

'Whereas,' George rubbed the side of his nose, 'if he was going up and then was pushed his position would have made sense. That was Florence's take on it. So why doesn't that seem to have occurred to the jurors at the inquest, or the coroner?'

'Perhaps because a second murder in one year was intolerable to the local constabulary, so not to be seriously contemplated. Not so easy to dismiss if there's a glaring motive, but in the absence of one it's frequently more comfortable to let sleeping dogs lie.'

'So that's what you want Florence to look into? Why anyone would wish Mr Tenneson dead?'

'She has her finger on the village pulse – as do you, Mr Bird, making your assistance also welcome, if you would be so good as to provide it. I have faith both of you would use the utmost discretion. May I change my mind and have that drink? Be damned to my Aunt Hermione's butler! I'd like to toast the first steps on the road to discovering whether someone has managed to get away with murder.'

'Meaning we're to be on the lookout for someone walking around pleased as Punch with themselves?'

For a man in his forties the inspector's grin was almost boyish. 'That would be a gift from the gods, but even handier is when we run up against a guilty party with a twitchy conscience. The sort of person of whom it is said he or she hasn't been themselves lately. Before too long they almost always fall over their feet to get caught.' His eyes sharpened. 'Have I just rung a bell?'

George hesitated, then nodded. 'In a manner of speaking, but it doesn't . . . couldn't have any connection with this business. His father explained the reason when mentioning it this evening. He, the dad, is an old man; deaf in one ear and can't hear out the other, poor old chap, so speaks in a bellow.'

'And he is?'

'Geoffrey Sprague. Used to be church organist. It has to be extra hard for someone like that losing his hearing. The son took over when he couldn't continue.'

'His name?'

'Neville Sprague. Decent, quiet chap by all accounts.'

'As is frequently said of many murderers.'

'A few months ago he saved young Rupert Trout from drowning.'

'Neither is heroism an excluding factor. What did Geoffrey Sprague say or bellow this evening?'

'Just personal.'

'Such snippets will mostly prove irrelevant, but we have to start somewhere. And I think I'd get more support from higher up if our quarry were not either of Mr Tenneson's sisters or his seventeen-year-old ward. The chief constable prefers not to go up against members of well-to-do families. It offends his sensibilities. All three women did very well by his will, but it has to be acknowledged that they had little to complain of financially while he was alive. Yet, again,' Inspector LeCrane lit another cigarette, 'what secrets a house named Bogmire might conceal.'

FIVE

Not only was Alf Thatcher a close friend of George Bird, he was viewed by almost all in Dovecote Hatch as a thoroughly good sort. He had been their postman for more than thirty years, and the sight of him coming to the door or pedaling his elderly bicycle (alas not his father's penny-farthing) up one street and down another gave the right sort of start to a morning – the equivalent of just the right amount of milk in a cup of tea or an egg boiled for precisely four minutes. This feeling of goodwill towards Alf was wrapped in remembrances of childhood birthday cards delivered and a willingness to remind Mrs Jones, next door but one, that there was a Mother's Union meeting that afternoon. On the rare occasions when someone else took over for him (usually the postmistress's son looking put upon), anxiety rippled up one street and down another that he was laid up with something worse than a bout of lumbago.

The morning after Inspector LeCrane's appearance in Dovecote Hatch, Alf did something unheard of and therefore unsettling. He put an envelope addressed to Miss Milligan at number twenty-two, Spinney Lane through the letter box of Mrs Marshall at number twenty-six. Being in her hall at the time, she spotted the mistake right away and stuck her head out the door. All she saw of Alf was a back view as he pedaled around the next corner, but it was enough to convince her something was wrong. Two minutes later she was in Miss Milligan's hall surrounded by several boxer dogs all displaying an eagerness to devour her from the feet up.

'Down!' roared their mistress to instant obedience. She was dressed in men's trousers old enough to have belonged to her late father, and a horsey sort of jacket. Mrs Marshall had always thought this sort of clothing on a woman unrighteous; not that allowances shouldn't be made. She held the married woman's view that a spinster's life was one long, sad march to the grave. But this morning her mind was entirely on Alf Thatcher.

'I'm worried. This,' handing over the envelope, 'and him looking all bowed over like he had the weight of the world on his shoulders, that's not Alf Thatcher. Not by a long chalk, it isn't.'

'Making mountains out of molehills!' Miss Milligan looked poised to clap her bracingly on the shoulder, but mercifully granted a reprieve. Mrs Marshall was of a fragile build. 'I'm always telling him to ride shoulders back, but he won't listen. That's men for you – the best and the worst of them! How about a cuppa?'

Mrs Marshall had only once drunk Miss Milligan's tea and vowed never to do so again. It hadn't put her in fine fettle. It had made her teeth curl. Or so she'd insisted to her husband. She declined the invitation on the grounds that she needed to get back because Miss Hatmaker was coming round to measure for new sitting-room curtains. Miss Hatmaker didn't make headwear, but would have done so if requested. She was an excellent, versatile needle-woman and, as the village seamstress, always in demand. Such were her dressmaking skills that word of them had reached Lady Blake at Large Middlington. Her Ladyship had considered having her make a couple of dresses for her daughter, but abandoned the idea when the lovely eighteen-year-old Lamorna went into hysterics at the prospect. Had she threatened to run away and never return, Lady Blake might have remained firm. Lamorna had been particularly difficult since the end of her very brief engagement to young Edward Stodmarsh. But getting herself pregnant by the gardener's boy was too dire a threat to be ignored.

Mrs Marshall explained to Miss Milligan that she'd already taken a back seat with Miss Hatmaker to Dr and Mrs Chester, who had needed four eiderdowns recovered. The same with the older Miss Tenneson of Bogmire House who, from the sound of it, had wanted half her wardrobe remade. She then returned to Alf Thatcher.

'Of course I've heard about the trouble he and his wife have been having with Ivy Waters over the dog they took in. The one she didn't want back when it was run over, but does now it's well again. Could things have come to a head, is what I'm wondering.'

'Hope they have, and someone's threatened to collar the wretched woman and have her put to sleep! Which I heard, by way of my charwoman, is what she told Doris Thatcher to do with the poor little blighter!' Miss Milligan snorted, surveying her four boxers with a tenderness kept for them alone. 'Some people should only be allowed bluebottles or earwigs for pets!' She would have gone on about this at length if Mrs Marshall had not cut her short. Her concern was genuine, not a mere means to gossip.

'I fear she may have decided to take them to court.'

Miss Milligan, emitting another of her snorts, slapped her hands on the sides of her waist. 'Just the vulgar sort of thing you'd expect of her sort, no breeding! I guarantee there's not an ounce of pedigree stock in her background. It's a pity I'm concerned about my little Flossie – sweetest little bitch you could ask for, and due the day after tomorrow for her first litter – otherwise I'd go this minute and have it out with the creature, make her apologize for the mountains out of mole-hills! Hate to think of Alf Thatcher being brought low . . .'

The man in question wouldn't have been surprised that the two women had accurately diagnosed his mood and the cause. That was Dovecote Hatch for you. People knew more about you than you did yourself. Last evening had been bad enough when it came to feeling down, given the upset with his wife about Rex. Alf and Doris rarely had words. And when they did it didn't take him long to decide he'd been the one in the wrong. Doris wasn't the quarrelsome sort. She'd have her say and let him have his. No going on about what he'd done yesterday or the week before as some women did.

He should never have started in on it making sense to give the dog back to Ivy Waters. 'Best for all concerned,' he'd said. That was when Doris had got worked up.

'It wouldn't be best for Rex,' she'd said. 'Any fool'd see that. It'd be back before long to him not getting proper feed-ings. Wandering the streets until he got run over again, by a car next time, like as not. And that he wouldn't get over so easy – if at all. Ivy Waters told old Mrs Weedy weeks before the accident that she wished she'd never saddled herself with the animal – she only did so because her young grandson had been staying with her for a fortnight and whined for a doggie. You know how it is, anything to shut the little buggers up. And there'd been this one at the market for half a crown.'

Now, of course, Ivy was claiming Rex had cost her several quid – first two, then four. Always out for a short cut to the lolly, was Ivy. Alf would have begrudgingly paid up, anything for a peaceful life, but Doris had refused to be squeezed.

'Give in to that game,' she'd said, 'and she'll not let up. Next time it'll be if we don't cut down our apple tree by her fence she'll notify the council. Besides, there's the principle.' And there lay the nub. Doris was very much a woman of principle.

Alf had apologized to her when he got back from the Dog and Whistle and they'd made up before going to bed, same as usual. Doris was never one to hold a grudge. Even that time he'd left her standing outside the pictures for an hour when they were courting, his excuse that his mantelpiece clock had stopped. Most women wouldn't have swallowed that one, true though it was. Could've been the end of things right there. A thought that always had Alf thanking his lucky stars. He didn't like to think for one minute what his life would have been from that point on without Doris. It would have been like going around with half himself missing.

They'd been in their thirties when they married twenty years ago, having met whilst on a week's holiday staying in a guest house on the front at Southend. The reason they'd each decided on a get-away was that after years of caring for ailing parents they were suddenly alone. In addition to discovering this, it came out on a walk down the pier that Doris had been born in Dovecote Hatch. The family had moved away when she was four to settle in Chelmsford, where her father had run a market garden. Alf hadn't previously put any stock in fate, but he couldn't go along with the ever-practical Doris when she insisted it had been chance – lucky, but no more to it than that.

She'd seen taking in Rex after the accident as the sensible, as well as the right thing to do. Someone had to get him well if possible. So why not her, being right on the spot? There was nothing noble or self-sacrificing about it. It wasn't like she'd been asked to give blood if he needed a transfusion! Neither was it a chance to get a long-wanted dog. Doris had never been one for pets – or hadn't been till Rex worked his way into her heart. But fond of him or not, she'd have returned him to anyone short of Ivy Waters. Alf had known all that last night. Trouble was, he'd turned coward, convinced that Ivy'd make good with her threat to take them to court and there'd be all sorts of expense ahead, let alone Doris's name getting in the papers.

And now all that seemed likely to come about. When sorting out the post that morning he'd come upon an envelope with her name on it – Mrs Alfred Thatcher – from a firm of solicitors in Kingsbury Knox, some fifteen miles from Dovecote Hatch. Hence the absent-minded act that had concerned Mrs Marshall and Miss Milligan, the bowed shoulders and his arriving at the gate to the Mullings woods without quite knowing how he got there. A thought occurred as he wheeled his bike through and closed the latch: he'd have a word with Florence. See if she had any ideas how to bring Ivy Waters to her senses before taking the letter home to Doris.

He was halfway along the path between the leafless trees when he saw Lord Edward Stodmarsh coming towards him with his yellow Labrador, Rouser. Alf still thought of him, as did most of the other villagers, as Master Ned, but deference for the young man must outweigh the affectionate informality that had existed towards the boy. The transition took adjustment on both sides. His Lordship at times longed for the carefree days when his paternal grandfather was alive, but the sense of the responsibilities that would be his when the time came had been bred into the bone. At twenty-one he was of wiry build and middle height, with reddish brown hair that had a tendency to spike up when tousled, green eyes and a liberal dusting of freckles.

'Hello!' He greeted the postman who'd dismounted the bike. A smile came and went on his angular face. 'I say, Alf, you're not looking your usual chipper self. Problem?'

'Nothing major, thank you kindly, Your Lordship. Just something me and Doris have to sort out.'

'Anything I can do to help?'

Alf repressed the urge to explain about the letter from the firm of solicitors; it wouldn't be right to put His Lordship in the middle of the carry-on with Ivy Waters. He straightened his back. 'Much appreciated, but no, sir. It will all come out in the wash. Bound to do. Well, there is something . . . if you don't object.'

'Of course.'

'I was hoping for a little chat with Florence Norris when I hand in the post, her and Doris being friendly. Get another woman's viewpoint, so to speak. That'll be all right, won't it? I won't keep her long.'

'You'd be welcome to do so, as at any other time, but she left for London yesterday afternoon to spend a week with her cousin in London.'

'So she did! Birdie . . . George Bird told me so last night at the Dog and Whistle. Can't think how I forgot.' Alf shook his head. His attempt to speak lightly was far from convincing. Ned Stodmarsh eyed him with increasing concern.

'How about Mrs McDonald?' he suggested. 'Would getting her opinion help?' He was speaking of the longtime cook at Mullings; a generous natured, understanding woman. 'No, I see that won't answer. But she'd gladly give you a cup of tea.'

'She's always ready with one.'

There was a pause, during which both men looked down at Rouser as if hoping for his contribution to the conversation. He continued to sit to heel, having been trained never to approach anyone beyond the immediate household unless invited to do so and getting a nod of agreement from his master. Alf thought of the little dog at home – the unwitting source of all the trouble – and was again tempted to unburden himself to His Lordship. Again, he resisted.

'Good boy,' he said belatedly to Rouser, who at the signal ambled up to him, tail wagging, to be patted, unaware that most of his kind despised postmen.

Immediately thereafter Alf parted from His Lordship and the Labrador, who were continuing on to the village, and pedaled along the path to where it opened onto the rear grounds of Mullings. They spread pleasantly – peacefully – before the eyes. The velvet lawns, herbaceous borders, sunken rose gardens and ornamental lake and tree-lined drive made the perfect tapestry placement for the more than two-hundred-year-old house. Its grandeur was matched by the welcoming aspect of mellowed brick walls, the differing shades of color amongst the roof tiles due to replacements over the years, and cheerfully twinkling windows.

Mrs McDonald, a tall, massively built woman with thick white hair, did offer Alf a cup of tea when he handed in the post, but he decided he'd better not.

'Thanks, but best get on home.'

Mrs McDonald was a little surprised but didn't say so to either of the kitchen maids. The only member of the staff in whom she ever confided was Florence Norris. Only a day gone and Mrs McDonald was missing her. No doubt Mollie, the head housemaid, would do a good enough job filling in as housekeeper, but the feel of the place wouldn't be the same for the next week. And Mrs McDonald didn't believe she was alone in thinking this. His Lordship would always regard Florence, whom he called Florie, as a mother figure, her having had so much to do with bringing him up as a child, and now Mrs Tressler, his maternal grandmother, had clearly become fond of her. As she bustled about readying for breakfast to be taken above stairs in an hour, Mrs McDonald hoped Florence and George Bird wouldn't tie the knot in the very near future. There'd been too many changes already over the past few years.

Meanwhile, Ned (he could never think of himself as Edward) Stodmarsh and Rouser had exited the gate at the village end of the woods and were angling left towards the green with its duck pond and scattering of oaks. Both the Dog and Whistle and the newsagent's stood on the near side facing it. Ned had hoped to see George Bird seated on a bench reading the newspaper as was his custom around this time of the morning, except during a downpour. Unfortunately today was an exception. No sign of George, although the day was dry if chilly. Ned wanted a casual word with him about Alf, but seeking him out at the pub would put too much emphasis on his concern. This was the sort of delicate situation his grandfather (*the* Edward Stodmarsh) had been so adept at handling. And

Florence – Florie always to him – wasn't here to advise. He could, of course, bring the matter up with his grandmother, Mrs Tressler. She was not as yet familiar with individual personalities, but she did understand village life; her own home in Suffolk (currently leased to an American family) being close to a hamlet that had existed since medieval times. Ned felt a pang of guilt that he still tended to think of her, fond as he was of her, as a secondary confidante. He had to change that.

He had stepped onto the green, intent on crossing over to the lane that sloped down to open country banked to the west by folds of hills, when he saw Miss Milligan and two of her boxers coming towards him. In addition to the ancient trousers and jacket that did not suit Mrs Marshall's sensibilities, she was wearing a hat that the most disreputable vagrant might have spurned, dragged down over her salt-and-pepper hair. Ned enjoyed his encounters with the forthright Miss Milligan. One never knew what would roll off her tongue. She'd once told him she had a girly pash for Major Wainwright of Green Trees. Got a thrill up her spine watching him stroke his regulation moustache while reminiscing about the Boer War as if it had been a case of sitting around in deckchairs over a bank holiday weekend. What to do with him should she reel him in was the question. She supposed she could take down her net curtains and do the dance of the seven veils. Ha ha! This had been accompanied by a poke in his ribs. Miss Milligan was no respecter of ribs, including titled ones. Ned's amusement on that occasion had sprung from picturing the ever-correct major's expression had he been privy to these remarks.

Bareheaded, Ned lifted a hand in greeting as he drew level with her. 'Good morning, Miss Milligan.'

She tipped the awful hat. 'Ah, Lord Stodmarsh! Didn't see it was you; lost in thought!' Miss Milligan had experienced no difficulty in dealing with his succeeding to the title; for her past and present slotted neatly into their respective places.

'Pleasant thoughts, I hope.'

'Sit, sir!'

Ned automatically looked around for a bench before realizing she was addressing one of the boxers who had nosed towards Rouser. 'Have to keep after Bruno's manners, or next you know he'll go to the dogs.' Miss Milligan brayed a laugh, then shook her head, brown eyes intent. 'No, Your Lordship, pleasant isn't the word for what's been going through my head. Bloody opposite, if you'll pardon my French! It has to do with Alf Thatcher.'

'Yes?' Ned's interest quickened.

'You may say it's foolish of me to get so worked up over the postman, but that man's the salt of the earth; sort that keeps the village ticking along in the jolly old way.'

'He's a great chap.' Ned smiled encouragingly. Patience was needed during conversations with Miss Milligan. Interrupting the flow only delayed getting to the heart of what she had to say.

'Not much of a brain, perhaps, but nice people so often don't; no offence intended, Your Lordship.'

'None taken.' A grin got the better of him.

'That Waters woman should be put in the stocks! I'd like to say burned at the stake, but that'd put her on a level with Joan of Arc. Heroine of mine. Often wonder if things would have ended differently for the gel if her suit of armor had come with a skirt, or been laced with ribbons. But back to Alf. Two things I can't stand.'

'Ah!' Green eyes sparkling, Ned awaited enlightenment.

'Cruelty and unsporting behavior. No wonder Mrs Marshall said Alf looked worn to the bone when she caught sight of him this morning.' She spelled out the word 'bone,' keeping an eye on the boxers so they wouldn't get excited, but even so the dogs could not restrain anticipatory glances up at her. Ned's expression reflected theirs. This might work out better than if he had found George Bird and eased into questioning him about Alf. Quite possibly George would not have been willing to confide beyond vague hints. Ned wasn't sure who the Waters woman was (his grandfather would not have been found so lacking) but they were bound to get to that eventually.

'Then of course there was his putting a letter to me through Mrs Marshall's door. Unheard of for him to make such a mistake. She and I agreed it has to be the dog business that's got him rattled.'

'Dog? What dog?'

Miss Milligan was only too happy to explain. Imparting information was meat and drink to her, especially when the recipient was as attentive as Ned. 'So there we have it,' she concluded, 'Doris Thatcher rightly refusing to give him back or cough up a penny to mollify Ivy Waters. As for Alf, if I have sized him up right, he won't want to go against his wife and has probably grown fond of the dog, but is shaking in his boots at the thought of being dragged into court before a judge itching to fine them hundreds of pounds. Load of rubbish! But that's often the mentality of those who've never so much as pinched a sweet as a child. They're petrified at the most distant prospect of the hand of the law coming down on their shoulders. It's the villains who sleep like babies.'

Ned wasn't so sure of that. Wouldn't even the most hardened criminals have moments of panic that they were being closed in upon? His spirits, however, had lifted at the thought there was something he could attempt on Alf and his wife's behalf – to intercede for them with Ivy Waters. He voiced this to Miss Milligan and she returned her glance to him after momentarily fixing it on the village street.

'Sporting of you, Your Lordship, but it wouldn't be the answer.'

'No?'

'It would probably bring Ivy round, but at a price of making her resent the Thatchers to the point of hatred. Don't want any more murders, do we?' No one had ever described Miss Milligan as tactful. Kind in her brisk way, yes, but not tuned to the sensitivities of others. Ned winced inwardly. The stain of what had happened at Mullings, the pain suffered by those he loved, was still raw for him. The cold breeze nipping at his face and neck felt like an irritant to be swatted away, but he kept his voice light.

'Anything else you can suggest?'

'Best leave it to me to get matters going in the right direction. It just came to me looking at the Dog and Whistle. Ivy isn't what you could call one of the regulars, not an every nighter, but she usually shows up once or twice a week. No,' preempting what she thought he was about to say, 'I'm not

thinking of getting a bunch of the tried and true joining me
in hauling her over the coals. Awkward for Alf if he was there,
which he usually is, and wouldn't have the desired effect any
more than your talking to her would. What I've in mind is the
complete opposite of a confrontation. Send her to Coventry.
Act like we don't see her – not so much as a speck on the
wall as far as we're concerned.'

Ned forgot she'd stung him on the quick. 'You think that
might work?'

'Confident! She's the sort of woman who can stand anything
but being ignored. Feeds on being the center of attention.
Accumulative silence will bring her to heel so fast she won't
care whether Alf or his wife Doris put us up to it or not.'

'Very wily! Do, however, bring her back into the fold, Miss
Milligan, once the point has been taken.'

Ned left her feeling quite sunny despite the breeze's deter-
mination to enlarge into a wind that would set the tree branches
rattling and scatter what birds hadn't migrated to the four
corners of the earth. He thought about returning to Mullings
immediately and regaling his grandmother with the story that
now seemed likely to reach a peaceful conclusion, but Rouser
would be disappointed if they did not extend their walk.
Crossing to the far side of the green, they took the lane that
wended down to the bridle path that ran between hedgerows
dividing a stretch of fields and pastures from the open
countryside.

They had been ambling pleasantly along, with an occasional
stick thrown and received, for some ten minutes when on
approaching a bend the clip-clop of a horse's hooves penetrated
the silence. A few further steps taken close to the verge gave
Ned sight of a young man astride a fine bay gelding. He was
familiar with both and was not particularly keen on a meeting.
The rider was Gideon Blake, only son of Winthrop Blake and
sister to Lamorna, with whom Ned had been very briefly
unofficially engaged in the days surrounding the murder at
Mullings. It was she who had ended things, but to no hard
feelings on Ned's part, having realized what he'd felt for
her was no more than a springtime infatuation arising from her
astonishing beauty.

Ned's lack of enthusiasm for now advancing towards Gideon (Giddy to family and cronies), who had drawn his horse to a halt and was looking beyond the brambles to his left, had nothing to do with any lingering discomfort on Lamorna's account. It was simply that he didn't relish being a captive audience for five, possibly ten minutes of drawling inanities. Beyond being an excellent horseman, Gideon had only one undeniable attribute – his golden-haired, blue-eyed good looks. In London it was likely his focus on them took a back seat for hours on end to gambling at his club or the racecourse and drinking himself insensible. Probably because his creditors were being difficult he'd recently returned to the country – where his thoughts need rarely stray from delight in the vision of physical perfection he bestowed on a fortunate world.

Ned did not think Gideon had seen him or Rouser, but good manners overcame disinclination and he was about to step forward and endure a snip by snip account of the fellow's latest haircut when he saw a girl with wind-whipped dark hair climb over a stile to Gideon's immediate left. His drawing to a halt and staring across the stubble field was now explained. He dismounted to strike an elegant pose, the reins dangling from his hand. His 'Hello, Mercy' drifted Ned's way but her response wasn't audible and her profile in shadow made it impossible to gauge whether she was pleased by the encounter or not.

At the time when Ned was re-crossing the green, Alf Thatcher arrived back at his home in the middle of a row of what had been almshouses. Having leaned his bike against the wall under the sitting-room window, he went through the front door into a tiny hall to be greeted enthusiastically by the small dog.

He stood staring helplessly down at it. 'Hello to you too, Rex.'

An appetizing smell reached him from the kitchen directly ahead. Doris, a neatly built woman of the same five foot four inches in height as him, was at the cooker frying pork sausages and streaky bacon. He never walked in after his early morning round without a cooked breakfast being less than ten minutes away from being put on his plate. He wondered if he should wait to give her the letter from the firm of solicitors until they'd finished eating, but that idea went out the window when she turned, took one look at him and wiped her hands on her floral pinny.

'Trouble?' She never beat around the bush.

Alf handed her the envelope, his voice cracking. 'Maybe it's not what we think. What if you had some relative out in Australia you never heard of that's died and left you a pile of money?'

She looked steadily back at him, her face as firmly controlled as her mousy hair under its net. 'You're a good man, Alf Thatcher, but you should know by now I don't need coddling. Ivy Waters has done what she threatened and much good it'll do her, seeing as she's not an ounce of right on her side.'

Alf wished he could feel as confident as Doris sounded.

SIX

Florence had settled comfortably into her visit with her cousin Hattie in the narrow, flat-chested terraced house in one of London's working-class side streets. It was named Hurst Street, but was known thereabouts as Hearse Street. Due to its proximity to a cemetery, horse-drawn hearses had been such a frequent sight some of the residents had joked they saved themselves the bother of drawing their curtains in respect by leaving them always pulled tight. That cemetery was no longer in use for burial and Hattie's next-door neighbor had said to her that a bit of life had gone out of Hurst Street.

The dim slice of hall at number twenty-two, with its steep staircase carpeted in a worn floral pattern, did not promise much for the rest of the interior beyond tired furnishings and old linoleum. But Hattie, who had been born in that house and spent her youth and much of her middle age tending her parents until their deaths, was a great believer that much could be achieved with a pot of light-colored distemper, cheerful hooked rugs and cushions sewn out of remnants. A new addition to the front room since Florence's last visit was the picture above the fireplace of a Scottish landscape. Hattie had found it in a second-hand shop and told Florence she liked to look up at it while listening to a record, worn scratchy, of Harry Lauder singing about the 'bonnie, bonnie, banks' of Loch Lomond.

Beyond family affection, the two women had a genuine liking and respect for each other that made spending time together deeply enjoyable. Each felt they invariably learned something from the other that helped clarify their individual paths. The pattern of their days that week had a cozy continuity. After breakfast they would either walk the mile or so to the little grocer's shop, not so different from the one Mrs Hewett ran in Dovecote Hatch, or take a stroll around the old cemetery squeezed in between grimly Victorian office buildings. In the afternoons they either worked on a jigsaw puzzle of the Eiffel Tower Hattie had started just before Florence's arrival, played drafts, read books from the library ten minutes away or simply sat and conversed.

On the day following her arrival in London Florence had made sure to listen for any further news reports on the wireless about the woman killed by the bus, but gleaned nothing more from that source. The next morning, on page three of the morning paper, there was a brief paragraph referencing the incident. It stated that the police were hampered in their attempts to locate persons related to or otherwise acquainted with the deceased by the fact she had been carrying no form of identification. An even shorter account of the same information appeared in that day's *Evening News*. After that, not a mention, which made dwelling further on the possibility that she might have been the woman in the headscarf who'd boarded the train at Large Middlington pointless.

It would also have been unfair to Hattie, who'd already shown more than sufficient sympathetic interest in the topic. A visitor preoccupied with gloomy thoughts would to Florence's mind be as welcome as a coffin going up and down stairs all day. Also, life had taught her the necessity of closing doors on indulgent speculation. Doing so had not been difficult concerning the recent death of Kenneth Tenneson – a man with whom she'd had no personal connection. She did not so much as know what he looked like. He had never been a visitor at Mullings and did not attend church. She had attended his funeral along with Mrs McDonald by way of representing Ned and Mrs Tressler, who were away at the time visiting her old home. Also out of respect for his two sisters, who were usually in their selected pew on a Sunday. Kenneth Tenneson's one friend (questioned at the inquest because they had been together for some hours on the afternoon of his death) was Major Wainwright; otherwise he seemed to have lived a very secluded life. Yes, the positioning of the body, his having landed on his back subsequent to his fatal fall down the stairs, had struck her as rather surprising if an accident.

George had agreed with her when she'd mentioned this to him, which he would not have done if he'd thought otherwise.

But the inquest had rendered its verdict of death by mis-
adventure. And who was she to consider herself an expert on
murder because of what had happened at Mullings? It might
have been different had there been a motive for someone to
do away with him that leaped out at one, but there was nothing
suggestive of this to set tongues wagging. He was by all
accounts a quiet, gentlemanly man. Admittedly the sisters, and
the young girl he'd taken into his home as a small child after
the death of her parents, had inherited the majority of his
estate, but they'd already been living very comfortably with
him at Bogmire House. Of course, at seventeen or so the ward
might have begun to want more from life than being cooped
up in the house with three middle-aged to elderly people.
Florence had thought when observing her profile at the graveside service that she was lovely in a dark, non-English rose
way. She had also noticed, as Mrs Trout the constable's wife
had done, the girl's reflective smile that had never faded from
her lips during Reverend Pimcrisp's creaky reading of the
verses with their inclusion of ashes to ashes, dust to dust. But
the most likely explanation for that was the contemplation of
happy memories of the man who had been a father to her.

If, as Mrs McDonald had said to Florence, it had been
Kenneth Tenneson's father found dead at the bottom of that
staircase, the situation might well have roused closer scrutiny.
Old Horatio Tenneson had been a glowering presence in top
hat and frockcoat, the terror of small children, and known to
have browbeaten his timid wife up to his last gasp. His passing
had occurred ten years previously, hers only a few months
before her son's. Of course it was always possible that Kenneth
Tenneson was not quite what he seemed – that he'd harbored
a guilty secret that had led to the making of a mortal enemy,
or that he was planning something that would have an unfa-
vorable impact on someone close to him, but Florence had
nipped such thoughts in the bud.

Her relationship with George was most frequently at the
forefront of her mind these days. She had never expected to
love again after her husband Robert had been killed in the Great
War. The same had been true for George, who'd been devoted
to his wife Betty, now gone for five years. The question troubling

Florence was whether her suggestion, made when he asked her to marry him, that they delay doing so for a year or so had been fair to him, her reasoning being that she wanted to feel better assured the household at Mullings could be managed perfectly well without her. Molly the head housemaid, now married to Grumidge the butler, would be a splendid replacement in the not-too-distant future, but she'd admitted to being unsure as yet of handling the accounts efficiently – adding that she wouldn't wish to depend too heavily on her husband's assistance in this regard. In this Molly was undoubtedly right. Doing so would diminish her in the eyes of the other staff members. In particular, trouble could be expected from Jeannie, one of the kitchen maids. She was a quick-witted hard worker but pert with it, and, as Mrs McDonald was known to put it: if given an inch of thread she'd sew you into a tangle you couldn't get out of easy even if someone handed you a pair of scissors.

George had agreed comfortably to Florence's wish in this matter, saying the last thing Lord Stodmarsh, his grandmother and indeed the staff needed was any immediate disruption of lives so recently shattered. Courting, he'd added with the smile that so endeared him to her, would make him feel young again along with having its own romantic charms. Had he, however, felt compelled to say that? Also, was she being completely honest with herself about the wait? Having worked since she was fourteen was she hesitant at the prospect of getting up each morning to a day not fully busy? She would be more than willing to help out at the Dog and Whistle, but that might be awkward for some of the regulars, feeling compelled to watch their language in front of her, former housekeeper at the great house. She could, of course, take over the book-keeping and learn to do the ordering. She knew George would be pleased for her to do so, having told her he wasn't all that keen on the arithmetic part of running the pub.

It was clear that Hattie, although she made no attempt to pry, was eager to hear how things were going between Florence and George. When Florence related her concerns she listened attentively as she always did, even over trivial matters, which this was not. Never having had a young man so much as hold her hand, she nevertheless, or perhaps for that reason, took matters of the heart seriously. She nodded before replying.

'I wouldn't worry, Florie, dear.' She was knitting a white lacy matinee coat with effortless speed. 'All will fall into place at the right time. I'm sure you can have complete trust in what George told you about being content to wait. Haven't you told me he's one of the most completely honest people in the world?'

'Yes.'

'Not one to talk to please, even with those he most cares for?'

Florence thought this through. 'No. He wouldn't; nor would he wish himself into my way of thinking. It's not in him, much as he might want to do so. He's not the man for peace at any price. And thank heaven for that. Oh, Hattie! I've been thinking like a muddle-headed schoolgirl!'

'I think that's very sweet.' They were in the front room with a fire burning in the hearth and the lamps turned on against the gathering dusk. 'And isn't it possible that when the time comes the new mistress, this nice-sounding Mrs Tressler, could have a part-time position for you; one that would allow you to come and go – correspondence to handle, that sort of thing? Lady's companion, I suppose you'd call it.'

It was an appealing idea. Mrs Tressler already sought Florence out for conversations unrelated to her work, such as who would feel snubbed if not invited to dine, or what families in Dovecote Hatch had needs she might help to meet.

Having conveyed this, Florence sat comfortably back in her easy chair, part of a three-piece suite Hattie had bought almost new from a neighbor emigrating to Australia, and turned the conversation to Hattie's knitting.

'Who is that lovely little thing for?'

'A couple round the corner's shortly expected grandchild.'

'First?'

'No.' There was hesitancy in the look Hattie returned her. 'Their son and daughter-in-law have three under five. Two boys and a girl. All dear little ones. It's her daughter this time.'

Was something not quite right with what should be an entirely happy event? A problem with the pregnancy? A threat to the life of the mother? Florence's concern was aroused, but she refrained from asking if all was going well, merely remarking that she always liked babies in white. Should Hattie wish to say more about the situation she would.

Florence had longed for a child during the years of her marriage to Robert Norris. They had not been blessed with one, but later she had held a close role in Ned's childhood. Their bond had been encouraged by his grandparents, Lord and Lady Stodmarsh, and his other grandmother, Mrs Tressler, had often expressed her gratitude for it. George and his wife Betty, also childless, had focused their affection on his godson, Jim.

Hattie agreed about the white.

Florence glanced up at the Scottish landscape above the fireplace and asked the question, not only as a means of changing the subject but because the thought had crossed her mind before. 'Would you ever like to go there?'

'Where, dear?'

'To Scotland.'

Hattie followed her gaze. 'You know, I think I would,' her smile was wistful, 'and not just because of Harry Lauder singing about it in that voice sounding like it has footsteps tramping through the ages in it. When I was about ten there was a girl in my class at school that came from Scotland; some little village in the Highlands. The way she talked about it – how lovely it was with the mountains purple with heather and the mists that would come over the lochs – well, I've never forgotten.'

'Perhaps one day we could go together.'

'That'd be nice. Still, I don't think it would do, Florie. It's one thing you leaving George to come here for a week, but a proper holiday without him – I couldn't feel right about it. Besides, you know me; I'm not one for stirring more than a few miles beyond the nest. And there are the lodgers – I know there's only one at the moment, and he's away quite a bit with his job these days, but usually there's two. Only I like taking my time picking the right person.'

'Couldn't a neighbor help out with them?'

'I suppose so, if ever I got my courage up to go – maybe on one of those coach tours.' Hattie picked up her knitting that she'd let rest in her lap. 'Vera and Gerry Carter down the road have made it clear they'd be more than pleased to pitch in any time if needed.'

'Well, there you are!'

Hattie finished a row and started another. 'They're the couple that's grandparents to this baby on the way. I didn't know whether to tell you or not, Florie – it could come off like gossip, but I think it says a lot about them being a special sort of people. You see, the girl, their daughter, isn't married.'

'It happens, Hattie.'

'Of course it does, though you wouldn't think so for the carrying on like the world's come to an end. All too often the girl's turned out onto the street and told never to darken the door again, sometimes after she's been knocked half senseless by her father for bringing disgrace on the family. But that's not the way Vera and Gerry took the news. Oh, they were sad, disappointed. Who wouldn't be? Then they sat down with Lizzie and asked her if she wanted to marry the boy – not what you could call the steady type, rather too keen on the drink. If she did, they'd support her. If not, they'd make sure she and the baby got along just fine without him.'

'What did she say?'

'That after the way he'd turned on her when she told him she was in a pickle she hoped he'd stay as far away from her as possible. She'd been worried Gerry would go round and order him to marry her, but he – Gerry – said no daughter of his was going to sign on for life with a man she didn't love.'

'That is a heart-warming story,' said Florence.

'Of course, they know it won't be easy-going, people being so judgmental. One way would've been for Lizzie to leave the baby with them while she went away to make a life for herself. Vera and Gerry offered that but it's not what she wanted. She's a very nice girl, as I'm sure can be said of a lot of unmarried mothers.' Hattie sighed.

'Has it been thought of that they should all move somewhere

new, have Lizzie wear a wedding ring and say she was widowed? Of course, she's very young for that to be entirely credible, but it would be hard to prove untrue.'

'It wouldn't be easy for Gerry to get another job, but that's not the reason they took that out of the picture. He says secrets have a way of coming home to roost and when they do the price paid is way too high.'

That night Florence had trouble sleeping. Murky thoughts of horse-drawn hearses passing along Hurst Street threaded into a dream of one stopping in the depths of a wood. A young girl with long dark hair stepped out of it and glided down a ribbon of pathway to a clearing in which a grave had been dug. Standing around it were figures garbed in black. One raised a heavy veil, revealing the face of the woman who had boarded the train at Large Middlington. A shadow formed behind her; that of the girl, pushing her with skeletal hands over the rim of the grave, now panting forth steam. Florence awoke to a voice crying out a word inside her head. The word was 'mercy,' and it came to her with slowly indrawn breaths that such was the name of Kenneth Tenneson's young ward. Mercy. So unusual, with overtones of Oliver Cromwell's Puritan times, she had thought when told of it.

No deep delving was needed to figure out that dream. Hattie's talk of Lizzie Carter's baby and the decision to make no secret of the truth as the best way of avoiding trouble down the road had connected in Florence's subconscious with a girl facing grief at the funeral of the man who had raised her when she'd been left otherwise alone in the world. As for the woman in the headscarf, it was inevitable she should put in an appearance. Before going down to breakfast Florence lay hoping that, whether alive or dead, she had known some mercy in her life.

That day Florence took Hattie to lunch at D.H. Evans as she had planned on doing and afterwards they had a pleasant ramble through the departments, lingering in Woolen Materials, where Hattie found a remnant in a pleasing blue and lavender plaid sufficient to make a skirt with a box pleat. Florence would very much have liked to buy it for her but was too sensitive to Hattie's pride to press the issue. A blouse to go with it would make the right Christmas present.

Hattie produced her purse, the purchase was made and they spent another half hour contentedly selecting a yard of lining, reels of cotton and two waist side buttons, the second as a spare, because, as Hattie said, it was in the nature of buttons – however well sewn on – to come off and get lost.

'In that library book I finished last night – *The Body in the Buttery*,' she told Florence as they wandered through the china department, 'it was a missing button that provided the vital clue to bringing the murderer to justice. I must say I was sad when he was hanged at the end, Florie dear; it seemed rather too severe. He was such a nice man underneath it all, so good to his family, and I did feel he was pushed to his limit. We all have one, though I can't say I've ever felt like murdering someone with, or without, a blunt instrument.'

Florence smiled. It was impossible to picture Hattie bringing a hammer down on the wickedest head, except, that is, in defense of a third party. Despite her gentle, spinsterish appearance she did not lack courage.

'But in this case the victim was a very trying woman, the sort that means well and in the process never stops talking, unaware of setting her listeners' nerves crawling from the strain because of being kept from things they just have to do.' Hattie stopped speaking, her expression stricken. 'Oh, dear! Here I am being just as insensitive, talking about death, even if a made-up one, when I know you must be worrying about that woman who went under the bus in case she was the one on the railway platform that traveled up to London with you in the same railway carriage. It's not that you've seemed preoccupied, but it wouldn't be in your nature not to wish to know if they were one and the same.'

Florence took her arm. 'I enjoyed listening to your story and agree with you about well-meaning people. I've never thought the description a compliment. Indeed, it seems to me a risky trait. And I didn't make any association between the fictional murder and that poor creature, whoever she was.'

'So kind of you to say!' Hattie brightened.

'But I do admit she was in a dream I had last night.'

'Even if we refuse to dwell, as is your way, Florie, our resting minds will push concerns to the surface,' Hattie continued as they walked on. 'Think me foolish, dear, but I've been wondering if there isn't some way you could find out? What about the police inspector you met during that difficult time?' Hattie was always delicate in her phrasing regarding the murder at Mullings. 'It sounded to me as though he liked you, Florie. Couldn't you get in touch with him and ask him, as a favor, to look into the matter? See if the sadly departed fitted your description? Of course, lots of women might in a general sort of way, but let's say she was six feet tall or extremely fat – that would let you know she wasn't your one.'

They emerged into the bustle of Oxford Street and Florence waited to answer until they had sidestepped a gentleman whose bowler hat and furled umbrella appeared to have endowed him with the belief he owned the entire pavement.

'That thought had crossed my mind. Inspector LeCrane's appearance and manner is deceptive, giving off an air of unapproachability, but he could not have been more understanding of how I was placed at the time – the tangled loyalties. Perhaps I should write to him.' They had a stretch of pavement to themselves; Florence took Hattie's arm. 'The only thing against it is the fear of coming across as a fool. And if there is the faintest chance of providing a link to the identity of the dead woman, I can't let that stand in the way. The one I saw must either live, or have lived, in or near Large Middlington to have caught the train there; or had some reason to visit the area – friends, relatives, or the opportunity of a job. So many possible reasons, making for people . . . at least someone who might know something of her history.'

Florence and Hattie stayed with this subject briefly before turning to other topics, including Christmas not being far off. On their return to Hurst Street they discovered that a letter had been delivered, from George. This was surprising, because he had suggested to Florence that they not write because he didn't want her taking time with paper and ink when she could be engaged with Hattie. She wasn't alarmed, but certainly eager to know the contents. Hattie left her alone in the front room with the letter, saying she would make a pot of tea. When she returned five minutes later with the tray and seated herself, Florence held out the two refolded sheets.

'I'd like you to read this – such a coincidence it coming right after our discussing Inspector LeCrane. On the evening of the day I got here he showed up at the Dog and Whistle. He wanted to talk to me about what he considers a suspicious death in the village – that of the Mr Tenneson I wrote to you about, killed from a fall down the stairs. George explained that I was away and after they'd chatted for a while Inspector LeCrane seemed to think he, George, might be of help too in uncovering anything suggestive of murder.'

'I imagine a lot gets said in pubs without people realizing what they've let slip,' said Hattie placidly.

'Yes.'

'And you've already shown the inspector you're a keen observer of human nature.'

'Only perhaps when it's about something right under my nose. George delayed letting me know about this till the tail end of my visit and would have preferred to wait until we were together. However, Inspector LeCrane would like the three of us to meet, if possible, the day after tomorrow upon my arrival back at Large Middlington. Apparently there's a hotel near the station where we could converse without attracting attention.'

'Such an opportunity to talk to the inspector about that other matter! As you say,' Hattie unfolded the letter, 'so coincidental, this, after our just talking about him.'

Florence agreed as she poured their tea while Hattie read. In the weeks to come when certain pieces began to fall into place, she was to remember much of their conversation from that afternoon and wonder if coincidences ever deserved to be called fate. So much could hinge on a button – one that could hang a person. One who, unlike the murderer in *The Body in the Buttery,* might be guilty of nothing more than descending a staircase at the wrong time.

SEVEN

On the subject of letters . . . the one Alf Thatcher
dolefully handed over to his wife the day after
Florence left for London was from a firm of solicitors
named Savage & Pritchard.

'You should've opened it,' said Doris, 'instead of worrying
yourself sick. You're every bit as pale as when you have it
bad with lumbago.'

Alf shook his head. 'I've never opened anything addressed
to you and wasn't about to start. Like I've said before, my
father used to read anything that came for my mother, even
birthday cards, and I vowed I'd never do that. It's the sort of
thing that takes a woman down, has always been my thinking.'

'And I've appreciated that.' Doris wasn't going to argue that
situations altered cases. 'You sit yourself down at the table,'
they were in the kitchen, 'while I pour you a cuppa.' The little
dog, Rex, having greeted Alf eagerly at the door, settled into
his basket by the domestic boiler, unaware he was the cause
of distress.

As feared, the letter requested that Doris present herself at
the offices of Savage & Pritchard at her earliest possible opportunity, there being a matter of considerable import to discuss
with her. An appointment time of three o'clock on the coming
Friday, 18 November had been set aside for her. A response
as to whether or not this was convenient would be appreciated.
It was signed by Henry T. Pritchard.

The letterhead provided an address in Kingsbury Knox, a
market town located on the far side of Large Middlington,
itself about eight miles from Dovecote Hatch. The quality of
the creamy vellum was such that it could have handsomely
papered the walls of Mullings, or so thought Doris, whilst
determined not to be intimidated. Alf cleared his throat after
she'd finished reading the contents out loud. 'Seems to me
that *yours faithfully* is downright cheek, him being on Ivy

Waters's side, not yours. But maybe,' he attempted a smile, 'we're better off with him than his partner, Mr Savage.'

'That's right,' said Doris, although she'd never put any stock in names. She'd known a Mrs Sweet who was anything but. 'There's no need for you to come with me, though I know you're willing.'

Alf looked shocked. ''Course I'll be there, backing you to the hilt; though I don't see you're forced to go Friday to suit Mr Pritchard.'

'Now then, Alf,' Doris responded briskly, 'you know delaying's not the answer if we want Ivy Waters to stop hounding us. Best to get it over with soon as possible. I'll let the man have his say; then I'll have mine. Better tell Mrs Hewett today she'll have to find someone else to do your afternoon round on Friday.'

'She'll want to know why.'

'Like that'll matter; there's not many in the village who don't know what's been going on and very few are on Ivy's side. Soon as we've finished breakfast I'll write back to Mr Pritchard saying we'll be at his office as requested. And this evening you go along to the Dog and Whistle and talk to George; that'll lift your spirits some. And he'll be especially glad for a chinwag with Florence away.'

'I wouldn't want to be overheard and have it get back to Ivy that this business has got us shaken.'

'Then ask if he'll meet you on the green tomorrow morning when he goes to get his paper.'

'That's the ticket.' It caught at Alf that Doris was boosting his spirits when it should've been the other way round, making him a pitiful excuse for a husband. He found himself wondering if Eliza Spellbinder – condemned and hanged for a witch when her neighbors turned on her – would've been spared if she'd had a man with an inch of spine standing up for her. And he'd only one to deal with, not a mob. The next morning he took Doris up a cup of tea before setting off on his early round, after which he did meet up with George for a chat. Getting the subject off his chest did help some, especially as his friend, with his access to village chatter, seemed to think Ivy Waters might already have started regretting her carry-on about Rex, and it would all blow over. He couldn't be pressed into saying more but he wasn't one to speak idly.

Even so, it seemed to Alf that Friday crawled round the long way. He and Doris allowed themselves extra time to get to Kingsbury Knox before three o'clock, because doing so required an exchange of buses and the second one didn't always come on time. Doris wore a red coat with a black astrakhan collar. Red wasn't a color she would normally have chosen. To her mind it smacked of trying to draw attention, which wasn't her way. It was the same with her spotlessly clean, uncluttered home; her taste ran to fawn and light shades of green. However, as she explained to Alf, she'd got the coat from the church bazaar in September, and at half a crown it was too much of a bargain to pass up – even after allowing one and six for Miss Hatmaker, the village seamstress, to shorten the hem.

'You look very smart,' said Alf when they were seated on the bus out of Dovecote Hatch, not letting on that he wished the coat wasn't so bright. 'Do me proud, you do, Doris.' He could see Elsie Trout, the constable's wife – two in front of them across the aisle – was looking over her shoulder at them. Another time, her mind on where she was off to, she might not have noticed them. It was silly to feel awkward, but there it was. His family had never had anything to do with solicitors and he'd certainly never dreamed he'd be the first. The horrible thought formed in his mind that he could murder Ivy Waters. Actually enjoy it. And him the sort who thought it unfair to label all conscientious objectors sniveling cowards, to say nothing of how he'd felt about that bad business at Mullings.

'And you look nice,' said Doris, handbag clutched on her knees.

He was wearing his one suit, usually reserved for funerals, weddings and very occasional church attendance in an attempt at smartening up his old tweed coat and cap. 'What you thinking, love?' he whispered.

'About leaving Rex on his own for however long this is going to take.' The bus lurched around a corner before its smooth run along the road into Large Middlington. It was a mild day for that time of year and usually it would have been restful

looking out at the countryside. 'What if he needs to go out
and he makes a mess?' This thought horrified Doris as much
as Alf's thoughts of murdering Ivy had appalled him. It wasn't
that she made a god of her home, as her late brother's wife,
Winnie, had frequently hinted she did; she just liked things
clean.

Alf attempted to reassure her that Rex could be trusted. He
knew she'd never have considered having a dog under normal
circumstances, which made what she'd gone through for Rex
heroic.

'If it'd been tomorrow, being a Saturday, we could have
asked young Rupert Trout to come in and stay with him. It's
nice he still comes round after school to see him and I don't
think it's just because he feels responsible, which he didn't
ought, for the accident.'

Alf hoped Elsie Trout wouldn't turn round again at catching
her son's name. She didn't, but that didn't mean she hadn't
heard and wouldn't ask before getting off the bus why they'd
been talking about Rupert – in a pleasant, conversational way
as any mother might. She was a nice woman. He had nothing
against her. He'd been sorry when Mrs Hewett had told him
Elsie hadn't been able to find a job cleaning after trying several
places. Probably, had been Mrs Hewlett's take, some people
didn't like the idea of the police constable's wife getting to
know the ins and outs of what went on in their homes. They'd
be worried she'd make something big out of small things
they'd just as soon be kept on the quiet, and fill her husband's
ears with it. Thinking about Constable Trout, Alf regretted not
being man enough to set aside his embarrassment about where
he and Doris were headed this afternoon and ask him to keep
an eye on the house while they were gone. What if Ivy, knowing
the coast was clear, decided to get in and take Rex? Easy
enough to break the little window over the sink, reach in to
open the larger one to the side and step down onto the draining
board. Alf's father had repaired windows and been kept busy
by customers who'd locked themselves out of their homes and
been forced to this way of entry.

Alf was still brooding over this dire possibility when the
bus pulled up at the stop he and Doris wanted. Fortunately

Elsie Trout had got off at the one before and only turned to smile and wave before doing so. A look at them made clear they weren't in the mood for chit-chat, let alone questions.

'Maybe we should buy a bottle of Dettol,' Doris said as they crossed the road to the stop where they'd wait for their next bus. 'The one we've got is only half full.'

'There's a spare in the pantry. I noticed it yesterday.'

'So there is. There's probably a couple. I never like to run out.' She added on a sigh, 'And no matter – he's only a little dog.'

Alf squeezed her hand. She was, and had always been, in his eyes, a remarkable woman. The bus arrived on time, leaving them a good half hour before they must present themselves at Savage & Pritchard. He suggested going into a café for a pot of tea, knowing he couldn't get a cup down, but Doris said she'd rather they just have a look in shop windows. Neither went often to Kingsbury Knox, but as the address they needed was in the high street, no wandering search was needed to find it. They eyed the department store's display of a three-piece suite and agreed it was smart but didn't look comfortable. Two doors down they paused to look at a peacock-blue satin evening gown tossed over a gilt chair. Doris said it should've been on a hanger. She didn't think being artistic an excuse for untidiness, but she could picture it looking nice on Lamorna Blake of the Manor at Large Middlington. And did Alf know that her wastrel brother was back at home for a spell? Alf said he had heard that was so because the lad had got into debt in London and was now hankering after some local girl, bound to be one of the society misses, but he hadn't attended to which one she was, not being interested. Doris replied it was a shame Mr Blake didn't take a leaf out of young Lord Stodmarsh's book and be a credit to his position in life.

By this time they had reached the premises of Savage & Pritchard. The building was two-storied above an iron-railed basement with a vigorously scrubbed white step and a black enameled front door, its brasses gleaming. Doris, who had pictured a shabby establishment of the sort likely to be occupied by a down-at-heel practitioner of law, liable to handle

cases a more successful solicitor would scorn to take, felt her
confidence dwindle.

Alf tried the door and when it did not open rang the bell.
Within seconds they were admitted by a woman in a gray suit
with a glimpse of a starched white blouse, wearing spectacles
and her hair wound into earphones. Her manner was that of
an efficient private secretary – crisply pleasant.

'Mr and Mrs Thatcher,' she beckoned them forward, 'thank
you for being punctual. Mr Pritchard is expecting you.' A
suggestion of his being a very busy man. 'Please be seated
while I ring up to him.' She indicated two leather chairs before
crossing to the desk at the far end of the room. It held a typewriter and a telephone and neat stacks of books and papers.
The staircase to the left was carpeted in a velvety maroon; its
brassy rods gleamed as if polished with sunlight, as did the
wooden floor, and bookcases and a couple of small tables
topped with crystal vases of chrysanthemums. It must once
have been the hall of a private home, thought Alf, holding his
cap between his knees. Doris hoped he wasn't about to fidget
with it. It wouldn't do to give away that they were intimidated.
The secretary had tugged at a bell pull and footsteps sounded
above. Probably another woman, or Mr Pritchard's clerk sent
to fetch them. Doris was suddenly glad of the red coat and
black astrakhan hat matching its collar. Both were quality.
Whoever had owned them first hadn't needed to buy on the
cheap.

A man was descending the stairs, nipping down them in
twinkle-toed fashion. A short, rotund man in a navy blue
pinstriped suit with a cherubic face and what little hair he had
left a circling of white thistledown. Amazingly, attached to
that face was a beaming smile. Alf and Doris exchanged looks
as they got to their feet. The same thought was in both their
heads. The clerk. Alf sought amusement in wondering if he
was paid a shilling every time he performed the task of leading
clients up to Mr Pritchard's or his partner, Mr Savage's office.

'Why, Mr Pritchard!' exclaimed the secretary. 'I was just
about to . . .'

'Oh, no, no!' He peeked over the banisters at her. 'You're
busy this afternoon, Miss Goodwin, even busier than usual,

and I know your bunions have been bothering you. I wouldn't expect . . . besides, with this being Mr and Mrs Thatcher's first visit I felt it incumbent on me to escort them up myself.'

First! That suggested they'd have to return. Oh, really! Doris would set him straight about that in a hurry. Mr Pritchard skipped towards her and Alf, smile expanding. 'Such a pleasure,' he said, pumping their hands.

'It may be for you,' said Doris. 'As for my husband and me, we'll have to see, won't we?'

'Oh, quite, quite,' returned Mr Pritchard with undiminished cheer, 'you have to be wondering, my letter coming out of the blue.'

'Can't say that.' Alf fidgeted with his cap. 'Bracing for it, so to speak.'

'Indeed, is that so? Well, my dear sir, I must say that comes as a surprise!' Mr Pritchard demonstrated his capacity for more than one facial expression by looking perplexed. 'I wouldn't have thought . . . but let us proceed to my office for a full and frank discussion.'

Doris and Alf followed him up the stairs to a gallery with a number of doors on the wall facing them. All were closed except for the one to their immediate left. Mr Pritchard led them through the opening into a largish room with dark green wallpaper. In some spaces it would have looked dismal, but here, coupled with wall lamps and framed old maps, it added coziness. Again came the rich smell of furniture polish. A large desk and a brown leather chair were positioned with their backs to the window overlooking the high street. Doris noted with begrudging approval that the contents of the desk top were as neatly organized as the secretary's had been. Angled in front were two chairs covered in a tapestry material. The wall opposite was lined with oak filing cabinets and in the middle of the far one was an iron-fronted fireplace with flames leaping from crimson coals. Above this hung a portrait of a man bearing a strong resemblance to Mr Pritchard. It was slightly askew, meaning Doris would need to avoid looking in its direction or the urge to straighten it would set her hands itching.

After closing the door through which the rapid clacketing

of the below-stairs typewriter had penetrated, Mr Pritchard gave a nod towards the painting. 'My late partner, Evelyn Savage. Also my first cousin. Most genial of souls, despite the surname. Families! Fortunate when members can get along.' It seemed to both Doris and Alf that he was eyeing them hopefully. Was he leading into suggesting it would be nice if neighbors – implying them and Ivy Waters – could do the same? Instead he invited them to seat themselves in the tapestry chairs, before enquiring tentatively if either of them would care for a glass of sherry.

Talk about trying to get on our good side, thought Doris. Reading her mind, Alf refused for them, but being the man he was he softened what could have sounded like a rebuff by saying it might have been different if the offer had been for parsnip wine, which Doris enjoyed a sip of now and then. To which she responded firmly, 'Not when I need to keep my wits about me, I don't.'

'Ah, yes, indeed!' Pausing at the side of the desk, Mr Pritchard picked up a silver box. Lifting the lid, he held it towards them. 'Does the same apply to cigarettes? Or don't either of you smoke?'

'Thanks ever so, but—' started Alf, again twiddling with his cap.

'We don't,' cut in Doris. 'He did when we met, but I told him I wouldn't marry him if he didn't stop. No offence, Mr Pritchard, but to my mind it's a dirty habit. Smell gets into everything.'

'Quite, quite! Couldn't agree with you more!' He returned the box to the desk before rounding it to position himself in a brown leather chair – of a size to devour him. 'One trusts, however, you'll understand the obligation to keep a supply of cigarettes on hand for those who have run out of their own and can't sit five minutes without lighting up. Now, let us come to the matter in hand. Your wedding took place in Chelmsford, Essex, I understand.'

'Well, now,' said Doris, beginning to lose patience, 'I can't see why Ivy Waters would feel the need to mention that. What's it to do with the price of tea in China? Unless she'd got the idea – with us not going to church regular – that it took place in a registry office, which might add proof that we're not proper Christians.'

Mr Pritchard blinked. 'My dear lady, I'm afraid I don't follow! Who, if I may ask, is this Ivy Walters?'

Doris returned the blink, momentarily incapable of speech.

Alf dropped his cap. 'Waters,' he corrected.

Mr Pritchard shook his head. 'Doesn't ping a triangle, let alone ring a bell.'

'She's a neighbor that's accused Doris of stealing her dog,' Alf pursued. 'All a load of rubbish – it's more that she didn't want him after he got knocked down in the street. She told Doris to do what she liked with him. Then after we'd got him well again she saw a way to squeeze money out of us for not returning him, anywhere from two to five pounds, depending on the day. And for him to be neglected all over again.'

'Shocking! Pedigree? Not that it makes a difference, except to her reasoning on price.'

'Mongrel,' said Alf, 'though she insists he's a wire-haired terrier. He could have some of that in him, though the vet said a lot else besides. Got him off the market for half a crown, was what Ivy told people when she first got him. Nice little fellow, name of Rex. He filled out after we took him; doubt if he'd had a proper meal one day out of seven beforehand. These last few weeks she's been threatening to go to a solicitor, so naturally we thought . . .' His voice trailed away.

'It's not like we couldn't have taken it from our post office book,' said Doris, 'but it's been the principle.'

'Certainly. Blackmail does not strike me as too strong a word for what you have been subjected to. But I fear we have been at cross purposes.' Mr Pritchard reached for a pair of gold-rimmed spectacles on his blotting pad and perched them on his nose, suggesting the situation had reached a turn requiring clearer physical as well as mental vision. 'The matter I wish to discuss with you, Mrs Thatcher, does not spring from any communication regarding a dog from this unpleasant-sounding woman. I can also assure you that no respectable solicitor would agree to handle such a case. As for less scrupulous members of our profession, which I am glad to say do not abound in this locality, their only inducement would be the opportunity to profit from a foolish woman's spite.'

'Well, then,' Doris patted Alf's arm, 'I must say that's a relief.'

'Unless,' he wasn't quite ready to breathe a sigh of relief, 'what you're about to tell us is going to put us in another kind of nasty spot. Not that we've anything on our consciences, but Doris and me aren't the sort to get letters from solicitors. I tried to make a joke of it when yours came, despite our worries about Ivy Waters, said maybe some distant relative of Doris she'd never heard of out in Australia had left her a bundle of money, but . . .'

'And let's back up a bit if you don't object, Mr Pritchard.' Doris squared her handbag on her knees, always a sign she meant business. 'If you didn't get it from Ivy Waters that Alf and me was married in Chelmsford, just how did you come by that tidbit?'

'Indeed, indeed! Ah, where to begin?' Mr Pritchard tapped his fingers on the desk. 'I suppose that is as good a place as any. I have been struggling over the past few days as to how best to broach what is bound to come as an immense surprise. Whether pleasant, the complete reverse, or a mixture of both has been the question.'

'Well,' said Doris, her head in a whirl, 'you certainly looked cheerful enough bringing us up here. Not to mince words, I thought, and I know Alf did too, that it was a case of welcoming a lamb to the slaughter.'

This received a nod of agreement from Alf, tempered by an apologetic look. 'No offence intended, seeing like you said we've been at cross purposes.'

'None taken, I do profoundly assure you both.' Mr Pritchard had now taken on the appearance of a stone cherub uncertain of his perch on a graveyard monument. He cleared his throat and adjusted the spectacles. 'One endeavored to be optimistic that the positive nature of what it is my responsibility to impart might counter the negative aspects, as you may understandably view them, Mrs Thatcher.'

'Best have the good bit first.' Doris's voice was steady, but she clutched at her handbag as if it were a life raft.

'Admirable, admirable! Your husband's suggestion, that the situation requiring your presence here might be in the nature of a bequest, however jokingly made, is in fact the situation. It is a sizeable one, made to you in a handwritten document by a recently deceased client of mine. Though not drawn up by myself, or other legal practitioners, it was duly signed by the testator and witnessed by two disinterested parties on the very day of death, thereby nullifying the one in my keeping thought to be in good standing at the time of his death.'

'Well, I never did!' was the best Doris could manage. Alf felt as though he'd suddenly come down with lockjaw.

'I need hardly say this new will set me back on my toes.' Mr Pritchard spread his small, plump hands. 'Dear, me, yes! It was brought to me on the afternoon prior to the date of my writing to you by one of those two witnesses, who had held onto it, as requested by the party concerned, until a private investigator, hired for the purpose of locating your whereabouts, Mrs Thatcher, succeeded in doing so. This had required discovering your married name, your maiden one of Green being sufficiently common as to extend the process a little longer than would otherwise have been necessary. Although I would have thought a visit to Somerset House should have made for an easy enough job of it, but I suppose the investigator may have been on other cases at the same time, or if charging by the hour – not that one wishes to cast aspersions . . .'

'So that's how you knew we'd been married in Chelmsford!' Doris was wishing she could set her hands on a cup of tea. She wanted to tell Mr Pritchard to stop going round the mulberry bush and give her the name of the person who'd gone to all that trouble to leave her something in a will. But it wouldn't do to look on the grab.

'The surprise was discovering you had returned after many years to live in Dovecote Hatch, where you were born at seven thirty-one a.m. on the seventeenth of September, 1880; your delivery having been assisted by a midwife by the name of,' he peeked inside the folder, 'Joan Liverwidge.'

'That's right. My grandmother.'

'I'm afraid not.'

'But Mr Pritchard, you just said—' Alf floundered.

'That Joan Liverwidge was present at your wife's birth, yes, yes, indeed! But,' the bespectacled eyes fixed mournfully on Doris, 'here is where I come to the difficult part of the revelation, Mrs Thatcher. Joan Liverwidge was in fact not your maternal grandmother. Neither were her daughter and son-in-law, Maude and Charles Green, your flesh and blood parents. The child born to them was a boy. At eleven fifty-five a.m. on that same date Mrs Liverwidge assisted at the birth of a girl.'

Doris, unaware that Alf had risen and was standing behind her, gripping her shoulders, spoke with incredible calmness. 'And you're saying that was me?'

'Yes, your parents were—'

'I'd as soon you don't call them that, if it's all the same with you, Mr Pritchard.'

'Please forgive me, Mrs Thatcher. I can only imagine . . . no, of course I can't! You were born to Irma and Horatio Tenneson.'

'Of Bogmire House, that creepy old place on the Little Middleton Road? And you're saying – though I'm taking it with a large pinch of salt – that there was a switch! Why on earth? It doesn't make sense. It's the sort of thing you hear said has happened with royalty when a male heir was all important, even if it meant passing the washerwoman's son off in the role if the King wasn't to chop off the Queen's head. But that's probably a lot of rubbish too.'

'The situation in which you have been placed is not dissimilar. The Tennesons already had two daughters, and Irma Tenneson was petrified that her husband, never an even-tempered man, would be enraged to the point of violence on being informed she'd produced another girl. She had spoken of her fear to Joan Liverwidge, whose daughter was expecting close to the same date. And the plot was hatched for the possibility of an exchange. Mr and Mrs Green were in much straitened circumstances: he was out of work and they'd been desperately wondering which way to turn. They already had a son, to soften the blow, in addition to a substantial payment, or such was Irma Tenneson's thinking as she confessed on her deathbed to the man who had until then believed he was her son.'

'Kenneth Tenneson?' Alf drew Doris back against him. 'Him who died just recent from a fall down the stairs! I've delivered the post to Bogmire for years,' he added. 'This is too much to take in! I think my wife could do with a good strong cup of tea.'

Mr Pritchard displayed relief at being able to supply a need. 'I'll have Miss Goodwin bring up a tray, and then to the reading of the will.' He reached for a bell pull at the side of the desk, his eyes lowered. 'I hope you will find the monetary portion of the bequest satisfactory, Mrs Thatcher.'

'Portion? What else is there?' A shaky laugh followed Doris's sharp enquiry. 'Not another dog, I hope.'

'No, no! I can imagine how ill that would sit with you coming on recent events.'

'Then what?'

'Mr Tenneson has left you Bogmire House.'

Alf, still standing behind Doris, went rigid. 'But he had two sisters, or I suppose I should say ladies thinking that's what they were – living there! And a young girl he took in when her parents died; leastwise that's how I heard it went. They're not going to like this one bit!'

'And I can't say as I blame them,' said Doris. 'Not their fault, any of this, is it? Got to be fair-minded!'

Mr Hendrick sighed. 'I don't feel I can venture an opinion regarding the young lady's reaction. I do, however, fear that the Misses Matilda and Lettice Tenneson will, far from embracing the news of a long-lost sister, go up in smoke when I break the news of the newly found will to them tomorrow morning. Ah, but here comes Miss Goodwin with the tea tray!' His features perked up. 'As my late partner Evelyn Savage used to say, there's nothing like a good cup of Darjeeling to banish nightmare eventualities.'

EIGHT

'Good day, Your Lordship.' Thus was Ned Stodmarsh greeted by Willie Griggs, one of the under gardeners, a lad of perhaps sixteen, as he set off across the rear lawn of Mullings at a little after seven the next day on his morning walk with Rouser the Labrador at his side. They were headed as usual for the earthen path leading into the village.

'And to you, Willie.' Ned paused in his stride on coming up with the lad raking fallen leaves into a pile, their having blown onto the lawn from the edge of the woods. Rouser sat without the necessity of being told to do so. Ned considered it important to have a pleasant word with members of the outdoor staff whenever the opportunity arose and time permitted. That had been his grandfather, the late Lord Stodmarsh's way, and he had instilled early in Ned the value of demonstrating appreciation for all who labored on the family's behalf. 'Everything going well?'

'Yes, Your Lordship; I enjoy the work.'

Ned sensed hesitancy. 'But something's troubling you.'

'I'm not sure that it should, but I've been wondering if I should say anything to Mr Brown.' Brown was the head gardener. 'Don't want him thinking me a dunderhead when Mrs McDonald could've asked for it for the pot. A chicken is what I'm talking about, Your Lordship. I noticed this morning one was missing from the hen house. A Rhode Island Red. There was seven of them and now there's only six. I wouldn't've thought anything about it, if I hadn't just noticed the door to the potting shed was left ajar and the sack of seed potatoes opened up.'

'Sounds like a tramp in search of a meal,' said Ned easily. 'And who can begrudge it? Go ahead and tell Brown. He won't think you a fool or that you're overstepping your position. He's a man who admires initiative.'

'Very grateful, Your Lordship.'

Ned had received good reports of Willie from Brown. The lad had only worked at Mullings for a couple of months, but his family had lived in Dovecote Hatch for generations. Old Mrs Weedy of Laurel Cottage, very much a local character and fount of otherwise forgotten lore, was in some way related to him. After asking Willie how he was settling in and receiving a beaming response, he enquired after Mrs Weedy's health.

'Remarkable for a body her age, though she bin a mite upset lately over Mr Tenneson's death.'

'The man who lived at Bogmire?'

'That's it, Your Lordship. What has her bothered most is how the young lady he brought up has to be feeling now he's gone and it's just her and his two sisters. Cousin Aggie, Mrs Weedy, that is, 'as always bin right fond of her, seeing how she often stops by at the cottage for a cup o' tea and has done since she were a nipper.'

'A shade grim, are the two older Miss Tennesons?' Ned was more interested than his casual tone implied. On his return to Mullings a few days previously after sighting Gideon Blake astride his horse on the bridle path below the green and hearing him address the girl who'd come across the field as 'Mercy', he'd gone to the kitchen and asked Mrs McDonald if she knew of a young woman with dark hair by that name. Had Florie not been away he would naturally have posed the question to her, but he and Mrs McDonald had been on excellent terms in his boyhood days, when he would seek her out for a treat straight out of the oven. She'd responded readily that he had to be talking about Mercy Tenneson, it being an unusual Christian name these days, though it might have been common enough once upon a time. She'd added as Ned reached into a tin for one of her rock cakes (prime favorites of his) that she could only claim to have seen Miss Tenneson once for sure, a few weeks back at her guardian's funeral, when she'd not been standing close enough to get a clear look at her. But she had heard through the grapevine that she was lovely in a haunting sort of way.

Ned now noticed that Willie, rake held inclined against his side, was looking at him hesitantly. It took him a moment to recall what he'd said to the boy. Oh, yes! It had been about the two older Miss Tennesons!

'I don't like to talk ill of nobody, Your Lordship . . .'

Ned felt his face flush. How could he have been so thoughtless? Grandfather would never have put a member of the staff in the predicament of asking his, or her, negative opinion of any of the villagers. 'I apologize, Willie; that was an unforgivable question.'

'Oh, no, Your Lordship! It's natural you'd be interested in how things are at Bogmire with Mr Tenneson not being there no more to look after Miss Mercy, her being like a daughter to him. Cousin Aggie do say Miss Lettice is cheery enough, too much so at times, but that the other, Miss Matilda, is a right sour puss, and nobody's at risk of getting sunstroke off a beaming smile from her.'

'Thank you, Willie. I do most certainly wish the young Miss Tenneson well.' Still embarrassed, Ned looked skyward. 'Appears we may be in for a clear day.'

It was the boy's turn to look awkward. 'Yes, Your Lordship, 'twill fair up decent after it's done showering on and off till evening.'

Ned smiled, not doubting in the least that Willie, born of generations of country men with internal barometers, was correct despite there being barely a cloud in sight and little to no breeze. Bidding him farewell and summoning Rouser to set off again, he headed down the woodland path. Why had he felt the need to discover more about how Mercy Tenneson was faring since her guardian's death?

His first glimpse of her climbing over the stile at the edge of the field the other day had not brought with it the sensation they were destined for one another. He didn't believe such things happened outside the stupidest of fiction. In addition to which, his disastrous infatuation with that golden goddess Lamorna Blake, from which he had mercifully been released when she'd ended their exceedingly brief unofficial engagement by telling him he was the last man on earth she would marry, had hardened his heart against entanglements before the age of forty. By the time he reached the gate to the village he realized what lay behind his concern for Mercy Tenneson.

Having been orphaned himself at an early age, it was easy to
empathize with her bereavement and the possible feelings of
intense vulnerability she might be experiencing. Ones that
could let her fall prey to the wiles of any young man free with
his flattery and of sufficient good looks and charm to disguise,
at least during the early stages of acquaintance, that he was
an empty vessel. Weak of character and a brainless twit to
boot!

Ned's mind filled with the image of Gideon Blake, so aptly
reduced to Giddy, dismounting his horse in the bridle lane to
address Mercy as she had climbed over that stile. Was it an
unexpected encounter? Or, Ned's thoughts darkened, a planned
one – at least on his part? If so, what could be going on in
that vacuous head of his? Anything of an honorable nature
would seem most unlikely if accounts of his maiden deflower-
ings were to be half credited. Also, his parents Sir Winthrop
and Lady Blake would surely not countenance such a pairing.
The daughter-in-law of their choosing (and from Ned's experience with Lamorna the decision would be theirs) must come
from an illustrious family. Also required was that she bring
with her a fortune sufficient to settle his current gambling
debts (of which word had spread) and ensure coverage of
future excesses.

Ned did not put much credence in Giddy's prowess as a
Lothario; village girls were not invariably simpletons eager to
allow the male members of the gentry to have their wicked
way with them in return for a sixpence. In all likelihood he
had created this image of himself by bragging of imaginary
exploits to his equally inane cronies whilst in his cups.

Nevertheless, he was weasel enough if sufficiently intrigued
to make an attempt at ensnaring the vulnerable Mercy Tenneson
. . . especially if she were as lovely as Mrs McDonald had
suggested. Ned's sighting of her had been too brief to form
an opinion, but she had climbed over that stile with a lithe
grace, and that long, flowing dark hair had brought a stray
image of Cathy Earnshaw in *Wuthering Heights* . . .

He did not return fully to the present until he reached the
green and heard himself hailed by Miss Milligan, as usual of
an early morning out walking two of her boxers. He couldn't

tell if they were the same ones she'd had with her the last time they had stopped and talked; she bred to the same color and standard of perfection and those she kept, instead of selling to carefully selected purchasers, were always the pick of the litter.

'Halloo, there, Lord Stodmarsh,' she bellowed again in a voice that would have carried to China, although she was now only a few yards away. 'I was hoping to catch sight of you. Sit, Sir Jasper! Sit, Ironside!' She barely paused to acknowledge Ned's return greeting before plowing on. 'I wanted to bring you up to date on that matter we discussed about Ivy Waters's persecution of Doris Thatcher.'

'Yes, of course. The business about the dog.'

'Remember I told you I'd handle the situation by urging the regulars at the Dog and Whistle to give her the cold shoulder next time she was in? I've made a point of putting in an appearance each evening since we talked, and struck lucky the one before last. In she waltzed around seven like Queen of the May. She went straight at it! Jabbering about her grievance, how much she'd doted on her little Rex and how it'd only been because she was so broken up by the accident she hadn't thought she could give him the proper care to get him well, et cetera, et cetera! What she got in return was stony silence. All backs turned on her. Delighted to report, Your Lordship, you could've wiped her up with a damp cloth.'

'One can't help feeling a little sorry for her, even though she brought it on herself. Not that I'm ungrateful, Miss Milligan, if her vendetta's ended.'

'No doubt of it!'

Ned feared for a moment she was about to slap him triumphantly on the shoulder, sending him flying across the green. But she'd merely reached out to adjust Sir Jasper's lead. 'How did George Bird react?' he enquired. 'He doesn't usually put up with altercations in the pub.'

'True! Peaceable man, without being a softie! But you have to bear in mind there was no scene. Not a squeak from Waters; she just slunk out into the night.'

'Maybe she'll apologize to Doris Thatcher. The whole business has had Alf very upset on her behalf.'

Miss Milligan was squinting down at Rouser. 'Good chap
you've got there! I hope you see he gets plenty of roughage.
Just read an article touting its importance to canine health,
disposes of the myth that it causes flatulence. Speaking of
George Bird, he had a fellow at the bar last night, a rough-
looking customer, the sort you could imagining knocking his
own mother into the middle of next week if she gave him any
backchat. I had the feeling I remembered him from somewhere,
and it came to me this morning – he'd knocked on my door
donkeys' years back and asked if I'd pay him to walk my boys
and girls. Gave him short shrift. Wouldn't have in any case,
but when he said his name of Stan something he was done
for. I had a cousin Stanley that was a bad lot from the cradle
on and I've known others since I wouldn't trust an inch. Call
me a Tomfool, but . . .'

'Shouldn't dream of it,' said Ned automatically. He was
thinking about Willie Griggs's missing chicken and the opened
sack of seed potatoes.

'Suppose me and mine should be toddling along.' Miss
Milligan paused, and then gave a half nod. 'Talk about getting
the old brain going! I've just remembered something else
regarding the Thatchers. Ran into Elsie Trout half an hour
ago, and she told me they were sitting behind her on the bus
early afternoon yesterday, and Doris was decked out to the
nines in a red coat with astrakhan collar that matched her hat,
and Alf had a suit on under his coat. Significant, she thought.'

'Why?' Ned had spotted two figures stepping onto the green
from the far side.

'I wouldn't normally put any stock in her opinions; she
imagines herself an arm of the law sniffing out mysteries on
account of being married to the constable. But I have to say
the woman may have had something this time. She asked me
if I didn't think it likely the Thatchers had decided to take
action by consulting their own solicitor for themselves instead
of waiting for Ivy to carry out her threats of having one contact
them.'

'I wouldn't think so. They're not the sort to add fuel to a
fire.' Ned was looking past her at two approaching figures.
Noting this without rancor, Miss Milligan turned her head.

'Ah!' she exclaimed in a fortunately reduced roar. 'Young Miss Tenneson in the company of Neville Sprague. One of the best church organists we've had in living memory according to Mrs Weedy, who could date 'em all back to the Ark. Decent if colorless chap! Though there has to be more to him than meets the eye, considering he dived into the river to rescue young Rupert Trout when he got caught in the current. Saved the boy's life, no doubt of it! He's also a model son to his aged father.'

'Yes,' murmured Ned.

'Frightfully convenient bumping into him like this, seeing as I've been wanting a word in his ear.'

The pair were now sufficiently in view for him to see that Mercy Tenneson moved with unaffected grace, that she was tall, possibly his own height of five foot eight, and slender. This morning her dark hair was tied back, revealing the suggestion of a fine-boned face. Maybe he was filling in that bit from his image of Cathy in *Wuthering Heights*. It wasn't like him to harbor such fanciful thoughts, though he had thought it a great book. Florie had read it to him when he was around nine or ten and they'd had lively discussions about the characters and plot, agreeing on the genius of Emily Brontë.

'Has the look of a thoroughbred,' rumbled Miss Milligan. 'I wonder why it was decided to change her surname from whatever it was originally? One assumes a formal adoption. Sensible. Simplifies things, but the name could have been left in deference to her family, even if none are left living. I don't believe in denying one's blood lines, unless there's some necessity for doing so, some blot on the old copybook.'

'Miss Milligan!' Ned could not prevent the outrage surging into his voice.

'Wasn't implying I heard anything detrimental in regard to her background, such as a history of blackguards or relationship to some frightful politician out to ban fox hunting. If everything was not up to scratch Kenneth Tenneson's sisters would have leaked it years ago. Matilda, the elder of the two, is known to have been furious when he took the child in; vicious temper by all accounts. On second thoughts, maybe she would have kept mum, to protect the family's good name, such as it is. It's different with Lettice – the woman's incapable of keeping her mouth shut about complete drivel even if it were to be taped over with Elastoplast. Noticed, did you, how she never stopped gabbling throughout the graveside service?'

'My grandmother and I were away and so didn't attend Mr Tenneson's funeral.'

'Ah, so you were, Lord Stodmarsh! I'm forgetful, unlike Lettice, who keeps a mental inventory of who said or did what day by day, week by week ten years back, and how adroitly she'd handled it all.'

Ned regretted not having any Elastoplast handy with which to seal Miss Milligan's lips. Mercy Tenneson and Mr Sprague were almost upon them. Fortunately they were talking intently between themselves, but broke off to acknowledge the encounter. Mercy smiled politely and Mr Sprague extended a hand to Miss Milligan and Ned, greeting each with a 'how-do-you-do?' His voice held a hint of diffidence, reflected in his light blue eyes. His face was thin, and his hair was so pale as to be almost transparent. It struck Ned as it had not done in past brief encounters that there was a lack of substance to him – here was a tall wraith of a man. Aged anywhere between thirty-five and fifty, liable to slip in and out of the onlooker's awareness without leaving the shadow of personality. Or did he merely seem that way momentarily because he was standing in close proximity to Mercy Tenneson?

Her old-fashioned gray flannel skirt and jacket, blouse of a lighter shade of the same and sensible walking shoes, could not detract from that quality of something . . . rare, setting her apart not only in her elemental loveliness but by something that lay within, at which he could not begin to guess . . . but found himself wishing to do so with an intensity that made no sense at all. She might not be at all a likeable person, one who had no care for dogs, though this seemed belied by Rouser's enthusiastically wagging tail. He always knew instantly who took to him and who didn't. The boxers continued to sit like statues, but it was possible their eyes had brightened.

He discovered he was holding her hand, saying in conventional form that he was pleased to meet her.

'And I you, Lord Stodmarsh.' Her voice was slightly husky. A smile touched her lips. Perfunctory? Why should he expect more?

'Oh, do please call me Ned.' He hoped his impish grin would meet with success. Her eyes were a dark gray. Characters in books were often portrayed as having gray eyes, but he didn't think he'd ever met anyone whose truly were, rather than an indeterminate shade, not fitting the usual blue, green, brown, or even hazel.

'That's very kind of you, but I'm sorry, I couldn't.' There was no protesting her firmness. His disappointment was edged by the hope she had drawn the same line with Gideon Blake. Should he offer his condolences on the loss of her guardian? Or would it reopen the wound she was endeavoring to heal, if only effectively in brief interludes of which this might be one?

But as it happened he was not to get in the next word. Miss Milligan was addressing the church organist.

'Ah, Mr Sprague! I've been intending to seek you out. The daughter of a cousin of mine's getting married next month. Lives in Hartsfoot – you may have heard of it, a tiny little hamlet outside Kingsbury Knox, church the size of a matchbox, no organist – but the silly girl insists she won't have the wedding anywhere else. It occurred to me you might be willing to help out. Not too much of a jaunt and you'd be paid, of course.'

'That would not be necessary. I'd be pleased to be of use, if, that is, doing so would not conflict with my duties here.' He did not so much stammer as group some words together and place a distance between others. Having had such little contact with him previously, Ned could not tell if this was habitual.

'Splendid! Why don't we toddle back to my house so I can fill you in on the details?' Typically Miss Milligan did not ask if she would be keeping him from matters to which he wished, or indeed needed, to attend. He looked uncertainly at Mercy Tenneson. There was nothing perfunctory about the smile she gave him. It was filled with warmth.

'Do go ahead, Mr Sprague. It was truly good of you to turn back with me on the bridle lane when I know you would have preferred to continue your walk. I behaved foolishly, getting nervous about nothing. I'm sure now it was my imagination playing tricks on me. I'm not usually that way, but things were a little tense at home this morning, my aunts not having slept well – worries, inevitable ones, relating to Uncle Kenneth's death. They'll turn out to be nothing of importance.'

Mr Sprague eyed her worriedly. 'Are you sure you wouldn't feel more comfortable if I accompanied you back to Bogmire?'

'You're always so kind, but I'm quite myself again.'

'No need to mollycoddle the girl.' Miss Milligan had summoned Sir Jasper and Ironside to rise. 'Besides, I'm sure His Lordship will be happy to walk back with her if that will ease your mind.' Miss Milligan was always confident of what others would do if it suited her thinking. A few drops had begun to patter down and Ned noticed the sky had darkened, confirming Willie Griggs's prediction of rain. Mercy Tenneson was looking at him enquiringly.

'Of course, I'll be delighted to escort you, Miss Tenneson,' he said with what he hoped was a suitable degree of enthusiasm, rather than the eagerness that was his internal response. He wanted to know what, or whom, had panicked her on the bridle lane. Another, this time decidedly unwanted, meeting with Giddy Blake, perhaps?

'Thank you, Your Lordship.'

He really would have to do something about her insistence on adhering to his title. Not now, but later. He was determined there would be a later. An immediate issue was the rain now coming down hard. Miss Milligan, Mr Sprague and the boxers had merged into the blur within moments of their departure. Ned didn't mind getting wet through, but he wasn't prepared to see Mercy drenched. Her apparent concern seemed centered on Rouser.

'Oh, the poor dear! And sitting so patiently! You should get him home as fast as possible and toweled off.'

'He's an all-weather dog. Labs are.' Rouser was Ned's Achilles heel; he would have paused in the midst of being shot at to brag about him. 'My grandfather had them his whole life. They're the best breed in the world. The muddier and splashier he gets the happier he is.'

'Or maybe you find it convenient to think so.'

Through the drumming rain a grin spread across Ned's face at the look from those cool gray eyes at an exact level with his own. 'Are we having our first disagreement, Miss Tenneson?'

'Impossible. We don't know each other.'

'I don't see what that has to do with anything. Complete strangers glare and shout at each other for the mere stepping on a foot. Meanwhile, we need to get moving. We can get an umbrella from George Bird at the Dog and Whistle; he always has a supply of ones forgotten and left behind.' Ned resisted the urge to take her hand as they started across the slippery green in the direction of the village street with Rouser neither lagging behind nor leaping ahead.

'By all means borrow one for yourself.' A good deal of her hair had come unpinned to stream in a dark river down her back. 'Don't think I'm being huffy, but there's no need for you to walk me back to Bogmire. I only agreed to pacify Mr Sprague; he's such a good man and was so admiring of my guardian. Mrs Weedy, a lovely old lady and friend of mine, says he hasn't been himself since . . . since . . .'

'Hard to talk about.' It wasn't put as a question. 'I do have some understanding. My parents died when I was very young, killed in a car accident, but I clearly remember not being able to speak their names for weeks afterwards.'

'I knew. And I'm sorry, Your Lordship.'

'About my title,' Ned continued in a lighter tone, 'it does have its obligations.'

'Such as?' They had reached the pavement outside the Dog and Whistle. Their eyes met through the rain. Again his irrepressible grin broke through.

'T'would sully the family honor should I leave you to drown for lack of an umbrella held nobly over your head. It's on our crest. "Leave none to perish in the rain."'

'Nonsense!' A laugh escaped her.

'Besides which, I can't imagine it would ease the tension you said the Misses Tenneson have been feeling were you to return dripping puddles on the floors.' Ned headed for the side door of the pub.

'But I'm not going straight home. I only said that for Mr Sprague. I intend to call in first at Mrs Weedy's house.'

'All the more reason. You'd feel compelled to mop her floors – the guestly thing to do, especially given her advanced years.'

The laughter was now in her voice. 'Your position in life would seem to have gone to your head.'

'Were you to add Ned, that would rhyme.'

'Certainly not. Aunt Lettice already has silly ideas because young Mr Blake has stopped to talk to me when I've been out walking – that . . . that I'm poised to be on speaking terms with members of the upper circles.'

'From my experience that can, in certain circumstances, be an unwelcome burden; naturally not to be held against me.' There had been no response to Ned's first knock at the pub door. He tried again.

A voice called out from the right; the newsagent had come out of his shop a couple of doors down. 'If you're wanting George he's not there. I saw him heading off with Alf Thatcher, after he delivered my post an hour gone. Did you and the young lady want to step inside till the rain slows, Your Lordship?'

'Very kind, Bert, but what I'd prefer is the loan of an umbrella – that's what I was hoping for from George.'

'Won't be a tick.' The man was back on the instant with the required article, which he raised before handing it over and vanishing back into the shop.

'So,' said Ned, shielding Mercy Tenneson from further damp beneath the black dome, 'I hope there's going to be no more nonsense, such as your insistence upon going on with this on your own, forcing you to be the one needing to return it. Also, surely you can tell from that melting look Rouser is giving you that he'd never forgive me if I failed in my duty to save your arm from the fatigue of lifting an object weightier than a handkerchief above your head for an extended period.'

'He has rain in his eyes, you . . .'

'Charlatan?'

'I was going to say exaggerator.'

'That still wounds. If, however, we don't get striding, he's going to get wetter still. Come up with an argument against that and make it pithy.'

She gathered her hair to the side, twisted it into a rope and wrung it out. 'I'm convinced. There's no getting rid of you short of shoving you into a lamppost,' she not only matched her steps to his but quickened the pace, 'and that would undoubtedly bring out your feudal subjects against me with pitchforks.'

'Very likely,' returned Ned equably, 'at a word from me, by divine right of lordshipness, or whatever, I'm sure Alf Thatcher would refuse to deliver your post.'

'I wish he had weeks ago.' It was a murmur.

'Why?' He was instantly solemn.

'I was just being silly . . . continuing your game.'

If this was not true, what else could it mean? They walked on in silence past the haberdashery and the bakery. The pavement was empty except for a woman on the other side of the street trundling a pram, with two children below school age scampering along behind. A couple of cars passed, windscreen wipers slashing. Ned knew the location of Mrs Weedy's home, Laurel Cottage. At the bottom of the village street he and Mercy Tenneson, along with Rouser, turned right into Spindle Lane, from which it would be only a five-minute walk, less at the clip they were going. He was readying himself to enquire casually, even though he doubted she'd tell him, what it was that had scared her just before Mr Sprague had turned up, but it was she who brought up the topic.

'I do hope you won't mention to anyone my getting wound up down on the bridle path thinking I was being followed.'

She hadn't mentioned that last part on the green, or he wouldn't have been left wondering about the cause of her distress, but she must think she had, in a still-rattled state of mind, slipped it in.

'Of course, I won't say anything.'

'If it were to get back to my aunts they would worry, needlessly.'

'I understand. Mr Sprague is to be counted upon?'

'Absolutely. He knows, none better, how things are with them.'

Precisely what was implied therein? They now took the fork that would bring them to Laurel Cottage. 'Have no worries about me either. Even so, are you entirely convinced it was your imagination at work?'

'I've said so,' the gray eyes met his, though shadowed – conveniently? – by the umbrella.

'Then what caused you to think there was someone about?' He spoke with mild curiosity. 'Where could he or she have been lurking?'

'I got to the bridle path by cutting across the field backed by that abandoned farmhouse; it makes for a short cut from Bogmire. That field hasn't been tilled in years and the orchard to the side of it left to go wild. There are always rustlings from it, but halfway down I stopped, thinking I'd heard footsteps. When I turned I thought I saw a figure . . . a silhouette close to the edge of the trees, and that it was frozen in place staring at me. And I had this sickening feeling it was going to spring to life and grab me.'

'Man or woman?'

'I don't know. Does it matter when it wasn't real? I ran the last few yards to the stile and within a moment or two Mr Sprague came along. I babbled to him about being watched and he went to look, but didn't find anyone.'

'Which doesn't mean your mind played tricks on you. There may well have been a flesh and blood somebody in that orchard. My guess is a tramp, afraid of being spotted and ordered to move on.'

'Yes,' she replied, flat-voiced. 'Either way it doesn't matter.'

Ned noticed two things. It had stopped raining and they were about to reach Mrs Weedy's whitewashed cottage with its green roof and garden gate. He lowered the umbrella as they came to a standstill. Rouser stepped aside to shake off the wet, then looked up as if interested to know what was to happen next.

'Here we are,' said Mercy Tenneson. 'Thank you, Lord Stodmarsh. I hope I didn't seem rudely ungrateful.'

'Independent,' he smiled, 'as you described Mrs Weedy, and she is viewed as a remarkable personality. I hope we'll meet again before long. It's amazing we haven't come into contact before.'

'I've been off at boarding school much of the time and I don't attend church. It's not that I've anything against them, but Uncle Kenneth didn't go, so it was a chance to spend special time with him, the aunts being gone. Mrs Tenneson had been more or less bedridden for years until her death in March, so we'd often go up and sit with her. He was a wonderful son.'

'He sounds altogether a very nice man.'

'He was. It would have been an honor to be his real daughter, but he said what we had was better because it was more of a gift. Goodbye, both of you.' Her smile went to Rouser.

Ned waited until she had gone through the cottage door before turning to make his way back to Mullings. He should feel satisfied having learned she was in no danger of losing her heart to Giddy Blake, but instead he felt more unsettled. It was her use of the word 'followed' rather than 'watched' when explaining her panic. What had put the former into her head if the concern had not already been there? He wished Florie were already back at Mullings instead of returning the next day so he could talk to her, see if she thought he was making a mountain out of a molehill. Of one thing he was certain: he wanted to get to know Mercy Tenneson better.

NINE

George Bird had been walking the few steps from the newsagent's back to the Dog and Whistle when Alf Thatcher rode up on his bicycle beside him.

'I was hoping I'd timed it right, Birdie, to meet up before you went back inside and took off your coat.' Alf straddled the curb with his foot. His face looked pinched, and that was unlikely to be from the chill in the air: the weather, hot or cold, never affected him one way or the other, he was proud to say.

No, thought George, something was wrong . . . more wrong than when they had talked a couple of days back about the letter Doris had received from the firm of solicitors in Kingsbury Knox that they were sure resulted from Ivy Waters suing them over the dog. The appointment requested had been for yesterday afternoon and George had been mildly surprised when Alf hadn't come along to the pub that evening to tell him how things had gone. Now he had the sinking feeling the news wasn't good. Maybe Miss Milligan had been overly optimistic in her assurances that Ivy had been persuaded by the chilly reception she'd received from the regulars in the tap room to see the error of her ways and drop the matter. For if that was the case, surely she'd have felt an urgency to get in touch with Messers Something and Somebody and tell them so in time to save Doris and Alf an unnecessary journey. One requiring him to take time off work. All this sped through George's mind in the blink of an eye. Alf was still speaking.

'Thing is, Birdie, I'd appreciate it no end if you'd walk back to the house with me so's me and Doris can get what's happened off our chests. Air our minds out, is the way she puts it. Says talking to you always helps her do that. It's not so much we're looking for advice; we've more or less decided how we're going to handle what's landed on our heads. The shock of it – her life being turned upside down all of an instant

– is what she needs to get past. That said, being Doris, she's taking it calmer than most would. Some'd be laid up in need of the doctor. Like we said to Mr Pritchard, things like this don't happen to ordinary people like us . . . and her growing up with never a hint of anything not sitting right . . .' Alf paused for breath.

Pritchard? The name rang a bell with George. Wasn't that the surname of the solicitor as signed that letter to Doris? ''Course I'll come along with you,' he placed a hand on Alf's shoulder, 'but instead of walking I could get out the car. It won't take a jiffy and I can put your bike in the back easy enough.'

'Thanks, Birdie. If it don't matter to you none I'd as soon wheel it and walk. It'll give me an extra fifteen minutes to fill you in some on the way. Like I said, Doris wants to talk things out, but from where she sees herself placed now, rather than going over the whole of it, from the moment we realized Mr Pritchard's wanting to see us had nothing to do with Rex. She'd as soon I give you the gist first. "You leave that to me, duck," I told her.'

'Then what was it about?' George halted the step he'd been about to take. Here was a possibility he hadn't thought of despite his wondering about Ivy Waters's behavior in not shutting down the situation.

'It's going to come as a shock.' Alf peered up at him anxiously.

'I've got round to that. But not a patch, whatever it is, on what it's obviously been for you and Doris. Spill the beans, old lad.' George gave his shoulder another squeeze.

'Well,' Alf clutched the handlebars tighter as he prodded the bike forward, 'it's . . . it's like this, see – you'll remember Doris's surname was Green before we married?'

George nodded. 'You've joked about it being a good thing the color suits her.'

'Trouble is, it was . . . and it wasn't, so to speak. It's what's on her birth certificate right enough – Doris May Green, daughter of Maude and Charles Green on the right date and all that, but it seems she wasn't . . .'

'Their flesh and blood child? She was adopted and never

had any idea until yesterday?' George stopped himself before saying he could imagine she must have felt as if the ground had shifted under her feet; he couldn't. It was the sort of thing you heard happened, safely believing you'd never be added to the list. He shook his head. 'Why on earth did this Pritchard have to tell her at her age, with her parents long gone?' The answer was in Alf's eyes. It was George who said the words. 'He had to – some strange, important reason.'

'Yes. No way would she ever have found out otherwise. Thing is, Birdie, she wasn't adopted. It was . . . this way.' Alf drew an unsteady breath, his eyes traveling up the six-foot-four length of George and settling fixedly at the top of his head. 'You're not wearing your cap.'

'Aren't I?' George felt for his cap. His hand met his bald dome. 'I remember, I didn't think it worth grabbing for the few steps I'd be taking to the newsagent's and back. It doesn't matter. Won't catch my death without it.'

'Not so sure about that. I wouldn't risk it if I was you. Better go back and get it.'

George was about to protest, then decided against it. Coming up hard against getting the rest of the story out, Alf needed a respite – the chance to slow his breathing, steady his voice before continuing. 'All right. Can't have you worrying about what I have round the sides being blown off. Back in a tick!'

Entering the Dog and Whistle, George discovered his own heart was pounding. He wasn't going to like what Alf was about to reveal. George wasn't a man to readily give way to queer thoughts – to a sense of ominous foreboding, but he was in the grip of one now. Something most unpleasant was on the horizon and not only for Doris and Alf. He couldn't pinpoint this certainty to anything definite, but there had to be something prodding it. He scratched his head before putting on the cap he'd retrieved from the wall rack; there were as usual several that didn't belong to him, ones forgotten by customers on leaving the pub, most of them close to matching his, but he always reached unerringly for his own. Closing the side door, he rejoined Alf on the pavement, glad to see his friend looking more himself. Even so, he would have liked to offer to push the bike. Unfortunately, being almost a foot taller, he would have had to bend over it, preventing eye contact. They were passing the haberdashery, a few doors down from the Dog and Whistle, before Alf picked up the conversation where it had left off.

'Like I said, Doris wasn't adopted. She was switched a few hours after birth with another baby born the same day.'

George's mind went numb, his voice wouldn't come; all he could manage was to stare blankly at Alf.

'A boy. Doris's grandmother – or I should say the woman she'd thought was her mum's mother – delivered both babies. They'd been due on the same date and each come right on time. Otherwise it could've bin hard to pull off.'

'Not easy, even so, I'd've thought,' said George after they'd stepped aside for two women who'd come out of the florist's, Alf shifting the bike onto the road to make room for them to pass. 'Who were the parents of the boy?'

'Irma and Horatio Tenneson.'

'Then that means . . .' George had thought he was done being amazed.

Alf nodded. 'The Greens' son grew up as Kenneth Tenneson. Old Mrs Tenneson told him right afore she died and left a letter with him confessing all. The reason she did it, she said, was her husband had let her know good and proper he'd be livid if she landed him with another daughter. Not hard to believe he had her scared witless, him being known to be a tyrant. She said he'd knocked her senseless more than once, and that'd be nothing to what he'd do to her if she failed to give him a son this time around. She confided in the midwife, who came up with the plan to make the switch if it was a girl, as long as the child born to her daughter was a boy. 'Course, everything would have to work out right. First thing that helped was Horatio being away on business, already gone for a fortnight and not expected to return for another week.'

The two men turned off the village street onto Hogwood Road, which wound around the front of Cold Wind Common before angling towards a series of lanes, one of which turned a corner onto the row of former almshouses where Alf and Doris lived, three down.

'But why would the Greens agree?'

'Well, for one thing they already had a son, Sid, around four years old at the time.'

'Even so, it had to be a horrific decision to face.'

'Boggles the mind, don't it? But they was in financial difficulties. Charlie'd lost his job in a factory not long after him and Maude was married. He'd always had a fancy to work the land and had talked his brothers and other relations into lending him the money on a five-year note to buy a smallholding out near Small Middlington. Trouble was, he weren't no businessman, didn't do more than scrape by. So when his family called in the loans he was forced to sell at a loss, and still not able to pay in full.'

'And Irma Tenneson promised them money?'

'She'd got a pile of jewelry left to her by her mother before she was married. Necklaces, bracelets and rings with diamonds and other fancy stones, most of them hidden away. She'd had the sense right off the bat not to want her husband knowing about them. The fortune she'd brought with her had satisfied him it paid to marry her. She promised the Greens she'd sell sufficient of the jewels to clear their debts and set 'em up for a new start in life. Doris don't blame them.'

'What are her feelings towards Irma Tenneson?'

'Sorry for her. Otherwise nothing one way or t'other.'

George felt cold under his coat, even though there was no deep chill or biting wind. His conversation with Inspector LeCrane kept fingering through his mind, along with Florence's puzzlement over Kenneth Tenneson's fall down the stairs having been declared an accident without more questioning as to the position of the body. He asked Alf if it was Mr Tenneson's conscience that had led him to write a new will with some provision made for Doris.

'That's what done it. He didn't get round to it till recent. Understandable. Bound to've been shaken up bad having a bomb like that dropped on him, and then Irma Tenneson dying before he could catch his breath. Whatever he thought about her pulling a fast one – her not being his proper mum an' all – he could've been right fond of her. Glad, even – same as Doris – he'd bin brung up where he was.'

'There's no telling,' said George as they turned another

corner. Or, he thought, the man could've been justifiably resentful. Angry. Sufficiently, perhaps, to speed on her death, feeling safe that he'd get away with it, since it wouldn't be looked into carefully, what with her being old and a long-time invalid. But what if his two sisters had their suspicions leading one or other, or both, to push him down those stairs? Something else was going through George's head. 'If Mr Pritchard had the new will, why'd he let the old one stand until now?'

'Tenneson had given it to his friend, Major Wainwright.' Alf explained about the private detective's seeking Doris's whereabouts. Then he explained the new will and how it differed from the first. Lastly, he told George Mr Pritchard had warned Doris and him that the Tenneson sisters would not take the news well.

'That would be understandable.'

'Oh, we can see it from their point of view, right enough, but he warned us the elder one, Matilda, was liable to turn nasty. Made it sound like we should look sideways and back when it come to her.'

George was pondering this when they turned up the path to the Thatchers' front door. Did Mr Pritchard have particular suspicions of Matilda – that she'd had a hand in Kenneth Tenneson's fatal 'accident'?

'Not that it matters,' Alf propped his bike against the wall to the right of the door, 'seeing as Doris has made up her mind not to take a share of the money, let alone a brick of that house. And I'm behind her all the way.'

George felt a rush of relief. Surely that'd secure Doris's safety. His mind cleared enough to wonder what Florence would have to say about all this when she got back tomorrow. He had one more question for his friend before they went inside.

'What about the young lady, Kenneth Tenneson's ward, or was she his adopted daughter?'

Alf shook his head. 'I'm not really clear on what the relationship was; if Mr Pritchard said, it went right past me; but the changes in the will don't touch how she stands money-wise. What Mr Tenneson set aside for her didn't come from family money. A well-off bloke he served with during the war had been injured bad and died not long after it ended. Anyways, being pretty much on his own in the world, what he had to leave went to Tenneson.'

'So that's what she gets.'

'And not to be sneezed at neither. Close on ten thousand pounds, I think was what Pritchard said.'

'No hint that this man, that died from war wounds, could've been the girl's father?'

'Not a dickybird. And I hadn't thought along those lines.' Alf led the way into the house's narrow hall. Two things reached them through the open kitchen door – the tempting smell of frying sausages and Doris's voice.

'There is no *if* about it, Ivy. You *did* upset me and Alf. No use pretending that wasn't your intention. Still, like I said, we'll be only too glad to put the whole business behind us if you stick to your word there'll be no more unpleasantness. It was good of you to come round, but now I need to get the sausages out the pan and start on the eggs. Alf should be back any minute if he isn't already. In fact, I think I heard him come in.' This received a low spoken response that Alf and George couldn't catch, followed by the sound of the back door closing.

'I suppose that's something; one small bright spot in the dark,' said Alf, 'not that Ivy's antics seem to amount to much now.' He hung his outdoor clothes and George's on the hall rack before leading the way into the kitchen. It was rather a cramped space, seemingly made more so by George's vast height and large build, but as with the other rooms it was immaculate. There was a table with a white enamel top placed close to the wall on their right. It was laid for three with a teapot and plate piled with toast in the middle. Rex, in his basket by the domestic boiler, cracked open an eye and went back to sleep. Doris had her back to them, cracking eggs into a frying pan to a hissing of hot sausage grease. She looked over her shoulder at them.

'Ivy Waters was here ten minutes reciting her party piece. What you heard was the tail-end of what I had to say. Nice of you to come back with Alf, George.'

'No bother, Doris. Pleased to. It isn't like both of you haven't been there for me, good times and bad.'

'Well, that's good of you to say. No need to've sounded so glum out there, Alf, seeing as our minds is set against taking a penny from that will, so there'll be no giving those two Tenneson women – that aren't and never will be sisters of mine – an ounce of reason to go up against us. Did Alf put you in the picture, George?'

'Did a good job of it. You must've felt you'd been hit on the head with a hammer.'

'Well, I have to say it took some taking in. And I'll be glad to know what you think of a few things going forward. You men sit yourselves down. Pour the tea while I dish up, Alf; it's just brewed.'

'Right you are, duck.' Alf took the chair with its back to the hall door and did as he'd been told, and George took the one facing the wall, leaving the one at the other end closest to the cooker for Doris. She joined them with her plate after placing oven-warmed ones of sizzling sausages, bacon, grilled tomatoes (Alf didn't like them done over the gas) and fried eggs in front of them.

'Talk can wait. Get that down you,' she instructed briskly.

Before doing so George told her he hadn't smelled anything so good in a month, and between the first few mouthfuls added that it all tasted even better. Second cups of tea were poured, toast plucked from the stack and buttered. A good five minutes passed before another word was spoken.

'Well, then,' said Doris, having sat back down after getting up to refill the pot, 'if that's put you in a better frame of mind, Alf, we can get down to asking George about those one or two things that's still bothering us some.'

'Can't say I'm cheery as a lark, but I don't feel quite so down in the dumps,' Alf admitted. 'First thing, Birdie, me and Doris is looking at that we don't much like is all the talk there's bound to be. Even if the sisters want to keep it under their hats, and seems to me they would, same as us, word's bound to leak out. They got servants, servants got ears, and give 'em a juicy morsel to spit out, they will.' He added hastily at a look from Doris, 'It's different at Mullings. Loyalty to the family's bred into the bone over a long history. And them that works there is trained proper. Florence and that butler

Grumidge wouldn't stand for anything as should be kept private spreading outside them walls. 'Course,' he added fairly, 'I don't hear naught beyond the odd word in passing about the housekeeper and couple of women what go in daily to clean at Bogmire. They don't have a gardener. Word is Tenneson took care of the grounds hisself, with help from the girl when she was home from boarding school.'

'Don't go getting away from the point, Alf,' said Doris.

He looked awkward. 'Forgotten what it was.'

'That human nature being what it is, word'll get out. And much of it will go back to my mum and dad. Their memories'll get the brunt of any nastiness. It won't take long for folks to shift all the blame to them. Rich people like Irma Tenneson are expected to have their funny ways – do things people like us wouldn't think up in a month of Sundays. It's different for our kind – step out of line an inch too far and there's no excuses; from our own as well as them that's a cut above.'

'This needs a think, all right.' George sat, musing. He didn't doubt she was right in that the Greens and the grandmother midwife would get the largest shovels of dirt thrown on their graves. That couldn't be stopped entirely, any more than could be the likelihood of Doris getting stared at on the street or in the village shops. To be fair, such curiosity was understandable. The same would've been the case with Kenneth Tenneson if he'd still been alive. And the talk would still make the rounds about him – running along the lines of *Never thought he resembled his father . . . Didn't look quite the gentleman . . . A touch of the peasant, there was – that's how I saw him.* Dead men, however, can't react to what's thrown their way. So there was little satisfaction to be got there. Certainly there'd be twitterings when the two Miss Tennesons were present, and they'd get their share of odd looks from the villagers, along with questions from their own sort. But there was no disagreeing that the upper crust was seen as having a glamour about them, which imbued their unusual doings (to say the least here) with a kind of romantic fascination that wouldn't be applied to the butcher or baker in the same situation.

'You've a lot in your favor,' he said finally. 'You're both well liked and respected in Dovecote. From what I've heard of them, the Miss Tennesons aren't big favorites one way or another. The older one has a hardbitten look and keeps to herself, except for showing up at church on Sundays; the younger's a windbag. Mrs Tenneson . . .'

'It's all right, George,' said Doris when he hesitated, 'you don't have to watch your words when talking about her. I don't have feelings about her one way or the other, except for being glad she gave me to Mum and Dad. That's what I can't stand, the thought of them being looked at bad. Nobody knows what they'd do themselves if they were down on their luck, wondering where the next meal was coming from.' Her eyes misted over, something that was quite unlike her. Alf reached to squeeze her hand.

'Maybe there'll be less of that than you think.' George spoke a little more optimistically than he felt. 'After all, they didn't live right here in Dovecote Hatch, did they?'

Alf agreed. 'They lived in a village – hamlet, really – a few miles beyond Little Middlington.'

Doris provided the name. 'Finch.'

George nodded. 'I know it. Tiny little place with only a few dozen inhabitants keeping strictly to themselves. Besides, didn't your family leave when you were very young?' Without telling anyone where they were going, as if bent on putting it way behind them, was his guess.

'I don't have any memory of it. But you're right about the way things are there, at least with the old timers. Bet my grandmother got it in the neck for taking midwife cases as far afield as Dovecote. All I remember Mum and Dad saying about it was they was glad to get out of there. Now, of course, I can see there was more than one reason for that.' Doris hadn't touched her second cup of tea.

George's mind had strayed to the Greens already having a child, a boy, when Doris was born, and whether that had made their decision easier. With so much else in his head he couldn't come up with her brother's name, only that he'd been around four years older and had been deceased some time. He felt compelled to be frank. 'The way I see it, there's bound to be some sympathy for Irma. Horatio Tenneson was a known tyrant. Easy to understand her being terrified of him, whatever her background.'

What he couldn't – wouldn't – mention was his feeling that the one who'd likely got the worst of the whole business was Kenneth Tenneson, brought up under the Bogmire roof. From the outside the place looked like something of a nightmare. What had been his feelings when he finally learned the truth? Had he concluded that a life of relative privilege was worth the deceit, or was he fiercely resentful of not being reared by his own?

It said something about him that whatever he'd felt, he'd made the decision to do right by Doris the best way he saw it. But it couldn't be wondered at if she wasn't at the point of seeing things from anything near Tenneson's side. George wished, not for the first time during this conversation, that he had Florence sitting beside him. She always had the knack of saying the comforting thing. Though she wasn't as close with Doris and Alf as he was – they'd been his closest friends in the village for years – she was fond of them. And they'd come to feel the same.

'Sorry to unload all this on you, Birdie,' Alf apologized. 'I know there's nothing you, or anyone, can do, but it helps knowing you get the ins and outs of what Doris is going through.'

'I'm not so sure there is nothing. A lot of the talk that goes on hereabouts takes place at the Dog and Whistle. I can pass it around that the last thing the two of you need is questions. Not to pat myself on the back . . .'

Alf nodded. 'People listen to you, Birdie.'

'It'd help, at least a bit,' agreed Doris. ''Course, they'd know you'd be in our corner whatever, us being friends.'

'I say that helps,' persisted Alf.

George thought of someone else who could do a power more good to ease what the Thatchers were facing, and similarly for the Tennesons. That someone was Master Ned. It was still odd to think of him as Lord Stodmarsh now, all grown up. Like his grandfather before him, he was not only respected and admired by the villagers, he had the knack of endearing himself to them. George held back from saying this. He'd bring it up with Florence; there were few closer to his young lordship than she was.

Doris started talking about her life growing up in Chelmsford. The reason the Greens, along with the grandmother, had moved there was because Charlie Green had a friend living there that wanted to start up a market garden and needed someone to come in on it with him. She'd never thought about it before, but probably Charlie had put money into the venture, which had been modestly successful. It had been a happy home. Always kept nice, and good, plain food. Like Alf would've told George, never a hint of anything not right. She'd been a lot closer to both parents than her brother was. He'd always been inclined to go his own way. She'd stayed living at home through the years, like most unmarried women did, and it had been a pleasure to take care of them when they grew elderly.

'You'll remember, George; it was right after they died I met Alf on that little holiday in Southend.'

George smiled; no reminding needed. It remained one of Alf's favorite stories and his face always glowed when telling it.

'Don't get me wrong,' Doris continued, 'Sid wasn't a bad son, or brother for that matter. He never did anything you'd call unkind or stirred up rows. He made a good job of the business after Dad and his partner retired. Made more money in half the time than they ever did. I wouldn't say he was generous with it, but then again it'd be wrong to accuse him of not doing right by Mum and Dad after his fashion. He paid them enough of a pension, I suppose you'd call it, to keep them going. Not to be nasty, but it didn't help that his wife, Winnie, was a cold fish.'

'Freeze your bum off if she come up behind you.' Alf absently buttered a slice of toast.

'Still living in Chelmsford?' George asked. He couldn't recall the last time this sister-in-law had been mentioned in his hearing.

'No, and that brings us to something else we're wanting to ask your advice on, George,' said Doris. 'And that's whether there's any need to tell Winnie what's come about. No obligation, is how Alf and I see it, what with Sid being gone along with Mum and Dad. The last thing we want is her poking her nose in, which she would if given half a chance. We'd have her round here ranting at us to grab all we can get from that will. And, as if that's not bad enough, I can just see her turning up at Bogmire, forcing her way in given half an inch and creating a scene, because, unlike Sid, there's nothing she likes more than a good bust-up.'

'It's the only thing able to put a smile on that mug of hers,' corroborated Alf.

'What's the likelihood of her finding out if you keep quiet?' asked George. 'Where'd she move after leaving Chelmsford?'

'Well, there's the thing,' said Alf. 'She's in Tuswall.'

'Ah!' It was a market town, about fifteen miles from Dovecote Hatch, in the opposite direction to Large Middlington, Small Middlington and Kingsbury Knox. 'What brought her there?'

'She said it was to be closer to us, now Sid was gone. Acted all sentimental, the pathetic widow, like their marriage'd been one long honeymoon – and that it wasn't by far. She'd sold the business and said she could go pretty much anywhere she chose, which was true enough, I suppose.'

Rex had risen from his basket and was sniffing the back door, and Doris got up to let him out into the fenced-in garden.

'The truth was,' Alf picked up where she'd left off, 'there was a woman in Tuswall as had grown up in Chelmsford. Her and Winnie had bin at school together and they'd kept in touch over the years, occasional visits back and forth. There was her friend's brother also in Tuswall, by then also widowed. Could be Winnie'd always fancied him, that there was blood in her veins all along. Anyway, wasn't more'n a few months after she moved there that they started seeing a lot of each other. Smooth type. They haven't married, but it's still going on. At the beginning we saw something of her, more than we wanted, really – we went out there when invited, made her welcome when she turned up here, always on the hop, but that soon died off after she'd done bragging about her fancy new house and posh neighbors. Nowadays, George, we don't see hide nor hair of her, unless we suggest it, Doris feeling we should for family's sake.'

'Anyone here know her, or even that you've a sister-in-law in Tuswall?' George realized as soon as the words were out that it was a foolish question. She and Alf were bound to have mentioned it over the years, if only in passing. Besides, there was Mrs Hewett in her position as postmistress, she'd remember any letters to and from.

Doris returned to the table after letting Rex back inside. 'We've no acquaintances in common, but I know your thinking; it's what's been nagging me and Alf.'

'I say you have to tell her, but along of adding if you sense she fancies stepping into the limelight that you'll get your solicitor to write and tell her to stay out, or he'll have a justice of the peace put in an order.'

'Didn't think of that one.' Alf brightened.

'Right you are,' Doris sounded back to her brisk self, 'we'll go to Tuswall tomorrow. She should be home, she's always gone on about never missing doing a Sunday roast in God knows how many years. Alf, you can stop by at the Trouts today after your next delivery and see if it's all right with them if young Rupert comes and stays with Rex while we're gone.'

When George left them ten minutes later to walk back to the Dog and Whistle he felt reasonably confident that both were in a more settled frame of mine. Not so in his own case. He was worried, ridiculously so, perhaps, that their lives could be in danger, despite the decision not to benefit from Kenneth Tenneson's will.

TEN

Although Florence had felt a pang at saying goodbye to Hattie after the pleasant week they'd spent together, she was glad to be on the train from London, due to arrive at Large Middlington at ten thirty-two that Sunday morning. She was looking forward to her return to Mullings. She'd missed not only Ned, whom she loved, but also her daily conversations with his grandmother Mrs Tressler on shared topics of interest in addition to those related to household matters. It would be good to be back with the staff, especially her friend and ally Mrs McDonald, and to discover how well Molly had fared in taking on the role of housekeeper in preparation for when she would do so permanently.

Uppermost, however, was her eagerness to be reunited with George, for the sake of being with him, which always felt so right – so meant to be, but also because there were matters for them to discuss. Foremost of these was his letter regarding Inspector LeCrane's visit to the Dog and Whistle in which he'd expressed the wish to confer with them about Kenneth Tenneson's death. That meeting was to take place an hour after George met her at the station. Less pressing, needless to say, but still important to her was the desire to talk to him about the woman who had died after stepping in front of a bus. Would he think it appropriate to ask, as Hattie had suggested, if the inspector would be good enough to look into the possibility of the deceased being the woman in the headscarf? There had been no word on the wireless or in the newspapers that she had been identified, but that didn't mean the police had written her off as one more suicide in a stream of them and given up on their attempts at discovery. Or, for that matter, that they hadn't already succeeded, but were keeping quiet about it for sound reasons.

Unlike on her journey to London, which had allowed little elbow room between passengers, she now shared the carriage all the way through with just two others: a thin, youngish woman who grimaced every time there was a bounce and a stout one engrossed in her knitting. Her thoughts went to the clergyman and his sister on that previous occasion and the children they were taking up to London on an outing to see Hansel and Gretel on ice. In particular her mind focused on the boy with red hair who'd sat across from the head-scarfed woman, at one point leaning forward to stare at her, until at a look from the clergyman he'd shifted back in his seat. The sister in chatting briefly with Florence had mentioned that the name of their parish was St Clement's. The clergyman had referred to her as Mary and she had been wearing a pince-nez. It wasn't much to give the inspector. And what of the idea that had formed in her mind following that dream she'd had of being at Kenneth Tenneson's funeral? Would it be advisable, or unfair, to bring that up?

The train drew in to Large Middlington station. The two other women remained seated, not even glancing out the window as Florence lifted her suitcase down from the overhead rack, opened the carriage door and stepped out onto the platform to see George coming towards her. She was struck anew, as if it had been months since parting from him, by his great height and large build, but then there was that smile, the warmth and kindness of him that never dimmed; would never do so if she weren't to see him for a dozen years. Neither was inclined to public displays of their relationship as a courting couple. A kiss on the cheek. No more. It was more than enough. They were enfolded in an invisible embrace that sheltered, strengthened and set them in a place where none other came within sound or touch.

His voice, his beloved voice. 'Glad to have you back.'

'It's wonderful to be with you again, George.'

'I've Bert Harding looking after the pub.' Having put his cap back on, removed on seeing her alight, he picked up her suitcase and they headed out of the station into the high street. 'How's Hattie?'

'Well and, as ever, such a dear. So pleased to have me there. Couldn't do enough to make the days enjoyable.'

'I hesitated to write that letter. Perhaps I should have said no to Inspector LeCrane's suggestion I get in touch with you so we can see him today, but after what's happened – what I found out yesterday – I think you'll agree it's important, even urgent, we do have a talk with him.'

Worried – close to alarmed – Florence looked up at him. He was good at masking anxiety, but she knew every line of his face. Her mind opened to a dire possibility. 'What is it? Has someone else died at Bogmire? Another accident?'

'No. Not that . . . and it didn't come from LeCrane, but there's been a development in the wake of Kenneth Tenneson's death.' George pointed to their left. 'There's a café two or three doors down – I spotted it driving up. I've parked round the corner. How about we go and have a cup of tea and I'll tell you about it?'

'Of course.' Beneath Florence's level voice anxiety quivered. George didn't get worked up without a reason . . . most likely one that involved a person, or people, who mattered to him. And that didn't include anyone at Bogmire. For either of the two sisters, or Mercy Tenneson, he would feel concern if they were faced with something unpleasant, but not this level of distress.

'Plenty of time before we need show our faces to LeCrane. That's to be at a hotel not much further down.'

The café when they entered it proved to be of the clean, plain-faced type with sufficient space, without the necessity of scraping past seating for the number of customers it looked likely to bring in. They took a table against a side wall as far from the nearest occupied one as possible. Florence restrained herself from saying anything until the waitress had taken their order of a pot of tea for two.

'Want toast or a scone with that, dears?'

Neither Florence nor George did. She couldn't have swallowed a crumb and it was obviously the same with him. They continued to sit in silence until the woman had returned to deposit the contents of a tray on the table and walked away.

'It's startling news, Florence, but it could be I'm letting my mind go places it shouldn't because of LeCrane getting it into his head, like you did, that Tenneson's fatal plunge down those stairs oughtn't to have been written off so quickly as an accident. I'm dragging this out, aren't I?'

'Some things can't be rushed. And this sounds like one of those times. Take every bit of time you need.' She poured milk into the thick white cups, but didn't reach for the teapot.

He smiled at her in that way of his that said more than any verbal expression of devotion. 'Always succeed in putting life back on its feet for me, you do, Florence.'

'That's how it is for me too. Whatever's happened we'll do our best to be of help.' She filled his cup. The tea looked strong to the point of stewed, but that was better than weak in the circumstances. She added two teaspoonfuls of sugar, the way he liked it, and passed it to him, poured her own, then sat back in her chair, willing herself not to display any sign that her mind was scurrying in circles, searching for the answer as to who had been caught up in a bad, possibly dire situation.

George sipped his tea; more to please her than because he wanted it. 'This has to do with Doris.'

'Thatcher?' It was a ridiculous question. A sign she was completely stunned.

He nodded anyway. 'And of course what affects her does the same for Alf. What it comes down to is a new will's come to light – left by Kenneth Tenneson in safekeeping with his friend Major Wainwright. In it Doris is mentioned. More than mentioned. He's left her a sizeable inheritance.'

Florence sat speechless.

'Neither of them was by any means pleased about it. They told me they've decided to let the solicitor know they're going to leave things as they were, not take a penny of the money, let alone move into Bogmire as by rights under the will they could. Though who'd want to live in such a grim-looking place beggars my mind. Naturally I didn't say a word about Inspector LeCrane getting in touch because of not being satisfied that fall happened from Tenneson turning giddy on those stairs, but if both you and he was to be right about that . . . well, you know what I'm getting at.' George mindlessly picked up his teacup. 'If he were murdered, it may not have been by a family or household member. Someone outside could have had a grievance against Kenneth Tenneson and gone to Bogmire to have it out with him.'

This sounded cold comfort to Florence's own ears, but she had been grappling to absorb what he'd told her so far. She wanted him to sort through it in the telling, suppressing the urge to ask what was behind the mind-jolting bequest. In a fictional world, Mr Tenneson's inclusion of Doris in his will might have resulted from some simple kindness she'd once shown him, long since forgotten by her. Seeing him drop his wallet in the street and returning it to him. Discovering him fallen in a ditch and fetching help. Such things possibly weren't all that rare in real life. Few things touch the heart like kindness. And, from what she'd heard, Kenneth Tenneson had been viewed as a somewhat isolated figure outside his home, mixing little with local people other than his friend Major Wainwright. That he should have left Doris a large sum of money was astonishing, but not utterly beyond range of belief, given time to sink in. His bequeathing her a share of the house inhabited by his sisters and ward required a compelling explanation.

George was explaining it to her now. His calm restored, he did so methodically, from Doris's receipt of the letter from the solicitor Mr Pritchard, and the assumption that his request for her to come to his firm's offices resulted from the matter of Ivy Waters and the dog Rex. Florence did not exclaim or otherwise interrupt the flow, which concluded with Doris's decisions of yesterday.

'She was in reasonable spirits, considering, though concerned, as I've said, with how best to avoid being beset by curiosity when word gets out – which it will all too quick, raising the question of whether to break the news to the sister-in-law. Do you think I was right in telling her I thought she should?'

'Absolutely. What if the story got into the newspapers and this Winnie found out that way? There would be the makings for a real upset. Who'd blame the woman for being angered at being left in the dark in the face of a revelation that involved her late husband? People she knew would press for information. Had he suspected as a child, or adult, that there was something amiss in his family? If not, what would he have thought of his parents giving away, or, to put it more brutally, selling off his flesh-and-blood brother?'

George nodded. 'The chance of the story getting into the

papers struck me too. It's just the sort to grab the ears of the
sort of fellows we had swarming round the village after what
happened in the spring. It's easy to imagine one, or more,
coming back with a plan to write about how Dovecote Hatch
is doing in the aftermath of Murder at the Manor. With me
having been caught up in the investigation, the Dog'd be one
of the first places they'd come, and cagey as most of my
regulars are with outsiders, there's some whose mouths could
be loosened for the price of a pint or two and this – about
Doris and the Tennesons – would drop into all too eager laps.
Have to hope it doesn't happen, but at least the sister-in-law
will have been forewarned.'

'It won't be easy telling her,' said Florence, 'especially if
she lays into the Greens, attacking their memories with Doris
not being ready to hear – let alone believe they did anything
deserving of blame. Which, whatever the reasons, a majority
of people might well consider the case.'

'You think that's something she's putting off facing?'

'Don't you?'

'Now you say it – yes.' George fell silent, partly because
the waitress was heading towards their table, but also to dig
deeper into what this would mean for Doris if she began to
feel sympathy for Kenneth Tenneson – a sense that he'd
paid the price for her happy childhood, had been deeply
wronged and yet on learning the truth had considered the
injury done to her and sought to make things up to her the
best he could.

The waitress moved away from the table after Florence
thanked her for enquiring, but no – they didn't want another
pot of tea; only their bill, please, when ready.

'Doris is a fair woman,' George was still sifting through his
thoughts.

'And a kind one.'

'She won't be able to shove the tie between her and Tenneson
out of her head much longer.'

'Then what?' Florence prodded gently, knowing what he
was going to say and that it wasn't easy for him.

'How's she going to take it if it turns out he was murdered?'
His eyes met hers. 'Oh, I know that's maybe putting it a mite

too strong. A shove down the stairs isn't guaranteed to kill anyone, but at the very least somebody may have been enraged enough with him not to think of the consequences.'

'You're afraid that anger could now spill over to Doris if it arose from the discovery that Kenneth Tenneson was making, or already had made, a new will providing for her.'

'Yes.'

'Not only leaving her a share of the family inheritance,' Florence continued, 'but the house. The Miss Tennesons's lifelong home, placing them – and let's not leave out his ward, who, if not his adopted daughter, bore his surname – in an extremely tenuous position if he were to die.'

They sat silent, thinking along similar lines. Neither had noticed the comings and goings of other customers, or that the café was empty of any but themselves. The waitress placed the bill on their table.

'There's no hurry.' She glanced down at the suitcase beside George's chair. 'Stay as long as you want; we get a lot of people in here passing time till they need to make for the railway station, or just back from a holiday and want to chat about it.'

Florence thanked her. When she walked away to clear off table tops, George took out his watch.

'Ten more minutes,' he told her, 'before we need to head for that hotel to meet the inspector. All right with you if we sit on here discussing?'

'I think we should. Let's say it happened the way you've suggested, which I agree could be a strong possibility. An altercation on the stairs indicates the discovery was made not more than hours, even minutes before Mr Tenneson headed up them in his outdoor coat.'

'That's the way I saw it.'

Florence's voice quickened. 'You mentioned in your letter that Inspector LeCrane pointed out what was testified to at the inquest – that Kenneth left his house at one o'clock to spend the afternoon of Tuesday, the first of November – the day of his death – at Major Wainwright's home playing chess, and left there at five o'clock. Which, considering the distance he had to walk, meant he should have arrived back at Bogmire, if not delayed for any reason, at around a quarter to six. A lot can happen in a space of almost five hours.'

George agreed. 'Although some of that time, not pinned down precisely, was spent by the younger sister in the music room with Neville Sprague talking about the Christmas day service at St Peter's. Something about a solo she was set on singing. And the older one was closeted for a period in her sitting room with Miss Hatmaker, the seamstress, going through clothing she required altering or mending.' He jolted in his seat, shooting Florence a startled look. 'That reminds me of what I meant to tell you straight off – about what I forgot to mention in my letter and didn't realize until I'd put it in the post! It might or mightn't be important. Possibly suggestive, when coupled with the position of the body, is the way LeCrane put it. Sufficient to make him decide to follow his hunch Tenneson's death needed a closer look.'

'I know why you forgot.' Florence smiled with love in her eyes. 'You were worrying with every line you wrote that you were intruding on my time with Hattie, perhaps spoiling a little the remainder of our time together.'

His gaze reflected hers. 'You know me inside out.'

'Tell me now.'

'LeCrane asked to see the police photographs taken of the body and when he looked at them he noticed something that might have been missed previously. It wasn't mentioned at the inquest. A missing button on Tenneson's coat sleeve.'

Florence wasn't fully present for her reply, something to the effect that this was certainly interesting, but could it have come off earlier? She was instantly transported to her afternoon at D.H. Evans with Hattie, listening to her cousin telling her about the library book she'd just finished reading, *The Body in the Buttery*, and how the solving of the murder had depended on a missing button. Her mind shifted to later that day, back in Hurst Street, when she'd admired the matinee coat Hattie was knitting. The response, delicately – non-judgmentally – expressed that it was for the granddaughter of a neighbor, to be born to a young, unwed mother.

This followed by talking about whether it would be best to allow the child to grow up knowing the truth, or to make up a story about a husband – a father – dying before she was born. How she and Hattie had agreed that secrets had a nasty tendency to come home to roost. As had just proved the case with Doris. And then the dream she'd had last night . . . of being at Kenneth Tenneson's funeral, looking at Mercy Tenneson's face – the profile, and how it had merged into that of the woman in the headscarf.

George had waited to speak. 'What are you thinking, Florence?'

'There's something I've wanted to talk to you about, to do with that woman on the platform the day I left. The one I thought was going to throw herself on the line. Now what I'm going to add is going to sound far-fetched, but I'm wondering if a different discovery may have occurred – a phone message, letters found in a drawer that had nothing to do with Alf and Doris, but led to sufficient distress to result in a fatal confrontation on those stairs.'

'Who are we talking about, Florence?'

'Mercy Tenneson. I'll tell you the rest on the way to the hotel to meet the inspector. It includes wondering if she was in all senses the daughter of the house.'

ELEVEN

Young Rupert Trout had been pleased as Punch when Mr Thatcher came round on Saturday to ask if he'd mind staying with Rex the following afternoon – say from noon to five – while he and Mrs Thatcher went to her sister-in-law's in Tuswall, depending, of course, on his mum and dad not minding. Elsie Trout, hearing Rupert talking to someone and wondering who it was, came out of the kitchen into the hall; she wasn't best pleased to be caught in her apron on the weekend, especially if it was by one of her more uppity neighbors, but when she saw who it was she relaxed. Her first thought was that Alf was there to hand in a parcel, though she hadn't been expecting one; but if that was so, neither he nor Rupert was holding it. There had to be some other reason, then. Perhaps he had come to see her husband on police business – something to do with the dog that had belonged to Ivy Waters. Before she or Alf could get out a greeting, her son burst into excited speech.

'Mum, it's about Rex!'

'Oh, dear,' she said. 'I'm sorry, Alf, Len's not here, but if you like I can tell him when he gets in you need him to go and soothe her down.'

'No, it's not that . . .' Alf began.

Rupert shot her a stupefied look. Here he was, bursting with impatience to know if he could go and look after Rex tomorrow afternoon or not, and she might as well have been talking Russian. 'Soothe who down?'

'Ivy Waters.'

Alf clearly knew what she was going on about. 'Thanks, Elsie, but all that trouble with her is fixed now. Come over this morning, she did, and apologized to Doris. Claimed she didn't know what in the world had got into her.'

'Mum!' Rupert begged her with his eyes to listen, but it was hopeless. He'd have had better luck standing within feet of an oncoming train and asking it nicely to stop.

'Flaming cheek! Spite straight from the Devil is what it was! And we all know what Reverend Pimcrisp would say about that!' Elsie Trout was not a particular admirer of the vicar, but his gloating views on the multitudes deserving of hell and damnation had their uses. 'Of course, it'll be Len who got her to see sense. He went about it like he always does – persistent, but cautious not to get her riled up worse. It takes years on the job to learn the do's and don't's of being a village policeman. All well and good the higher-ups coming in when there's big trouble, but what I say is who keeps things ticking along peacefully the rest of the time?' She gave the apron a tug, a sure sign she was getting worked up. In this case it came from thinking about all the praise heaped on Florence Norris for helping the county inspector get to the bottom of the Mullings murder. Still rankled, that did.

'You're right, Elsie.' Alf was growing just a little impatient to get off home, but being him it didn't come through. 'Anyone around here that doesn't know we're lucky to have Constable Trout needs a good talking to.'

'Mum! Mr Thatcher wants to—'

'Now as for me, Alf,' she whisked on, 'there was the other worry – that Ivy Waters would get her claws into Rupert here.' A nod in his general direction.

Hah! So she could at least see him, even if she didn't notice he was ready to pop like a balloon, thought her undutiful one and only. Alf was again quicker off the mark than he was in getting the next word in. Doris would be wondering what was holding him up.

'I can see you being bothered, Elsie, but like they say – all's well that ends well.'

She was an unstoppable train. 'After all, it was him ran over the dog. Why not drag him into court, have her whole pound of flesh that way? That's where my mind's been these past few weeks.'

Instantly Rupert couldn't have spoken if he'd tried. His throat was closing, squeezing shut, as it always did when remembering that terrible moment on the bike . . . Rex dashing out immediately in front of him, the impossibility of stopping, not even time to swerve, and then the horrible feel of impact, of being thrown sideways onto the road with the bike landing on top of him. Mum had said, after, that he'd likely have been seriously injured or even killed if he'd gone over the handlebars. And Dad had growled back at her that going on about what could've happened but didn't was just like a woman. He'd hated them right then because it wasn't him that mattered – his scrapes and bruises were nothing – it was Rex. Would the dog make it, let alone get better? His parents hadn't been there to hear Rex's squeals of agony or see him crawl inch by inch to the side of the road, but he'd told them he'd never get the memory out of his head. So just how thick were they?

And they expected him to be good in school! That thought followed him back to the here and now. Mr Thatcher was telling Mum about him and Mrs Thatcher – how the only person they'd feel comfortable looking after Rex while they went out tomorrow was him, Rupert.

'It says a lot about your boy that he didn't blame the dog for running out in front of him, pitching him off his bike. Not only that, but he's come round faithful at least twice a week after it happened to see how the little fellow's getting along.'

'Well,' said Mum, looking chuffed, 'that's nice to hear.' Of course, she had to spoil it. 'Better than being told he's been up to larks with his friends. What time do you want him round?'

''Bout noon, if that's all right with you and his dad. Doris and me should be back no later than five. More like four.'

'I don't usually speak for Len, but I'll make the exception seeing it's you and, therefore, no reason why he'll mind.' Mum sounded all puffed up with importance and still looked it when Alf left almost immediately afterwards. Though still rubbed raw by her bringing up the accident, Rupert admitted to himself she'd done a brave thing. He wasn't so sure his father wouldn't get his nose out of joint when he got home because she'd gone over his head.

'Thank you, Mum.' The words sounded forced, which they were, but he followed them up by offering to make her a pot of tea.

He should've realized she wasn't silly enough to get Dad going by telling him up front she'd agreed to let their son spend tomorrow afternoon at the Thatchers'. She didn't even mention that Alf had been round till he'd taken off his coat and was sitting at the kitchen table drinking his second cup of tea and finishing off a plate of thickly buttered malt bread.

Then when she did bring it up she sounded resentful, saying it would be nice to have Rupert do something helpful for Doris and Alf, but charity did begin at home. She had a couple of skeins of wool she needed to wind into balls and she didn't see why Rupert couldn't put her first by sitting opposite her on a Sunday afternoon, when families were meant to be together, with the skeins wrapped round his parted knees to make the job easier. They always got in such tangles if she tried to do it on her own. She didn't have to go on. Dad went all red in the face and said he'd never heard the like. When good people asked a favor there shouldn't be no ifs, ands or buts.

'I'm surprised at you, Elsie! You tell that boy to get on his bike this minute so he can tell Alf and Doris he'll be there.'

Rupert, listening from the hall, presented an expressionless face on entering the kitchen.

'Hear that?' growled his father. Probably thinking he'd kicked up a fuss about being stuck with a dog on a Sunday afternoon and had managed to twist his mother around his finger.

'Yes, Dad. Anything you or Mum need from Mrs Hewett's shop? I'd like to stop in on the way back and get some dog biscuits to take tomorrow.' He knew this would sound like he was buttering up, but that was life for an eleven-year-old! And he was singing on the inside. He'd try to teach Rex to beg, if his leg was mended enough. No risking that.

At half past eleven the next morning, quite a nice one for November, he set off wearing last year's winter coat, which was just the right length when riding his bike. He had his mother's string bag hung from the right handlebar, the cord handles wrapped round to stop it banging against his leg. Inside was the sixpence-worth of dog biscuits he had bought from Mrs Hewett. He'd used his pocket money. He got fourpence a week, but had some saved. Mrs Hewett had wanted to know whose dog they were for; she always wanted to know everything, down to what time you got up and when you went to bed. When he told her they were for Rex, she'd got even nosier, wanting to know how that business was working out. He'd said he thought things was fine now, and hurried out of the shop before she could say how horrible the accident must've been for him. Inside the string bag was also a book he'd taken out of the library yesterday morning.

It was a tiny library, but the children's librarian knew what boys and girls not old enough to borrow from the adult section liked to read. She'd encouraged him to try one of the William books by an author named Richmal Crompton, because they were about a boy of eleven – same as him. She said some people considered them penny dreadfuls, but she thought them loads of fun. Rupert thought so too. He'd told his friend Timmy about them, how William and his friends, known as the 'Outlaws,' were always getting into trouble – not to mention terribly dirty – just from trying to do good deeds. Timmy said he'd already heard of them, but they weren't ones he'd waste his time on because they were written by a woman. Rupert hadn't believed this. He said Richmal had to be a man's name, and anyway, how could a woman tell stories about boys like she knew them inside out? But the children's librarian had said Timmy was right. Rupert was tempted to give him a thump next time he saw him, but decided best not to seeing he'd no intention of stopping reading about William and the Outlaws' adventures. He just wouldn't mention the books to Timmy again. The one in the string bag was *William the Bad*. He'd already read the first two stories. He pictured himself reading out loud to Rex, and Rex looking really interested, even like he wanted to laugh at some of the really funny parts.

He pedaled cheerfully along lanes and around corners. It should only take him ten minutes or so to reach the Thatchers', but he hadn't been about to take a risk on being late. What if he should come upon a horse-pulled farm cart blocking the road, or a bus gone the wrong way? It wouldn't do to have Mr and Mrs Thatcher worrying. He wished they were special friends with Mum and Dad so he could've called them Auntie Doris and Uncle Alf. At first it'd been all about going to see Rex, but he'd grown fond of them too. He couldn't help it.

They were that nice to him. He hadn't gone to see them yesterday afternoon like Dad told him to, but it wasn't because he couldn't be bothered or wanted to be deceitful. He'd thought Mr Thatcher might want some peace and quiet with his wife after Mum talking on and on at him like she'd done.

She hadn't used to be like that with people, more on the short side, really, when it came to conversations outside of him and Dad. He'd been surprised when she'd started talking about thinking she'd like to look for a job cleaning a few mornings a week. Dad had thundered on at first about no wife of his – like he had others! – needing to go out to work. But he'd come round surprisingly quick for him, saying if she was set on it he'd let her have her way so long as he wasn't the one to suffer. Let him return to a neglected house and meals not ready on time just once – not twice – and that'd be the end of it.

This was not what you'd call encouraging, but Rupert had wondered why his dad had given in. He didn't think it was about the extra money she'd bring in. It wasn't like Dad ever complained about Mum not doing a good job managing on the weekly housekeeping money he gave her, and decided it served her right having to pitch in the difference, which is what Timmy said his dad told his mum when she started cleaning in the mornings for Mr Sprague and his father. If asked if his parents were fond of each other, he'd have said he supposed so, but not in the way Mr Thatcher was of Mrs Thatcher. Still, could it have sunk in with Dad that Mum was getting fed up with having no one to talk to most of the day? He was only just beginning to see that himself. That stuff about winding wool – she'd asked him to help her with it a few times lately, whilst before she'd almost always used the back of a kitchen chair to hold the skeins. He told himself it wasn't his fault if she wished he was four instead of eleven and still wanted to spend lots of time with her. It was her showing she minded that got him all resentful and what she called rebellious. Perhaps he now thought his mother might ease up on him if she got out of the house more. But so far she hadn't been lucky getting work. Every time she went after a job Mrs Hewett told her about, either

someone'd got there first or it seemed she didn't suit. Timmy
said his mother didn't think everyone would want the local
constable's wife snooping through their house, causing
Rupert to wonder with a grin if that's what she did at the
Spragues'.

He decided upon rounding another corner, fair curls ruffled
and blue eyes sparkling, that he'd try to show Mum he thought
she was all right – as mothers went. She'd surely see that was
a lot coming from a boy of his age. He was now on Church
Road, with St Peter's to his right. Across from it, the walled
and gated rear grounds of Bogmire separated a scattering of
cottages. Three or four minutes from the Thatchers' now. About
to pedal faster, a plaintive meowing caught his ear, coming
from high up; it had to be an upstairs window, unless . . . this
was going to be one of those times! He stopped, feet on the
ground straddling the bike. A few feet ahead to the side of
one of the cottages stood a large elm. Way up, a furry ginger
face poked through the naked branches. Except for Rupert,
the street was empty of life. And not a net curtain twitched.
Another meow, more of a demanding screech this time, the
cat having obviously spotted him. Bother! There was nothing
for it but to climb up and rescue the little wretch, otherwise
its owner or a Good Samaritan would get word to Constable
Trout that he needed to come right away and get it down.

Rupert had often suspected that what some people liked
best about living in Dovecote Hatch was the opportunity to
watch his stout father inch up a tree, getting redder and puffier
in the face with each branch, to grab at a cat that the closer
he got to it went up higher, or suddenly decided it was perfectly
capable of skimming down on its own. There were times after
Dad had been jawing on at him about leaving his bedroom
light on, or something equally stupid, when Rupert would've
enjoyed seeing it too. But deep inside him was the nagging
thought, put there by Mum, that Dad would go up after a cat
once too often and have a heart attack. He'd even had a few
bad dreams and had woken in a panic that it'd really happened.
Leaving the bike propped by its kickstand alongside the curb,
he stood in front of the elm and called up to the cat in a cooing
voice.

'Here, puss, puss! Good puss! You can do it!' This resulted only in more meows, irritated sounding ones at that. Rupert felt like yelling that it'd got up there without help, so could just lump it, but that would only send it scampering onto a higher branch, and there wasn't time to waste. In the ordinary way he liked climbing trees and mounted this one nimbly. In next to no time he was within reach of the cat and managed to grasp hold of it without meeting resistance. He had it under one arm, then, turning slightly to steady his position, he was able to look out over St Peter's churchyard with its tombstones, some of them dating back hundreds of years, beyond to the folds of hills and woodlands. Gladness that he lived here bubbled inside him, if not for more than a second. The cat hissed, squirmed and snaked out a sharply clawed paw, catching Rupert on the neck.

But for his grip with his free hand on a sturdy branch (there were some dead ones that should've come down in a high wind), he'd likely have toppled to the ground. And he wasn't so sure he still wouldn't, the miserable beast continuing to struggle. A voice hailed him from below. A man's voice.

'Let him go and come down.'

Rupert wavered in place and in his mind. *William and the Outlaws* wouldn't have given in so easy. It'd be a point of honor with them to win the Battle.

'I'll get him. I'm wearing gloves.'

It was enough. Rupert let the cat go as it went for his face. He reminded himself as he went down the tree backwards that *William and the Outlaws* hadn't had Mr and Mrs Thatcher waiting for him. The ground once more beneath his feet, he turned to see Mr Sprague.

'Your neck's bleeding,' observed the church organist. 'Otherwise all right? I'll get it.' He looked and sounded hesitant, but then he always did. It was the only really noticeable thing about him. He was tallish and rather thin, and his face looked like one in a faded photograph. What no one looking at him would guess, but Rupert knew and would never forget, was what was inside him. Courage. If Mr Sprague hadn't plunged into the swiftly moving river to save him that day when he'd come close to drowning, Rupert didn't think he'd be alive. He'd be buried in the churchyard – one more tomb-stone. And here was Mr Sprague, again offering help.

'Saw you from my bedroom window,' he was saying. Church Road was a short street, ending with a right turn into Old Bridge Lane. Mr Sprague's house was just round the corner; its back garden bordered the churchyard. 'This cat is from Bogmire and doesn't have the best disposition, but it may remember seeing me there and give me a less difficult response.'

He went nimbly up the elm, talking gently to the creature as he went. Moments later he was back on the ground with it under his arm. His reward on setting it down – a hiss, then a leap over the Bogmire wall.

'How rude!' Rupert shook his head. 'But thank you, Mr Sprague.'

'Belongs to Miss Tenneson – Miss Matilda Tenneson, that is.'

'Oh! I hope it has better manners at home.'

'From what I've seen of it there, I wouldn't think so. Where are you off to, Rupert?'

'Mr and Mrs Thatcher's. I'm looking after their dog while they're out.'

'Does he have good manners?'

'He's a great little fellow.' Rupert was anxious to be off, but didn't want to show it. That would've been rude. Mr Sprague's uncertain expression had intensified. He was shy, that's what it had to be. Rupert had never suffered from this problem himself, but he knew from school that being shy often meant no friends and being picked on by bullies.

'How've you been, Rupert?'

'Fine, thank you, Mr Sprague.' He was about to ask how church had gone that morning – if the hymns had been good ones – but Mr Sprague had another question for him, spoken with a more focused look. Perhaps conversations got easier for him as they went along.

'How did your Guy Fawkes night go? Plenty of fireworks?'

'Didn't buy any. Some of our group got bad colds, making it worthless to celebrate.'

'So what did you do with the money? Treat yourselves to sweets?'

'No. It's still in the collecting tin on the wardrobe shelf, waiting for next year.' Rupert slid a glance towards his bike.

'I mustn't keep you. Good day,' said Mr Sprague, his voice diminished as if about to vanish back inside him after its airing.

'Goodbye, and thank you again.'

With a lift of his hand, Mr Sprague crossed the road. Rupert, getting on his bike, saw him enter St Peter's and wondered how much time he spent practicing on the organ, or just playing for the enjoyment of it. Was he lonely? He had no wife or children, and perhaps not many friends, just his father, who Timmy's mum said had grown very crotchety in his old age. It didn't seem much of a life, but Rupert stopped thinking about him once he turned onto Old Bridge Road and picked up speed, freewheeling on reaching the point where it sloped steeply downward before curving into the lane where the Thatchers lived. As a rule he would have reveled in the rush of air on his cheeks, but he was too anxious about being even a few minutes late to enjoy it this time. Would they be watching him in coats and hats from the front window?

Dismounting outside their house, he nearly forgot to take the string bag off the handlebars. Once inside he felt a lot calmer. Mr Thatcher had opened the door for him with a smile, saying: 'Right on the dot, Rupert. Knew you would be.' Behind him came Rex in a welcoming rush, suggesting his bad leg was back to normal, and Mrs Thatcher appeared in the kitchen doorway, also smiling.

'Well, if this isn't kind of you, Rupert, I don't know what is.'

'I'm glad you asked me.' He straightened up from crouching to stroke the dog to a delighted tail thumping. 'Rex and me'll have a grand time.' His eyes glowed. 'Anything special you need to tell me?'

'Only that we usually let him out into the back garden every couple of hours,' responded Mrs Thatcher with a smile. 'There's plenty of water in his bowl and he won't need feeding because we give him his night meal at six, though he likes a biscuit every now and then.'

'I bought him some as a present.' Rupert jiggled the string bag.

'Well, I never! That is kind of you. The nicest thing we've heard all week,' said Mr Thatcher, looking as pleased as if he'd just heard he'd won the football pools. 'Don't you think so, Doris?'

'I do! We feel lucky to have got to know you, Rupert. Maybe one day you'll feel comfortable enough to call us Uncle Alf and Auntie Doris.'

'Could I start now?'

''Course you can,' they replied together.

'Thank you; that'll be splendid!' Rupert's eyes now had the shine of tears. 'I don't have any real ones and I'm sure I'd like you better anyway. One more thing: would it be all right for me to take Rex for a walk? Cold Wind Common's only a few minutes away, but I'd keep to this road if you'd rather.'

Rex gave an enthusiastic woof. He really was clever.

''Course it's all right, and I'm sure he'd enjoy being out on the Common,' said Uncle Alf. 'We'll give you the spare key. It's on a shelf in the kitchen, behind a little jug with *A present from Southend* on it. That's where me and Auntie Doris met on holiday.'

They all moved to the kitchen, where Rupert was shown the key, informed there was a jam sponge in the cake tin on the table baked especially for him and he was to help himself from the pantry to anything else he fancied. Five minutes later the Thatchers left – Auntie Doris looking very smart in her red coat and black hat – leaving him and Rex to decide what to do first.

'How about that walk?'

Rex woofed approval. Rupert took down the key, attached the lead, and on their way out of the house set the string bag on the radiogram in the front room. He took out the book and bag of biscuits, pocketing one of the latter. It would be good to come back here, settle into one of the easy chairs with a slice of sponge cake and cup of milk and plan with Rex what to do next. The walk to Cold Wind Common took no time at all. Once there, Rupert removed the lead and suggested a race. It was growing nippy and it'd be good to warm up, but he was careful not to run too fast on account of the dog's injured leg, though there'd been no sign it wasn't as strong as ever.

They had the common to themselves and romped happily for ten minutes, Rupert letting Rex win on every circling, not worrying that he'd get too far ahead or wouldn't come when called. On past occasions he'd always done so immediately with or without the reward of a biscuit. They slowed to a walk. Rupert wondered what Timmy and the rest of his friends would think of the pleasure he'd taken in Mr and Mrs Thatcher wanting him to call them Auntie Doris and Uncle Alf. Probably decide he'd gone dotty. He didn't care. On returning to their house with Rex back on the lead, he practiced addressing them in this new way so it would come easy instead of sounding awkward. Back inside, he hung the lead and his coat on the hall tree. Looking cozily tired, Rex went into the kitchen to curl up in his basket by the domestic boiler.

Rather than getting himself a cup of milk, Rupert put the kettle on for tea and, while waiting for the kettle to boil, cut himself a slice of sponge cake. He'd just put it on the plate set out by the tin when the doorbell rang. Rex roused his head to woof but did not get out of the basket. Rupert turned off the kettle. Could it be one of the neighbors? Or his mother come to see how he was doing? Don't let it be her! It would make him feel that he'd shrunk back to being six. He walked to the front door, but before reaching it the bell gave another jarring ring – impatience vibrated. You'd think whoever was outside had been locked out of their own house. Suddenly Rex was at his side.

He could see two people through the glass insert, but whether one was his mother he couldn't tell. Not his father, that was one thing at least, because the helmet would've shown. To his surprise he found himself facing the Misses Tenneson from Bogmire. He recognized them both from having seen them in church. What on earth would bring them here? He couldn't imagine an acquaintance, let alone a friendship, between them and Auntie Doris and Uncle Alf. They were upper class, for one thing, besides not looking the sort too many people would want to get pally with.

'Out of our way, boy!' The shorter one poked him in the

middle with a walking stick. She was stumpily built with the face of a gargoyle – bulging forehead, baggy skin and popping eyes – glaring at him. 'We've come to see that woman who has destroyed our peace of mind. Whether her peasant of a husband is on the premises or not is a matter of no interest to us.'

Rupert bristled along with Rex. 'Do you mean Mr and Mrs Thatcher?' Could it be they'd come to the wrong house?

'Who else?'

'They're not home, so I can't let you in.' He went to close the door without saying he was sorry – it would have been a lie, and he only told those when he considered them to be strictly necessary, but it made no difference. He found himself propelled back down the hall.

'Let that dog continue to growl and I shall be forced to silence him with my stick.' This was wielded to such effect that Rex did not need the threat to be repeated.

'My dear Matilda, might you not be somewhat cajoling? Whoever this boy is, he can hardly be held accountable for your irritation of the nerves.' The other one had followed the gargoyle in and pressed the door shut behind her. She had a long, foolish-looking face with projecting teeth and a froth of mousy fringe in front. 'Wouldn't want to let the doggie out.'

Rupert's reaction was one of being trapped in a cage. He'd never felt so strong a need for his father. They were potty, both of them. Should be in a lunatic asylum. He managed to find his voice: 'My dad's Police Constable Trout; I'll fetch him if you don't leave at once.'

'Impudent urchin!' Another jab with the stick. 'Summon whom you wish. It will make not a whit of difference to us. We shall not depart until that woman apologizes for being born into our family.'

Rupert could only gape.

'What Miss Tenneson is endeavoring to explain, child,' the other one cooed at him, 'is that Mrs Thatcher is our long-lost sister, given away at birth because poor Mamma was concerned that Papa might be touchy when confronted with another girl when he was intent on a son. Dear man though he was, it never took much to set him off.'

The gargoyle rounded on her. 'How dare you, Lettice, speak of him so? He was the best of fathers! Not a day went by that I did not revere his every word.'

They were, without Rupert's realizing how, in the front room.

'Dearest,' cooed the one with the teeth and silly fringe, 'have we not disagreed sufficiently since Mr Pritchard brought us the news of our brother's new will?'

'Never again speak of him, as our brother, in my hearing! He was a changeling, brought up above his station and competence; but for the shaming of the situation I would disown him from the rooftops of Bogmire!'

Rupert was not only bewildered but in a fix. He supposed he should suggest they sit down and make themselves at home, even offer to make tea and bring it in for them. But that'd be encouraging them to stay and he didn't have that right. He already felt he'd failed Auntie Doris and Uncle Alf by allowing them inside. He wasn't worried they'd be cross with him. They'd understand; he was sure of that. They might even think it was all for the best – the women getting the chance to have their say. Perhaps they'd even be relieved he hadn't offended them.

The one named Matilda had sat down in the chair with Uncle Alf's slippers beside it and was staring grimly in front of her. 'No piano! What an existence! I'd prefer to have been born dead!'

The other, the Lettice one – stupid name – was wandering around the room picking up ornaments and inspecting them. Cheek!

When she started babbling on about being reminded of the dear little doll's house in the nursery at Bogmire, Rupert slid off to the kitchen with Rex at his heels to have a think and eat the slice of sponge cake he'd cut before the Invasion. He now knew how the English in 1066 must have felt when the Normans showed up at Hastings. It was cowardly of him to turn tail, but the women weren't going to burgle the place because he wasn't keeping an eye on them. Everything here was too far beneath them, and if they wanted to kill each other that was all right with him.

Aunty Doris, their sister? He shuddered on her behalf, and Uncle Alf's too. It went against nature, her being so nice. He wondered how long she'd known. If it was true, that is. Maybe something hard and heavy had crashed down on their heads when they were out walking. All in all, that seemed the likeliest explanation.

TWELVE

During their short walk from the café on Station Road to the Gladstone Hotel where Inspector LeCrane had requested they meet him to discuss Kenneth Tenneson's death, Florence and George had agreed not to say anything to him about the idea which had entered her mind. This was the possibility that Mr Tenneson might have been the father of the girl he had reared under the guise that she was the orphaned daughter of a friend of his. It was merest speculation based on the lack of clarity as to whether he had legally adopted her; an action that was highly likely to have necessitated producing her birth certificate and possibly other documents.

What could not be left out of the telling was Florence's belief that the woman in the headscarf, despite what had seemed to be the ravages of a hard life, bore a strong resemblance to Mercy Tenneson. It might mean nothing at all above coincidence. But what if it did provide a link between her and Bogmire? It would then be left to the inspector whether to explore that avenue or not. Florence admitted to George her nagging concern that she might have been influenced in her suppositions by her desire to discover for her own peace of mind whether the woman on the train and the one who had stepped fatally in front of the bus were one and the same.

'That's not your way, Florence,' replied George. 'You're what I'd call a cautious thinker, you don't go imagining things to be the way you'd like them to be. If Inspector LeCrane didn't know that, he wouldn't be asking for your help.' They rounded the corner onto the street where they should find the hotel halfway down. 'Before we show up, I've been thinking – it was only because he didn't get talking to you that he filled me in on what was on his mind, so's I could pass it along. It wasn't till further in he said perhaps I could be of help too.

Could be he felt he had to for politeness's sake after taking up my time.'

'I'm certain you're wrong about that. I can't imagine the inspector doing or saying anything out of concern of offending. He has charm, but he wouldn't extend it to the detriment of his job. If he hadn't trusted and respected you he'd never have taken you into his confidence beyond asking if you'd let me know he'd like to talk to me. The realization that you're in a position to pick up snippets of information at the pub may already have been in his head, or it suddenly struck him what a useful source you'd be of possibly pertinent information. More so, in fact, than I, seeing that talking out of school by the staff is discouraged at Mullings. The only exception with me is Mrs McDonald. She and I have been friends for a long time and her tales are never even approaching the malicious. It's possible she may know more about Bogmire and its inhabitants than I do.' Florence mused on this thought before adding that she wouldn't have felt as agreeable to getting involved in the Bogmire affair without George.

He smiled down at her. 'It is wonderful to have found each other at this special time of life. Have to pinch myself sometimes to believe it.'

'Yes, dearest George.' She found herself wishing there were no reasons to wait to marry, that they could do so tomorrow.

The Gladstone was a severe-looking red-brick building, dating from the days of that prime minister. They went in, entering a foyer steeped in hush, gloomy despite being lit by an overhead fixture and a scattering of lamps. It presented a decidedly masculine ambience, due in part to dark paneling and cumbersome furnishing, but also because of the stale cigar smell and the dustiness that came from it. The ideal haunt, no doubt, thought Florence, for middle-aged to elderly gentlemen whose main pleasure in life was sitting in roomy leather chairs with footstools for gouty legs whilst taking snuff and drinking vintage port. No such persons disturbed the silence by their comings or goings. If on the premises, they must be shuttered behind closed doors.

The only person present was the man standing behind the reception desk, and he might well have been the ghost of a contemporary to the Victorian prime minister. There was a suggestion of a prim, moldering dark suit giving off a faintly greenish hue, possibly retrieved from relics in an attic. Otherwise, until they came within a few feet of him, he seemed liable to vanish into a wisp of shadow cast by the ponderous staircase rising on his left into the gloaming. His shoulders hunched, he peered at them through wire-rimmed spectacles and bade them good afternoon in a quavering voice as if mystified as to why they were standing looking at him. George gave their names and explained they were here to meet a gentleman by the name of LeCrane at noon. It lacked five minutes to the hour, but the inspector wasn't the sort to keep them waiting unless unavoidably detained.

'What's that you say?' A wrinkled hand cupped an ear.

George repeated his inquiry. 'Do you know, sir, if he has arrived yet?'

The ancient appeared to rack a befuddled brain in the manner of someone asked to reel off the names of all the capitals of Europe in twenty seconds. 'Let me think . . . meeting someone at the Grange, did you say? I knew a fellow who was a butler there. We were in the Crimean War together. I'd get in touch with him on the . . .' he wavered a finger at the telephone on the wall alongside the desk, 'but wouldn't wish to disturb him. I believe he's dead.'

This was undeniably frustrating, but George had boundless patience; his heart went out to the man, as did Florence's. At his age he'd surely earned the right to spend his days in complete relaxation without any demands being put on him. They both hoped another staff member would appear to assist them. But astonishingly, he blinked behind the spectacles and emerged out of his fog to adjust his watch chain and cuffs before enquiring with aloof dignity how he might be of service. Had he been in a doze on his feet?

George explained again and received the reply that the gentleman in question was awaiting their arrival in the Green Room. He had requested one where he might be private with them.

'I thought that one best suited for such a purpose. He was gracious in his appreciation. My name is Stevens. If you will kindly accompany me I will take you to him.'

Having thanked him, Florence and George followed in his tottering wake beyond the foyer into a corridor lined with doors. Only one room was open to view through a velvet-swagged archway – a large, bookcase-lined apartment with the deep leather chairs Florence had imagined, positioned singly or in pairs. A dozen or so were occupied by the sort of men she had also pictured – she even saw one take a pinch of snuff and another with a leg supported by a hassock. Conversations were muffled under wheezing bronchial coughs and irritable snorts. Not at all an environment for elegantly gowned ladies daintily partaking of afternoon tea, though they must in former times have stayed at the Gladstone. It certainly appeared better suited to its current incarnation as a club for gentlemen inclined to the dour.

'The Green Room, sir and madam.' Stevens located the doorknob after only two attempts and preceded them inside. There could be no uncertainty as to why the apartment had been so designated. The walls were papered heavily in a dark olive matched by carpet and window hangings in the same color, and featured prominently in the fabric of four armchairs grouped before a fireplace which was belching out smoke but limited heat. An oil portrait of Mr Gladstone with a blackish-green background hung from the picture rail above it. Inspector LeCrane rose to his lean height from one of the chairs with a view of the doorway, coming forward to greet Florence and George, his thin face expressing pleasure. He then thanked Stevens for escorting them.

'My privilege to be of service, sir. Will there be anything else you require?'

LeCrane glanced enquiringly at his guests. 'Sherry? Tea?'

'Tea, please,' said Florence, knowing it would also be George's preference. Unusually for a man who ran a pub, he rarely drank anything stronger, and they presently needed especially clear heads. LeCrane nodded at Stevens.

'I will convey the information to the kitchen maid directly, sir.'

'And a plate of sandwiches, a variety if it can be managed.'

'I will speak to Ethel, sir. Regrettably standards are not what they once were.' Whether he was referring to sandwiches, kitchen maids or both was unclear. Upon his austere, tottery departure, the inspector urged them to be seated; they settled themselves in the two chairs across from his, to which he now returned.

'So very good of you both to agree to see me. Am I correct in thinking you are aware of the very recently discovered new will signed by Kenneth Tenneson?'

Florence eyed him in surprise. 'Yes, George has long been friends with Doris and Alf and I have come to know and like them. How did you find out about it, Inspector?'

'With little expenditure of effort, given that I am a godson to Walter Halfhide, the chief constable, who is acquainted with the late Mr Tenneson's solicitor, Henry Pritchard of the firm of Savage and Pritchard. I had already used the connection on encountering him, seemingly by chance, at the restaurant where he lunches daily, and casually elicited information about the will existing at Tenneson's death. There being no legal reason why he should not do so, he promptly sent me a copy, along with a copy of his mother's will as I'd requested. In the latter I found a point to ponder, but if you don't mind I will address that further into our conversation.'

Florence and George murmured accord.

'Given the dramatic nature of the new version of Tenneson's final earthly testimony, Mr Pritchard could barely contain his eagerness to discuss its contents. I need not have bothered remarking that his good friend Walter takes a minute interest in everything happening in the county. Which, if Mr Pritchard had thought about it for a second on either occasion, he would have recognized as far from the truth.' The inspector's smile curved in cynical amusement. 'My esteemed godparent possesses no such absorption in any topic save for shooting pheasants and dining upon the spoils. Most assuredly never in matters of crime, having only agreed to accept the pesky job of chief constable after a great deal of arm-twisting by his friend Lord Sunderby. Unless, that is,' the inspector's smile deepened, 'when confronted by the demeaning prospect of having to bring in Scotland Yard. But let us get to what is of primary importance. How are Mr and Mrs Thatcher reacting to . . .?'

He was interrupted by the arrival of a maid, presumably Ethel, wearing a worn black dress and dingy white apron and cap, and staggering under the weight of a loaded but not excessively heavy tray. Both men rose to assist her. Before they could do so she told them sourly she didn't need no help in the adenoidal voice frequently attributed to dim-witted female servants by Agatha Christie in her books.

Having planted the tray with a rattling thump on the low table in front of the chairs, she straightened up and gave them a resentful stare. 'Hope that suits, but if it don't there's nothing else that isn't saved for our gentlemen, and very touchy they gets if it's not what they like. Them sandwiches is roast beef with horseradish and chopped egg in mayonnaise. It's of no mind if you turn up your noses. You won't be back. Nobody comes a second time, 'cept for the members. And that's only 'cos they've nowhere else to go that don't cost a pretty penny.' She ended with a sniff. Agatha Christie maids, thought Florence, were invariably given to sniffing, making no return to their expressed gratitude.

'How utterly cheering,' remarked Inspector LeCrane on her departure. 'Would you kindly be mother, Mrs Norris?'

'With pleasure.'

How very handsome she looked in her brown hat and green coat, he thought, and what an intelligent, aware face she had. He not only admired her gifts of perception, but liked her . . . and George. They would make an ideal couple, bringing out the finest traits in each other. They would marry, he had no doubt, when the timing was right. Mrs Norris would wish to feel assured that young Lord Stodmarsh had sufficiently recovered from the emotional shock of the murder at Mullings before leaving her position of housekeeper. The union would be an entirely happy one in the inspector's opinion. He considered his own bachelorhood; it suited him entirely at the present, but possibly . . . one day in the future he'd rejoice in finding the ideal lifetime companion. By mutual accord, conversation on the topic of prime interest was not resumed while they drank cups of tea and partook of the surprisingly tasty sandwiches.

George began by saying that the Thatchers had rallied

remarkably well, all considered. ''Course, it all came as a terrible shock to them both. But Doris has always had her head screwed on good and tight and Alf's the sort of husband that's behind his wife every inch of the way, even when push doesn't come to shove. Besides doting on her. Not a woman to compare as far as he's concerned. Don't you agree, Florence?' He turned to her.

'Absolutely. They're a prize couple and you couldn't meet nicer people.'

'That's reassuring to hear. Do either of you object to my smoking?'

'Not at all,' said Florence, 'George enjoys a pipe occasionally.'

'It would be more often if it didn't keep going out while I'm serving up drinks.'

'I appreciate your indulgence.' The inspector reached into his inside pocket for his slim silver cigarette case and lit up. 'Have your friends decided on how to handle Mrs Thatcher's inheritance?'

George nodded. 'I was telling Florence before we got here that they want no part of it – the money or the house. They'd certainly never dream of moving in there. It sounds kind of odd, I know,' his voice rippled with mirth, 'but they'd see it as a come-down, not the opposite, leaving their comfortable little home to live in a barracks turned into a prison. That's Alf's view of Bogmire. Says his deliveries there've always given him the creeps; that if he was a Roman Catholic he'd cross himself before starting down the drive.'

'He has my utmost sympathy; I drove past it on my last visit to Dovecote Hatch, the one when I came to your pub, and seasoned as I am to grim-looking abodes and the evils within, I experienced the fanciful notion that if I'd been on foot and anywhere close to the front door an invisible hand might reach out to drag me over the threshold.'

'I've never seen the house, Inspector, but I take your word for it,' returned Florence.

'No concern on either of your parts that the Thatchers might change their minds about moving in, even temporarily?' Inspector LeCrane's eyes followed the wispy coil of smoke headed for the ceiling to merge into the mesh of cobwebs.

'Not on your Nellie!' The words were out before George could decide they might not be best suited to the ears of a man of such elevated good breeding and education as the one seated opposite him.

Florence added vigorously to this statement. 'Even if they were tempted, which as we've said they absolutely are not, Doris would consider it an insult to her parents – the ones that brought her up – to set foot inside for as little as five minutes. And that's a huge relief to me and George.'

'Worried for their safety?' Inspector LeCrane disposed of his finished cigarette in the ashtray.

She answered, 'How can we not be, given even the slightest possibility that Mr Tenneson's death resulted from his two sisters having learned of the new will? George has been fretting about that from the moment Alf filled him in on what he and Doris had learned at Mr Pritchard's office on Friday.'

'I confess to being in complete agreement with your fears.' The inspector withdrew another cigarette from his case. 'If the information given to Constable Thatcher by the two Misses Tenneson is correct, they were alone in the house except for the housekeeper, who was the one to discover the body. Anything is possible, but it seems unlikely she would have become so overcome with rage at her long-time employer that she'd be moved to dispose of him.'

'Surely the advent of an intruder cannot be discounted,' said Florence, her thoughts returning to the woman in the headscarf. 'And what of Mr Tenneson's ward? Where was she at the time of death?'

'Visiting an old lady by the name of Mrs Weedy.' Inspector LeCrane applied his silver lighter to the cigarette. 'Yes, she could have slipped back to Bogmire unnoticed, done the deed and speedily returned to Laurel Cottage – if I remember the name from my notes correctly. Old people do have a tendency to doze off. Mercy Tenneson may have waited for Mrs Weedy to drift off and grasped her opportunity, confident her absence would not have been noticed and she would still have her alibi corroborated. There is, however, the question of motive.

If there should be one, it seems unlikely to have sprung from discovering a change to his will. Her inheritance is a large one, Mr Tenneson having invested wisely the money left to him by a friend from his war days, and it has increased substantially to very nearly ten thousand pounds. Of course, if outraged on the Misses Tennesons' behalf, who knows? She may be unbalanced.' Inspector LeCrane shrugged a shoulder.

'I know it's reaching at straws,' said Florence, 'but was there anyone else at Bogmire during the day?'

'Who might suddenly have happened upon a reason to do away with Kenneth Tenneson?'

'Maybe it isn't so far-fetched,' put in George. 'You never know what goes on in the heads of people you wouldn't think would hurt a fly.'

'Indeed. I cannot count the times where the cases with which I've been involved have proved that truth. We do know that two people were present during that day at Bogmire. I'll begin with Neville Sprague, the church organist. The housekeeper says she admitted him to the house at two o'clock in the afternoon and took him up to the music room, where Miss Lettice Tenneson awaited him. According to that lady, she had requested he come and accompany on the piano whilst she went through the hymn she was to sing as a solo at the church service on the following Sunday. "Jesu, Joy of Man's Desiring," I believe.'

Florence and George exchanged glances. 'Oh, dear!' she exclaimed involuntarily.

Inspector LeCrane surveyed her with the quiver of a smile. 'You dislike Bach?'

'Oh, no! It's that . . . unfortunately Lettice Tenneson has a . . . poor singing voice.'

'Excruciating?'

'I'm afraid so.'

'Whilst laboring under the delusion, given the intended solo, that she's been bestowed with a heavenly gift worthy of the archangels? One encounters such thinking oftener than one would wish. Is it necessary to ask if she considers herself a soprano?'

'I'm afraid so.'

'God forbid!'

'That's putting it about right,' said George, seeing that Florence wished she'd never set this conversation going and needed rescuing. 'Screeching; worse than any knife on any sink. Sets my teeth on edge and I'm not what you'd call halfway musical. It's bad enough when she just sings with the choir. The others can't drown her out, but it helps some. Poor Sprague! I can't imagine what that session was like for him.'

'So small a church as St Peter's is very lucky to have him as church organist.' Florence was relieved to be back on more comfortable ground. 'He's extremely accomplished. Takes private students for piano and, I believe, violin lessons.'

'How often does Lettice Tenneson perform her solos?'

'I don't make it to morning service every Sunday, but I would think from . . .'

'The subsequent murmurings of complaint?'

Florence could not refrain from returning the inspector's deepening smile. 'Yes, which occur three or four times a year. Do you know what time Mr Sprague left Bogmire that day?'

'The housekeeper did not let him out, but according to Lettice Tenneson it could not possibly have been later than four thirty, if that late. An eternity, we can presume, for him; although she thinks they may have talked for half an hour or so before his departure as she always likes to be congenial and would have welcomed his staying longer had she not become aware he was on edge to go, on account of it being his father's birthday, as he had mentioned.'

Florence wondered how many times she had needed to be reminded, given that she was an incessant talker. 'What does Mr Sprague say about when he left?'

'I have not heard that he's been asked.' The inspector directed a question to George. 'Does he ever stop in at the Dog and Whistle?'

'Only on his father's account. Two or three times a week he'll see him inside, usually around eight, and return for him ten minutes or so before closing. The old man's very deaf and growing a little addled. Sits gnawing on his thumb until it looks raw. I remember,' George hesitated, 'once overhearing him shout at the person he was talking to, that his son had once tried to poison him by putting something wicked tasting on it. Probably bitter aloes, is what I thought – you know, that stuff mothers sometimes put on their children's thumbs to stop them from sucking them. I could see why Sprague'd feel he should try it. I don't think the old man'd be of any reliable help as to what time his son got home, but that's not why I brought up his grumbling about his son. It wouldn't have been only me in the Dog and Whistle that evening that heard him, leaving alone those he was talking to, and now I'm concerned that if it turns out Mr Tenneson's fall wasn't accidental and that the younger Mr Sprague had been in the house that day, word could get round unfairly that he'd tried to murder his own father.'

The inspector nodded. 'Opportunity trumping the lack of perceivable motive.'

Florence asked him who was the other outsider at Bogmire on the day of Kenneth Tenneson's death.

'A seamstress – Miss Hatmaker, from around nine in the morning until four. She is quite certain it was no later because she never stays longer, it being her one firm requirement, as she eats her evening meal punctually at five.' The inspector tapped his cigarette over the ashtray. 'She'd been there the previous day too, attending to the mending. She came again because Miss Matilda Tenneson wanted her to alter some clothing and was closeted with her in that regard for what she is sure was more than a couple of hours until her departure.'

Florence eyed him thoughtfully. 'She was not summoned to speak at the inquest,' she said.

'No reason was perceived for her doing so.' Inspector LeCrane returned her look with an equally level one. 'Please do proceed, Mrs Norris.'

'That missing coat sleeve button?'

'Neither Constable Trout nor the doctor noted it.'

'So George told me.' She could have reminded the inspector that Dr Chester had been insufficiently observant on one vital occasion at Mullings, but to do so wasn't in her character. Besides, she liked Dr Chester and thought him otherwise a very good doctor. 'They could have seen it was gone, but thought it unimportant; buttons come off all the time and don't get sewn back on right away. If they're lost, a matching replacement has to be located.'

'I've gone around with missing buttons often enough,' agreed George. Something was niggling at the edge of his mind . . . something that might be important, but wouldn't come. 'Not when my wife was alive, of course, but before I married and after she died.'

Florence touched his hand, and then turned her gaze back to the inspector. 'But Miss Hatmaker having been at Bogmire the day before working on the mending does make the absence significant. She was in the habit of coming to Mullings once a week when the late Lord Stodmarsh was alive to inspect his attire for needed repairs; he didn't have a valet. I know her to be an extremely punctilious woman. If she did the same for Mr Tenneson on a regular basis, I cannot imagine her allowing that button to come loose. Perhaps you might talk to her again, Inspector.'

'May I entrust that task to you, Mrs Norris? My object at the present being to remain well in the background, so as not to put a particularly interested party on notice to be on his or her guard.'

'I understand,' George said. 'You want us to see what we can discover by exercising a subtle approach on your behalf. I could try for a word with Major Wainwright.'

'Ah!'

'He isn't one of my regulars but he does come to the Dog and Whistle fairly frequently. He was in last Monday evening and I noticed he didn't seem himself. I hadn't been aware he was a friend of Mr Tenneson, which would be enough in itself to have left him feeling low; and now we know about his involvement in the new will, that would explain it even better, because either he'd already handed it over to the solicitor, Mr Pritchard, or was about to do so.'

'Thank you, that could prove helpful. Mr Tenneson may well have shared other potentially important confidences with him. I realize I'm imposing, asking a great deal of you both.' Inspector LeCrane eyed them ruefully. There was also, however, a grimness to his expression that augured ill for the killer of Kenneth Tenneson, if indeed such a person existed. In what state of mind that individual might now be – gloating, panicked to the point of striking again if deeming it essential – it was impossible to guess.

'We're willing to do what we can to help,' Florence assured him.

'I have to say the idea didn't sit all that well with me first off, even though I know it isn't right to look the other way when obligated to do your bit,' said George. 'It doesn't feel nice asking people questions on the sly, listening for what they could let slip talking at the pub, watching them – comparing their behavior to what it'd been in the past, in case there was something they thought they should've told and made a difference at the inquest, or didn't even realize they knew about, that doesn't fit the information as you have it. Making for someone being mistaken or telling a deliberate lie about that day. But it's different now, with Alf and Doris having been brought into the picture.'

'I understand completely,' returned the inspector.

'Although maybe I've overreacted some, worrying so much about Doris's safety if one of the Misses Tenneson was involved because of the will,' George included Florence in his thoughtful look, 'but she might not feel the need to act so drastic with Doris if a loophole was to be found that'd let her and the sister contest the will successfully.'

'Ah, but alas for them, I think that highly unlikely, bringing me back to the point I found curious in their mother's will. I should start by telling you that the wealth at Bogmire came from Irma Tenneson, not her husband; he brought little to none into their marriage.'

'I wonder,' mused Florence, 'how much that contributed to his bullying of her. Doubtless he didn't need the incentive, being an arrogant and thoroughly bad-tempered man, but it must have stuck in his craw.'

'Indeed! Her father was a rich, self-made man. Brains, but lacking the niceties of the upper class. To counteract this imbalance on his daughter's behalf, he had her educated at an excellent school, besides having her privately tutored in elocution, music and art, and later having her chaperoned on a year abroad. Bogmire was their home. And you will see how that explains the jewelry she sold to pay the Greens.'

Florence and George had no wish to interrupt. Inspector LeCrane continued fluidly, 'The marriage was convenient to both parties. Irma's father wanted a husband for her of established background, and Horatio Tenneson fitted that requirement. He was out for a rich wife.'

Florence did now have a question. 'But wouldn't her fortune and Bogmire have become legally his after the wedding?'

'Given an archaic system, yes. However, her father held different views on women's rights – at least as applied to his daughter. He tied everything up so his son-in-law had no claim on the house and access only to the annual income derived from the capital. Everything was hers to dispose of as she wished in her will.'

Neither Florence nor George asked how he'd come by this information. He had his sources, including the chief constable, amongst the movers in county society. 'This brings us to what drew my attention upon reading it; without having done so, I might have decided not to pursue matters – the position of Kenneth Tenneson's body and the missing button being interesting but open to question as to their significance.'

'How did she bequeath her estate?' enquired Florence. George was leaning forward.

'Ten thousand pounds to each of her daughters. All else,' Inspector LeCrane stubbed out his cigarette, 'to Kenneth Horatio Tenneson. No mention of his being her son to provide the now needed loophole. But as the Thatchers are not going to rock the boat, I think you may relax on their behalf.' An interruption came with the opening of the door and the tottering advance of Stevens from the reception desk.

'I thought it right to tell you,' he said in his quavery voice, 'that with the evening being advanced I shall be going to bed.' The mantel clock disagreed as to the time of day but refrained from chiming in.

'My word!' The inspector regarded him equably. 'How one does lose track of the time. Will you have any objection to our remaining a little longer?'

'As you wish, sir, though I should warn you it may be unwise to linger. Marauders abound in the streets with their cudgels. But you are still young and can perhaps fend them off without suffering too grave an injury. The maid should still be about here if you should require anything further. I believe her name is Ethel.'

'I seem to remember that was it.'

'Possibly, though she may have been the one who ran off with the traveling salesman. Or was it a circus clown? These young girls today! Comes from knitting themselves jumpers. Never used to be such garments. The very word "jumpers" does not sound respectable to my ears.' Stevens shook his already shaky head before making his inch-by-inch departure.

'Poor old fellow,' remarked Inspector LeCrane. His face sobered. 'I sense from your intent expression, Mrs Norris, that you wish to disclose something to me.'

George looked startled.

Florence smiled. 'You could have said wish to ask, tell or explain, but of course you've had years of experience reading faces.' She proceeded, as exactly as she could, with an account of her encounter with the woman in the headscarf. The fear she was about to throw herself on the railway line. What she, Florence, could see of her on the journey to London – the nebulous impression that she might be foreign, that she might have aged before her time due to a hard life. On to the presence in the carriage of the clergyman, his sister, wearing a pince-nez, and the children they were taking to see Hansel and Gretel on ice. The name of the clergyman's parish – St Clement's. The way the red-haired boy seated opposite the woman had stared at her. Then hearing on the wireless after reaching her cousin Harriet's about the woman who had walked in front of the bus and the questioning in her mind as to whether she and the one in the headscarf might be the same person. Only then did she mention the perceived resemblance to Mercy Tenneson.

Inspector LeCrane had listened intently. He now sat silent for what had to be a full minute, before responding, 'Thank you, Mrs Norris. Compelling; providing much food for thought.

I do have a piece of information for you. The woman killed by the bus has been identified by a neighbor who'd begun to worry about her absence, and as it happens, mentioned that there was something not quite English about her, though not speaking like a foreigner.'

He was interrupted at that juncture by the maid, Ethel, entering the room. If she were a girl who giddily knitted jumpers, Stevens's views on what constituted a girl were elastic. Ethel, had he given her name accurately, looked to be forty at least, with hair more gray than brown. Eyeing them sourly, she asked if it was all right for her to remove the tea tray, making it more than plain she'd be glad if they did the same with themselves. Given the possibility that she was eager to begin giddily dusting or getting out the carpet sweeper, she had a point. Inspector LeCrane assured her they required nothing more and would be leaving within ten minutes. George, being closer to the door than he, lifted the tray and carried it out into the passageway, where she took it from him with begrudging thanks.

Florence had been inwardly on tenterhooks waiting for the inspector to continue; hopefully with further revelations. He did so as soon as George was reseated. 'I'm afraid I can't give you the name of the woman identified by the neighbor, my interest in the matter being cursory, but I believe Christian and surname were ordinary. I will, of course, get them to you. What I do recall is that she lived alone in the top flat of a converted house in a decent district. The neighbor has the ground-floor one and provided the information that the woman rarely had visitors apart from a man who had started showing up recently, described by the neighbor as looking a thoroughly bad lot. The night before the bus incident she had seen him go up the staircase and afterwards heard what sounded like a violent altercation. After seeing the man leave shortly afterwards she went up to find out what had happened and saw bruising on the right side of the woman's face.'

Florence thought the inspector had remembered a great deal. 'If she was the one on the train that could explain what the boy with ginger hair seated opposite her was staring at.'

The inspector acknowledged this. 'The neighbor said she saw the woman from the top flat leave early the following morning and when she did not return that day or in the ones following, thought she had sensibly gone away for a while. But considering she hadn't been carrying a handbag, let alone a suitcase, the neighbor began to worry, which is when she went to the police. You may well be on to something, Mrs Norris. If so, what we need is a trail to Bogmire.'

THIRTEEN

Florence and George decided some twenty minutes later when seated in his car to take a detour to visit the textile factory town of Westbridge. She had grown up there until leaving to start working at Mullings. Her father had died many years previously, but her mother still lived there, now at the home of her other daughter Ada and son-in-law, Bob. Persuading her to move in with them had not been easy, Mrs Wilks resisting every inch of the way. It had, however, become abundantly clear that she was no longer able to manage on her own. Ada and Bob were being bricks about her still disgruntled attitude. Fred – Florence and Ada's brother – was of no help, rarely coming to see his mother, although he lived close by and had no family, wife or children, to put claims on his time. Florence regretted not being able to shoulder more of the load. She sent money once a month and went with George to Westbridge once a fortnight, taking with them a basket of food, including Mrs McDonald's wonderful bread, but that was little indeed in lifting the burden borne by Ada and Bob.

Florence was not expected back at Mullings until early evening. Her mind had been so caught up in other directions that it hadn't occurred to her until she was in the car that here was the perfect opportunity for the visit. George agreed wholeheartedly. She had bought Ada a tablecloth and Bob a pipe rack in D.H. Evans, along with a napkin ring for her mother, unable to think of anything else she might be likely to use. Even so, it wouldn't be well received. Nothing pleased Mrs Wilks these days.

'What makes it seem so unfair,' said Florence as George turned onto the road to Westbridge, 'is that Mother was never really fond of Ada.'

'Unfortunately that's so often the way of things; you can't let yourself feel guilty,' he answered soothingly.

'I know. It doesn't help anything. What might is for her and
Bob to have a break, go away for a holiday. I've suggested it,
offered to come and stay with Mother, but Ada won't hear of
it. She says what does more than anything to keep her and
Bob's spirits up is having the grandchildren – the ones living
down the street – come round every day.'

'Maybe she'll have a change of heart and agree to your
offer.'

'Perhaps. What I'm sure of is they won't mind our showing
up on the hop. They've grown very fond of you, George.'

'I feel the same in return. They made me feel welcome right
from the start.'

There was not much traffic on the road. George was a
careful whilst not a dawdling driver, and they headed for
Westbridge in comfortable silence. Florence, as always, felt
embraced by security in having his solid bulk beside her,
knowing that their thoughts were frequently in tandem. They
had said very little since leaving the Gladstone Hotel about
what they had learned from Inspector LeCrane, knowing each
would want to first mull over the information in their heads.
Her first task would be to talk to Miss Hatmaker the seamstress, and his to discover what if anything he could find out
from Major Wainwright.

They were greeted warmly by Ada and Bob on reaching
their spotlessly kept home. It reminded them of the Thatchers'
in that regard, as well as being unfussily comfortable. Mrs
Wilks's reception of them was lukewarm despite George's
paying particularly close attention to what she said, which was
little. She lived in a world of her own, focused on her days
in service to a noble family in the north, the grandeur of whose
estate far outshone Mullings. She mentioned this again to
Florence before relapsing back into silence.

Ada, standing behind her chair, shook her head. She'd just
told Florence in a lowered voice that she'd purchased the chair
out of the money Florence sent, it being just the right size and
comfortable support for an elderly person sitting for much of
the day. Florence had agreed, but now on following her sister
into the kitchen to get tea ready, she added the hope that Ada
and Bob would treat themselves next time to something they

wanted. She again brought up the idea of the two of them going away, if only for a few days.

Ada shook her head. 'It's kind of you, Florence, but we're the home and slippers kind.' She took a fruit cake out of its tin. 'I'd much rather have that nice tablecloth you brought, and Bob's thrilled to bits with his pipe rack. So stop worrying. My lot's not as bad as you'd think. In a funny sort of way, it helps that Mother was never fond of me; I got used to her criticizing me years ago and now it blows right over my head. Do you know, I used to wonder when I was little if I was a foundling, but that idea went out the window, because she'd never have taken one in.'

Florence instantly thought of Doris and Mercy Tenneson and what made for a real mother or father. She put out flap-jacks, lemon curd tarts and mince pies, and made the tea while Ada sliced tomato and cheese sandwiches and added a dish of pickled onions. The result, eaten in the sitting room, was perfect, the bread not the least bit stale as Mrs Wilks complained it was. Afterwards she fell asleep in her new chair, and it was possible to fully enjoy the remaining hour or so of their stay.

George made no comment on her mother's behavior when they were back in the car. She'd explained to him after he'd met her for the first time that it was nothing new, only exaggerated by age. Now, as they drove away, he spoke only of what a good sense of humor Ada and Bob both had and how much he liked being with them. Florence didn't tell him what else Ada had said to her in the kitchen – that she hoped they wouldn't take too long about getting married, or at least not wait until they were in bath chairs. It wasn't that he'd think Ada interfering; this just wasn't the time to attempt to focus on their own lives. They discussed their meeting with Inspector LeCrane, though not at length, because both their minds were chiefly occupied with concern for how Alf and Doris had fared on their visit to her sister-in-law. The last thing they needed was any kind of upset, however minor, to add to what they'd gone through over the last couple of days. It was nearing six o'clock when the car reached Dovecote Hatch. Doris and Alf should be back by now; they'd talked of returning between four and five. Ordinarily Florence would have felt the need to return at once to Mullings, but when George suggested they call in at the Thatchers' on the way there she was as anxious as he to do so. He had stopped the car at the curb outside and they had just got out when a woman whom he recognized as an occasional customer, along with her husband, came hurrying across the road to them, speaking in gasps.

'I was at the window and saw your car turning the corner, Mr Bird. I've been back and forth looking out ever since they set off an hour ago – the Thatchers! Saw them with me own two eyes, getting into a taxi, both of them with a suitcase. I'd just that minute stepped outside to fetch in the screwdriver my hubby had left lying there after fixing the shed door.'

They stared at her blankly. The woman appeared to belatedly notice Florence.

'Oh, hello, Mrs Norris, I'm Mrs Hardy. Sorry for ignoring you, but I've been asking myself ever since what on earth must have happened.' The woman's breathing was beginning to slow down. 'I've talked to others in the street since, and all to a one told me neither of the Thatchers said a dickybird about going away. Oh, another thing! They had that little dog with them. Do you think it could have anything to do with him and the trouble Ivy Waters has been giving them?'

'I'm sure not,' answered George. 'That's been settled. She even apologized to them. There has to be some other reason.' Florence, who nearly always managed to remain calm in the face of possible cause for alarm, was impressed by how unperturbed he sounded. 'They said yesterday they were planning on going to Tuswall early this afternoon to see Doris's sister-in-law; perhaps they discovered on getting there she was ill and felt they should go and look after her until she felt better.'

'Suppose that could be it,' said Mrs Hardy doubtfully, 'but it seems queer they didn't explain before taking off.'

George and Florence couldn't have agreed more. Before they could respond, another woman appeared, also from across the road. She was stout, red-faced and clearly agog. 'You talking about the Thatchers leaving in that taxi?'

'Nice of you to bother asking, Miss Dobbs,' Mrs Hardy snapped back. 'I was round your house not half an hour gone, knocking on your door to see if you knew anything about it.'

The reply was smug. 'I heard you. Banging is more like it. I didn't bother opening up because I was having my supper, and I don't like being interrupted once I'm sat down at the table. I guessed what it was about. Two taxis showing up outside the same house on one afternoon is something that hasn't happened before in my memory, and I've lived here most of my life.'

'Two taxis?' Mrs Hardy echoed, her surprise obviously too great to bother looking affronted.

'That's right. The first was a couple of hours earlier. I couldn't see who or even how many got out of it or who let them inside, because I didn't have my glasses on.' She wasn't wearing them now. 'But it's easy enough to find out who came and where the Thatchers were headed. There's only one taxi service in Dovecote and that's Mr Wood's. We only have to ask him.'

'Talk of stating the obvious!' scoffed Mrs Hardy.

'I don't think it right to do that; indeed, I'm very much against meddling and creating a stir,' said George firmly, 'If Alf and Doris had wanted anyone to know their business they'd have shared it. For all any of us know, they could be back early tomorrow.'

Once they were back in the car and around the corner, he glanced at Florence. 'Of course I'm worried, as I know you are, but I couldn't let those women know that.'

She agreed. 'Though you were right in what you said. Otherwise I'd advise we go and talk to Rupert Trout and find out from him who arrived at the house while he was looking after the dog and whether they were still there when Doris and Alf got home. But that would be the worst thing we could do, with his father being Constable Trout and perhaps feeling compelled to make enquiries.'

'No, that wouldn't do at all; they're already dreading the tongue-wagging to come without adding to it. I'm hoping they left a phone message waiting for me.'

'Maybe. Although they wouldn't have expected us to stop by as we did and be anxious. They knew you were picking me up at the railway station and would assume we'd have a lot to talk about and want time to ourselves until I needed to return to Mullings.'

'And they've no idea we've been concerned for their safety.'

'What if they found out by way of their visitor, or visitors, that they may be at risk? Let's suppose it was the solicitor, Mr Pritchard, in that first taxi, come to warn them to be careful because he had suspicions, increased by talking with Inspector LeCrane, that danger lurks. I know that sounds dramatic, but I can't think of a better way to put it.'

George thought she looked and sounded tired; it had been a long day for her, with the train journey the least of it. 'Neither can I, dear.'

'Yes.' Florence was remembering Hattie's recounting of *The Body in the Buttery*. 'But we're bound to hear from them very soon.'

''Course we are.'

Presently they arrived at Mullings, George driving in through the rear grounds with their ornamental lake, herbaceous borders, rose gardens and fountains. With its purity and symmetry of line, the house was an exquisite example of Queen Anne architecture. Lamplight gleamed through, casting a golden glow upon the mellow brick that was beautiful and inviting.

'You're going to be very much occupied,' said George, drawing up close to the side entrance leading to the kitchen and other rooms used by the staff. 'Would you prefer to telephone me rather than the other way round if there is a message waiting?'

'I think that would be best. I'll do so at the very first moment I get.'

They got out of the car and he kissed her cheek after leaning into the back seat for her suitcase. Florence experienced an intense pang at the necessity to part from him even for the evening. His expression told her he shared it. He went in with her and deposited the suitcase in the passageway as he deemed proper and knowing they were of like mind on this. Not that Lord Stodmarsh or his grandmother would mind how long he lingered. Indeed, His Lordship had encouraged him to come to Mullings as often as he liked, but in his view and hers it just wouldn't do. She felt she was already stepping over the line in continuing to call His Lordship Ned in private, but he had insisted he'd be wounded if she didn't.

No sooner had the side door closed behind George than Grumidge emerged from the butler's pantry with a warm smile of greeting for Florence. He was a man in his late thirties to early forties, neatly built, with smooth, dark hair and keen eyes in an intelligent face. He always presented an impassive demeanor in the best tradition of the ideal butler when required above stairs and a firm, if fair one with the staff exclusive of Florence and Mrs McDonald. His outward manner to head housemaid Molly had always been strictly correct, before and after their recent marriage.

'Welcome back, Mrs Norris. You have been much missed.'

'Thank you, Mr Grumidge.' Florence hoped her voice and manner were sufficiently bright, that there was no hint of being distracted by what had happened. 'It is good to return, but I'm sure Molly has done extremely well in my stead.'

His face lit up as he would only have allowed with her, their relationship having been an excellent one over the years, besides being fully aware of her desire for Molly to take over as housekeeper in the relatively near future. 'I believe you will feel reassured, Mrs Norris, by how she has handled the opportunity to stand in for you, and her confidence in dealing with the household expenditures and recording of them.'

'I'm so pleased and grateful to hear it.'

'She will appreciate that. Before I take your suitcase up to your room I have a message to relay from His Lordship.'

'Yes?'

'It is that he deeply regrets not being on the premises to greet you, but he felt it incumbent upon him to leave not fifteen minutes since to go over to Farn Deane.'

'Is there a problem?'

'Tom Norris telephoned to inform him that there is a horse suffering from colic which he and the stableman had managed to get standing after finding the creature writhing on the ground, but now it must be kept walking in circles, in all probability for hours, if it is to have a chance of recovery. Unfortunately I know nothing of horses and hope I'm conveying the situation accurately. His Lordship may not be able to return until the middle of the night, or even the morning, but will see you as soon as possible.'

'I understand completely and why Tom felt compelled to get in touch with His Lordship. They'll both view it as tragic if the horse has to be destroyed. I shall be anxious to know how the poor animal does.'

'Of course. I'll take your suitcase up now. Molly will be down momentarily; she is taking a final look to ensure you'll find your room exactly as you would wish.'

'You're both very thoughtful.'

Tom Norris was Florence's deceased husband's younger brother. They'd shared a boundless love of the land and had planned to manage the Stodmarsh home farm between them on their father's death. There'd been Norrises at Farn Deane for centuries and the late Lord Stodmarsh had highly respected and valued those working it during his lifetime. He and Her Ladyship had been delighted when she'd married Robert. Ned had been in the habit of going there with Florence for Sunday tea ever since he was a small boy, frequently on encouragement from his grandparents.

Florence had maintained a close relationship with Tom and his wife, Gracie, and did so to this day. Childless, it had grieved them that his passing would bring the end of an era.

That sadness was lifted by Ned's wish upon leaving school, and having decided against going up to university, to make Farn Deane his primary occupational interest in the estate. He spent most of his daytime hours there, the bond between him and Tom deepening into an affection close to that of father and son. Florence rejoiced in this and was glad Ned was there now to physically assist and emotionally support her brother-in-law at Farn Deane whilst Gracie provided sustenance for them by way of quick but heartening food breaks and drinks. She also acknowledged to herself that she felt relieved that Ned was not present to welcome her back to Mullings. He knew her too well not to recognize that she had something distressing on her mind which she did not feel free to confide in him.

She was about to turn from the passageway to go into the Mullings kitchen, where she knew she must be at the ready to provide her own welcome, when Molly came down the stairs. Dark-haired, prettily plump and rarely out of temper, she was now beaming.

'Oh, Mrs Norris, it is good to have you back! The place isn't the same without you.'

Florence expressed her pleasure at seeing Molly. 'Mr Grumidge told me how well you managed during my absence and that's so very reassuring, knowing that when I leave Mullings for a different life, it will be in your capable hands for many years to come.' She indeed believed this would be so, because Molly had told her she did not want children, having done her share of mothering in helping rear her numerous brothers and sisters. A decision with which Mr Grumidge, now her husband, was in full agreement.

'I expect you're ready, if not positively gasping, for a cup of tea. I'll take your hat and coat and hang them up for you. They're much too smart to lay on a chair or even hang on a hook down here. Mrs Tressler asked me to tell you that after you've settled yourself, taking all the time over it you like, she'll be pleased to see you in the drawing room and hear about your visit in London. What a lovely lady she is, Mrs Norris.'

'We're all very fortunate having her here.'

'Such a blessing, especially so, of course, for His Lordship.' Molly vanished up the stairs with the brown hat and green coat.

Florence hesitated a moment before entering the kitchen to be greeted by the delightful smell of baking gingerbread. Mrs McDonald was not only a dear friend but a sensible woman inclined to view disturbing matters from the most reasonable of perspectives. It would have been at the least a temporary comfort to confide in her. She was standing by the vast, scrubbed table on which a teapot sat on its trivet along with the accompanying crockery and a Madeira cake. In build, she was the female equivalent of George, a massive woman over six feet tall and broad of girth without being fat. She had a fine head of snowy white hair and blue eyes, now sparkling.

'Florence! The past few minutes I've been counting till you were free to come in here.' Her voice was suited to her size, for which she said she thanked God, because a reedy let alone squeaky one would have been laughable. It held no hint of a Scottish accent; understandably, because she hadn't so much as spent a day there, her grandparents on her father's side having been the ones to move to England. Mrs McDonald was the only member of the staff to call Florence by her Christian name. It was only because she intensely disliked hers, which was Minnie and had never fitted right, that Florence didn't use it.

'I've missed our times together, Mrs McDonald, particularly our late evening chats over cups of cocoa,' she said when they were sitting at the table.

'So've I. Best part of the day for me. Funny how these little rituals come to mean such a lot. If you're wondering where Jeannie and Annie are, I told them they could have a short break while you and me caught up on things. Oh! Here's a piece of news for you. Don't know if you saw it coming – I didn't – but Jeannie's getting married.'

Florence put down the morsel of fruit cake she'd been nibbling to please her friend, not because she felt like it. 'No, I didn't. Who to?'

'Mrs Hewett's nephew, Billie Anderby.'

'The one that works evenings at the cinema?'

'That's him. I think it must be quite a recent romance, but they're not waiting to tie the knot. Jeannie's given a fortnight's notice. Says she's getting a job there too. I hope it all works out. You know what they say about marrying in haste, repenting at leisure.'

'On the other hand, Jeannie's the sort of girl who knows her own mind.'

'For the moment, maybe.' Mrs McDonald didn't sound convinced of a happy ever after. 'She'll be a loss here; I'll admit that. For whatever I say about her being snippy, given half a chance she's a hard worker. And it's not so easy these days to find someone new. Girls aren't as keen as they were about going into service. They used to be grateful for a roof over their heads and their meals found. Now they'd rather be typists or shop assistants, given the chance. Oh, well, we'll see.'

Florence forced herself to set aside her eagerness to telephone George; that would have to come after presenting herself to the mistress of the house. 'Could you manage with Annie and someone coming in daily?'

Mrs McDonald pursed her lips, obviously thinking. 'I don't see why not, now that there's only His Lordship and Mrs Tressler when it comes to meals above stairs, and it's only rare they entertain for dinner. It'd likely have to be an older woman, but that could be all to the good, being past the flighty stage.' She paused. 'It'll be your decision, Florence, but what do you say to Elsie Trout? I've heard she's looking for a domestic job, but hasn't had any luck so far. I suppose that could be because she's Constable Trout's wife and people are nervous she might snoop and rush home to tell him if she came across something she thought fishy.'

Florence had managed to swallow down the last of her fruit cake. 'I wouldn't be surprised. Even with nothing to hide they wouldn't relish her poking around on the off chance. The ones that are nosy themselves would be the quickest to think that's what she'd do. I'll get in touch with her and have a word if you'd like.'

'I'd appreciate it. But I do apologize; here I am rattling on and I haven't asked about your stay with your cousin. I've always liked the sound of her from what you've said.'

'Thank you and I will tell you all about it, but would you mind waiting?' Florence got to her feet. 'Mr Grumidge told me Mrs Tressler would like to see me in the drawing room when I have the chance.'

'Away you go. It'll give me the chance to put Annie and Jeannie back to work and I'll be right here all evening. And later we can have those cups of cocoa if you're not too tired.'

'I won't be, and it'll help me sleep.' Florence hoped her smile wasn't frayed. Her anxiety had returned. She made a decision. 'I'll go by the passageway because I'd like to take a moment to telephone George.'

Mrs McDonald's face lit up. She wasn't incapable of believing in happy-ever-afters. Not when the couple were obviously so right for each other. 'Missing Mr Bird already?'

'Just something I didn't get the opportunity to ask him.'

Florence hastened into the housekeeper's room and lifted the telephone receiver. A woman from the exchange enquired what number she wanted; she gave the one for the Dog and Whistle. To her surprise, George answered at the second ring. 'It's Florence.' She breathed in relief. 'You must have been standing right there. Were you talking to Alf or Doris?'

'Sorry, dear. There was no message left and they haven't rung. I'd just hung up after talking with the inspector, but I'll get to that in a moment. I've been thinking about what I said to those two women outside the house – how maybe they'd gone back to the sister-in-law's in Tuswall. Maybe that wasn't hopelessly barking up the wrong tree. I don't mean that business of finding her ill. If that was the case, knowing them like we do, they wouldn't have left her, especially having to turn right back. If things was that urgent they wouldn't have bothered about suitcases.'

She didn't delay things by reminding him about the dog. 'That's true, so what do you think could be the reason?'

'Well, I know it sounds a stretch after them telling us the sort of person she is, but what if she was surprisingly nice about the whole business and invited them to come and stay with her for a little while, till the worst of the gossip's over? Or, it being hard to credit a leopard changing its spots, only pretending sympathy in the hope she could persuade them to change their minds and accept the legacy, and then feel they ought to cut her in with a nice bit out of loyalty to the Greens.'

'Anything's possible.' Florence was ready to clutch at straws. 'Though it doesn't explain the first taxi. There has to be a connection.'

'You're right. All I can come up with is it *was* Mr Pritchard in that one, and he'd left a message with Rupert to warn them that the Tenneson sisters had taken the news about Doris extremely badly, and they'd best get as far away as possible from Bogmire till he could put precautions in place.'

This sounded plausible. Florence's spirits lifted. 'What did Inspector LeCrane have to say?'

'That the name of the woman killed by the bus was Betty Taylor. And with it being such a common one and not knowing her date of birth it may be difficult to track her down.'

'Betty like your wife.'

'Yes, and like I told you, hers was shortened from Elizabeth, but this one might not have been.'

George promised to telephone Florence back if he heard from Alf or Doris that evening. They agreed that otherwise they would talk in the morning, and she went with somewhat lightened steps to see Mrs Tressler.

FOURTEEN

The drawing room was a gracious, elegant apartment without being overtly grand. With the exception of a few sofas and chairs, it was mainly furnished with pieces dating back to the time when the house was built, and the muted colors of the finely woven silk carpet were echoed in the wallpaper and fabrics. Upon her entrance, Mrs Tressler rose from her chair beside the glowing fire. She was of a similar height and slim build as Florence, with a slight wave to her bobbed, graying hair. Although she could never have been considered to be beautiful, the plainness of her face was illuminated by the character that showed through – that of courage in the face of adversity, sound commonsense and good humor. On their first meeting Florence had been put in mind of a competent, caring school teacher to whom even the most unruly students would respond positively. She had come to like and respect her.

Now, after expressing pleasure at seeing her again, Mrs Tressler invited Florence to sit across from her so they could have a comfortable talk.

'Would you care for a sherry?' There was a decanter and two glasses on the table beside her chair, obviously placed there at her request so that she could make this offer.

Florence thanked her but declined. 'It might make me a little sleepy, as I don't often have it.'

'That's understandable. Even the smallest port has the same effect on me, Mrs Norris. And I imagine you might not get to bed as early as you would like after your journey. I do hope your days away were highly enjoyable.'

'Very much so, Mrs Tressler.' On further prompting, Florence sketched an account of her daily doings with her cousin, mentioning Hattie's enjoyment of listening to recordings of Harry Lauder singing Scottish ballads.

'Is she very fond of Scotland?'

'She's never been, but would like to do so one day.'

'Then she must. I have a small house in the Highlands – a lovely spot. It's a little remote, but there's a village nearby and buses pass through, so there's no difficulty getting to a railway station. Perhaps you could persuade her to accompany you there on a holiday. Your doing so would please me greatly.'

Florence thanked her, knowing the offer was not motivated merely by courtesy, and said she would definitely bring it up with Hattie. She then turned to Molly's account of how comfortable she had been managing during her absence, expressing her own pleasure on hearing this. Mrs Tressler was fully aware that Florence wished to leave Mullings in the not-too-distant future, and that her reason for waiting was not simply to give Molly enough time to find her feet, but was primarily due to her own reluctance to walk even a short distance from Ned's life until she felt assured he'd recovered sufficiently from the sorrows that had come with the murder.

A woman other than Mrs Tressler might have found this incomprehensible coming from a housekeeper, but she understood and valued the deeply fond relationship that existed between Florence and her grandson, appreciating that it was forged out of the care Florence had provided from his early childhood onward, helping him to overcome the lost feeling of being orphaned at so young an age he could barely remember his parents. His other grandmother, though devoted, had been unable to spend as much time with him as she would have wished due to her prolonged invalidism. Mrs Tressler also knew, without resentment or envy, that he still had a tendency to lean on Florence when necessary.

Now she reiterated how disappointed he was not to have been there to greet Florence himself that evening. 'As you well know, Ned' – she never made any pretense of not knowing Florence addressed him as such when they were alone – 'felt compelled to go to Farn Deane. And I sense that he was particularly anxious to talk to you about the Tenneson girl and his concern for her safety.'

The thought that passed through Florence's mind was how

the situation at Bogmire kept becoming more personal. She leaned forward intently. 'I hadn't realized he knew Mercy Tenneson other than perhaps by sight, Mrs Tressler.'

'He didn't. He'd never so much as met her until this past week. If you remember, he and I did not attend Mr Tenneson's funeral due to our being away staying with friends whilst I made arrangements to let my house to that very pleasant American family. It is such a relief that they expect to remain in England for the next five years, so the matter is settled, at least for the foreseeable future. It's the home I left on coming to Mullings. It has been in my husband's family for many years, and I might possibly one day wish to return there. It will be part of my grandson's inheritance.'

'Yes, Mrs Tressler. As you know, I was at the funeral, since you had requested before leaving Mullings that Mr Grumidge, Mrs McDonald and I represent you and His Lordship.'

'So I did. Was there an opportunity for you to speak with Miss Tenneson?'

'No.'

'How did she look to you, Mrs Norris?'

'I wasn't close enough to see her expression, but someone mentioned to me when people began leaving – I think it was Mrs Trout, the police constable's wife – that Miss Tenneson had smiled during the graveside service, which I attributed to fond reflections on her relationship with the deceased.'

Mrs Tressler adjusted her hands on her lap. 'Yes, any other reason seems unlikely at such a time. What I was actually wondering, however, is whether you thought her especially good looking in a way likely to bowl a young man over at first sight?'

'His Lordship?'

'I feel guilty about doing him an injustice, but I can't help remembering how he was swept away by Lamorna Blake's beauty to the point of rushing into a proposal. He has only encountered Miss Tenneson on two occasions, the first being no more than a glimpse, and now he's showing this intense interest.'

Florence looked thoughtful. 'My view of her was limited at the funeral and I had not come across her before that.

Even so, I'd say there was something arresting about her that would draw the eye. I found myself thinking of Cathy in *Wuthering Heights*, as if she belonged to the elements in a wild landscape. Perhaps not in England, but somewhere starker; but that could be because she reminded me of a young Russian woman I once met.' Florence was seized by a sharp twinge of unease. This recollection had only now filtered to the surface of her consciousness. Had it inaccurately biased her impressions of Mercy Tenneson and the woman in the headscarf, leading to her creating in her own mind a physical resemblance between them beyond one of a more general sort? She forced herself to focus on Mrs Tressler and her concern for Ned.

'I can well understand your concern after His Lordship narrowly escaped what would have been a disastrous marriage to Miss Blake. However, I believe that episode will have left him extremely cautious of succumbing to blinding infatuation and mistaking it for love. He discovered for himself very quickly after that proposal that he and Miss Blake had nothing the least meaningful in common and, worse, he did not like her. He knows he was extremely fortunate in being able to extricate himself, and I'm convinced he realizes he might not be so fortunate another time. Of course, it's not to say that Miss Tenneson's looks play no part in his taking an interest in her. He is a young man, and it is not to be wished he may never again find any woman attractive in her person, but I think you may feel more comfortable, Mrs Tressler, if his concern for her well-being is not driven by perceiving himself as her knight in shining armor.'

'Which is exactly what was concerning me, Mrs Norris. I do thank you. How well you have put this in perspective for me. There is a reason I chose to discuss the subject with you, at the risk of seeming to be disloyal to Ned. It is my fear that I failed him by not expressing a willingness to do what I could to be of support to Miss Tenneson, by welcoming her to Mullings and endeavoring to get to know her.'

'Mrs Tressler, your devotion to your grandson could never lead to any action on your part that might be misconstrued by those who have witnessed it.'

'Again, thank you. It is so good to have a confidante who also has his interests so much at heart.'

Florence smiled. 'I'm honored you feel that way. As for your unease, did His Lordship suggest, even hint, that he wished you to befriend Miss Tenneson?'

'No. He said he felt fortunate that he'd got her to talk to him at all, that she was resistant to doing so beyond responding to his greeting when Miss Milligan, the woman who breeds boxer dogs, introduced them on the village green.'

'Then it seems highly questionable that he would risk the chance of getting to know her better by rushing overtures of friendship including an invitation to Mullings.'

'How foolish of me not to have realized that, Mrs Norris. The result of my clouded thinking.'

'Did this occur during His Lordship's second encounter with her?'

'Yes, if the first could even be called such a thing, since as I think I mentioned, it involved little more than catching sight of her. He was taking Rouser for his early morning walk when he saw Gideon Blake stop his horse to talk to a young woman with long dark hair.'

'Lamorna Blake's brother.'

Mrs Tressler nodded. 'Not unreasonably from what I know of his irresponsible antics, he is frequently referred to as "Giddy." He addressed the girl as "Mercy," and Ned observed them talking together before he retreated with Rouser, wondering if it had been an arranged meeting. In other words, an assignation.'

Antics, thought Florence, was a politely lenient term for young Mr Blake's riotous mode of living, which included racking up gambling debts and involvement in drunken skirmishes and loose morals. The latter was unacceptable, even amongst the gentry, who might believe themselves to be entitled to have their way with village maidens, but considered seductions, crude ones at that, of sisters and daughters of their own class, as being a step too far.

'His Lordship would have been concerned for any young woman, pretty or plain, that Mr Blake appeared to have his sights on, Mrs Tressler. What intense relief he must feel at not having married into that family. Did he know Miss Tenneson's Christian name at that time?'

'No. He told me he asked Mrs McDonald on his return about a dark-haired girl of that name. It is an unusual one, is it not? And she told him who she was. On the morning when he spoke to her he'd just been talking with one of the under gardeners who coincidentally mentioned the Tenneson family. He is related to a Mrs Weedy.'

'That will be Willie Griggs.'

'Yes, that was the name. He said she had taken an interest in Miss Tenneson.'

'Mrs Weedy is a very old lady and a fount of village lore, still with her wits about her.'

And, thought Florence, someone from whom she might get useful information for Inspector LeCrane. She chided herself for not thinking of Mrs Weedy before now. 'What happened, Mrs Tressler, after Miss Milligan introduced Miss Tenneson to His Lordship?'

'Ned overheard her expressing her thanks to Mr Sprague for rescuing her – from what occurrence she did not say. But in the course of Ned's conversation with her, he discovered that she thought she had been followed on crossing a field by a shadowy figure in the outlying woods.' Mrs Tressler continued her account, ending with Ned's leaving Miss Tenneson entering Mrs Weedy's cottage. She then apologized to Florence for keeping her so long when there must be other things she wished to do, including relaxing prior to getting back into action.

Florence got to her feet. 'I will of course keep what you've told me in confidence, Mrs Tressler, but if it's all right with you I'll ask Mrs McDonald in a general way what she knows about the doings, past and present, at Bogmire. It can be done easily enough, if I enquire if she's heard how the family there has settled back into life following Mr Tenneson's death.'

'An excellent thought.' Mrs Tressler also rose. 'I do hope you will consider spending some time here as my companion after your retirement as housekeeper, though there's no need to make up your mind about it until the time is ready.'

Florence thanked her. The fire in the grate needed replenishment, but she did not presume to mention this to Grumidge on seeing him moments later in the hall. His reason for being there was likely due to his intention of entering the drawing room as soon as possible without intruding on Mrs Tressler's time with Florence. He had doubtless arranged for new logs to be brought in when he gave the word.

She made it her first task to request Molly to gather the maids together and bring them to her so she could express her appreciation for their keeping things running smoothly during her absence, singling out Molly, of course, for special praise. The footman and the fifteen-year-old boy who performed odd jobs, such as fetching in the logs, were officially Grumidge's province, along with the outside staff. However, Florence thanked them both when they passed her way. It was good to see a beaming smile appear on the boy's face.

She then went up to her bedroom to tidy herself and unpack her suitcase, which she could have done later, but it gave her an occupation while she sorted through her emotions, which were decidedly mixed. Being valued as a confidante by Mrs Tressler meant a great deal to her; additionally, it had provided her with information that might well bring results. Against that, her anxiety as to the Thatchers' whereabouts was growing stronger.

It had struck her, as it should have done when she'd been talking with George on the telephone, that Doris and Alf were not at all the sort to have fled Dovecote Hatch on being given some dramatic news – even that their lives were in danger – especially if it had come from a solicitor of whom they'd been unaware before the last couple of days. In their place she would have questioned Mr Pritchard's motives. It would hardly have been surprising if, whatever he might have said to the contrary, his sympathy leaned towards the Tenneson sisters. Perhaps he had acted from self-interest. They might have offered to reward him financially for frightening off the woman who had undermined their inheritance under the new will, and embarrassed them vastly in the process. These conjectures might be an injustice to Mr Pritchard but could not be summarily dismissed.

Florence went downstairs and entered the housekeeper's room with the intention of quieting her mind by going through what Molly had written in the order book for last week and this. She also wished to be ready to pick up the telephone instantly if George were to ring back with reassuring news of Doris and Alf. She didn't doubt he'd momentarily believed what he'd said about their having allowed themselves to panic unreasonably, but nonetheless, something serious must have happened for them to take off in that taxi. Did it involve trickery?

George did not phone again. At ten o'clock, having finished writing to Hattie and knowing herself incapable of concentrating on other tasks, Florence went to the kitchen in the hope of finding Mrs McDonald alone. It was usually around this time that they sat down to their cups of cocoa.

'My, you do look worn out, and no wonder after your long day,' said this good friend, looking round from pouring milk into a saucepan. 'You sit yourself down while I get us our nightcaps.'

Florence didn't need to remind Mrs McDonald that they were both well used to being on the go from very early morning till bed. She said she'd been sitting for hours already and was told not to bother about that – more of the same wouldn't hurt. Mrs McDonald placed a cup of cocoa in front of Florence and fetched another for herself before joining her at the table, eyeing her sharply.

'Now you start in on that. It's not just tiredness, is it? There's something serious bothering you – I saw that the moment I set eyes on you earlier. I hope nothing's wrong with Mr Bird.'

'No. Other than he shares my concern.'

'To do with your cousin?'

'She's perfectly well and content, and it doesn't involve my own well-being or that of anyone at Mullings. It isn't my story to tell, Mrs McDonald, though I'm sure you'll find out soon enough. The one thing I feel I can share with you, knowing that you will keep it in confidence, is that it has to do with Bogmire.'

Mrs McDonald sat silent, not taking a sip of cocoa, before saying, 'Well, this doesn't exactly come like a bolt out of the blue, seeing as His Lordship asked me about the Tenneson girl, wanting to know if I could tell him anything about a dark-haired young lady named Mercy. I didn't think anything of it at the time, as it's an unusual name. But then he asked me about her again, and this time he sounded anxious.'

'What did he say?'

'Asked what I knew of her circumstances at Bogmire. All I could tell him was that I wouldn't want to live under the same roof as that pair of old biddies now their brother's gone. They can't be suitable companions for a girl her age. She should be seeing a bit of life. And the house – such a gloomy monstrosity from what I've heard! Though I haven't seen for myself, I'll admit.'

'Mrs Tressler mentioned that His Lordship had met Miss Tenneson and asked you about her. It's interesting, and I'm eager to speak to him about those meetings, but as I've said, my disquiet about Bogmire was already there, heightened earlier this evening by . . . what I can't tell you about yet.' Florence took a sip of her cocoa.

'Rightly so. You've known from when you were a girl starting out here at Mullings to keep your lips buttoned when needed. I remember thinking back then: there's one that wouldn't gossip if her life depended on it. But my guess is it has something to do with Mr Tenneson found dead at the bottom of those stairs. I'm not one with an overly suspicious mind, but when that sort of thing happens any reasonable person would wonder if it was an accident or if he'd been given a shove into the next world. It didn't take a word passing between you and me to be certain that if I'd thought it, so had you, and it wouldn't be the first time a coroner's inquest got it wrong.' Mrs McDonald took a deep swallow of her cocoa. 'I'm not probing.'

'I know that.' Florence gave her an affectionate look.

'Just putting you in the picture from my end, before I tell you about a talk I had with Jeannie.'

'Yes?'

'It was after that second time, the one when His Lordship seemed worried. Jeannie's not like you were at her age, Florence. Now, that's not to say she'd talk out of school about anything to do with Mullings, but she is always ready and willing to spill the beans about this, that and the other in the village. I brought up Bogmire by saying I'd heard it was haunted, which I haven't, and asked if she'd ever heard such foolish stories, because to my way of thinking they'd sprung from those living there being an odd bunch. Except for Mr Tenneson, who seemed to have been a nice, quiet gentleman, no more peculiar than any normal person.'

'Yes?' said Florence again, not wanting to waste words.

'Off and running was Jeannie. She told me her mum has a friend, Mary, that was in service for a couple of years at Bogmire, and says she got out of there fast as she could by marrying the first boy that asked her. Happily it turned out all right, though that's neither here nor there. This Mary said old Mr Tenneson was a right so-and-so. He treated his wife terrible, poor, languishing woman. He'd rage at her over the least little thing, and it would have been no surprise if he struck her too. She'd thought the younger Miss Tenneson potty, but said that the older one was the worst of the lot.'

'In what way?' Florence set aside her now drained cup.

Mrs McDonald continued in her methodical way. 'There was another girl working there at the time. She could have been a beauty if she'd been born upper crust and got to wear lovely clothes and have her hair dressed like she was a debutante. As it was, so says this Mary, she was a looker, no doubt about it. But she wasn't so caught up in her appearance that she wasn't a hard worker. She could turn out a room and do a good job of it in next to no time. Now, it seems that the older Miss Tenneson found out that the girl had been slipping off on the sly in the evenings to meet some fellow in the abandoned farmhouse that's still there.'

'I think I know the one you mean. It's about ready to fall down now.'

'That's it. Easy enough for her to get there quick by way of the field across from Bogmire just a little further down the road. Mary says she'd warned her to be careful, because she'd seen him lurking outside and thought he looked a bad lot, grabbing at the girl's arm when she hadn't been able to get out of the house till a little later than usual. As to how Miss Tenneson got on to it, Mary's guess is it came through the younger sister, the one that never shuts her mouth, with the silly name – she might as well have been christened Cabbage as Lettice, to quote Jeannie.'

Eager as she was to hear the rest, Florence felt compelled to say in fairness that it could have reached Matilda Tenneson by way of a dozen other people.

'Of course, there's bound to have been plenty of gossip. Whatever the case, she came storming into the kitchen one morning, grabbed the girl up by the hair and shoved her against a wall. Then she snatched a plate off the table and threw it at her, catching her in the throat, all the while screaming she'd beat her senseless if she didn't cease her sluttish, filthy foreign ways.'

'Foreign?' Florence was startled into exclaiming. 'Was she a foreigner?'

'According to Jeannie, she'd been born in this country and her father was from here, but her mother had come from one of those other places, like Hungry or Checkosaliva.' Mrs McDonald's lips twitched. 'That's how she pronounced them; she thinks that's what Mary said.'

'Did she have a foreign-sounding Christian name?'

'I can't remember what Jeannie said it was, something quite common, though shortened from something else. I'll ask her.'

'Do, please, and if you can, Mrs McDonald, get the surname.'

'Easy as wink. I'll find out first thing tomorrow morning.'

Florence drew herself back to the scene just related. 'What happened next?'

'The housekeeper came in and went to fetch Mr Tenneson, the brother. He arrived and pulled Matilda away from the girl, just as she was about to claw her face, and hauled her out into the hall, where he could be heard raging that if she ever acted in such a way again it would be him beating her senseless. And him mild as milk, is how Mary put it to Jeannie's mum. A short time later he fetched the girl into his study, and when Mary was about to go past it minutes later, the door was open enough to see the poor thing crying on his shoulder. Miss

Lettice asked Mary what all the ruckus was about and when she was told said it was a bit naughty of Miss Matilda to get so cross. Mary told her parents what had happened and they insisted she leave Bogmire at once, which she did, as fast as she could get her hat and coat on.'

'What about the other girl, the one that Matilda Tenneson treated so brutally?'

'From the sound of it, her father was a brute.' Mrs McDonald shook her white head. 'Mary said she reckoned he'd have told her to stay and lump it, but she did hear – Mary, that is – that the poor creature left a couple of months later and went off to live in London.'

'Is there anyone hereabouts she might have kept in touch with, other than her own family?'

'I asked Jeannie that, and she said that according to Mary the only one would be Mrs Weedy, who'd been very kind in inviting her in for cups of tea and a chat after seeing her stop to admire the flowers in the garden at Laurel Cottage. I've also heard from Jeannie that it's been the same case between the old lady and Mercy Tenneson.'

'There's food for thought, Mrs McDonald, even if it is somewhat overshadowed by the discovery that Matilda Tenneson has a violent side to her nature.'

'Strongly suggesting that a shove down the stairs would be nothing to her if she got her knickers in a twist, if you'll pardon my language, Florence.'

After clearing the table and washing up, the two women parted to go to their beds. Florence's mind was a ferment of activity. So much to tell George and pass along to Inspector LeCrane. If not for Alf and Doris's inexplicable absence, she would have judged it a good day, in that progress was being made towards discovering the truth of how Kenneth Tenneson had died. As it was, she expected she'd have trouble getting to sleep, but in fact she went out like a light, not waking till dawn.

She went downstairs, wondering who would deliver the post in Alf's stead. At six thirty she was at her desk in the house-keeper's room when none other than Alf himself walked in. She could only stare at him speechlessly.

'I have to talk to you, Florence,' he said in a wretched voice, gray-faced and his body sagging as though half dead on his feet. 'Me and Doris went to Bogmire last night – I'll explain why in a minute. But there's something else that can't wait. I think they tried to poison Doris with parsnip wine.'

FIFTEEN

Florence took hold of Alf's arm and led him to the armchair across from her desk. 'Sit down, Alf, dear, before you drop. Just tell me, is she all right?'

It took a moment for him to be able to speak again. 'Yes, if you don't count being what she calls a trifle upset. More annoyed, like. "The cheek of it, pulling a stunt like that the very first evening," is what she said. It's me that's frightened to death.'

That would be Doris, thought Florence; she'd never let on to Alf even if she was in the worst panic imaginable.

'Is she in hospital?'

'No, still at Bogmire. Any other woman would've got out of there fast, but she wouldn't hear of it when I said we should go home. Insisted that if there'd been funny business it was our duty to help get to the bottom of it. She wouldn't let me even fetch the doctor. Said it wasn't like it'd left her feeling desperately ill, just queasy, like, with a bit of a headache. And she insisted that could've just have been from it tasting so nasty. It did give her a bit of a scare, she did admit that. But what I've been asking myself is how much worse it'd have been if she'd taken more than a sip. I was all for asking Mrs Hewett to get someone to do my rounds, but Doris didn't want me to do that and I was afraid to make a big thing of it, letting her know I'd properly got the wind up. So I told her to lock the bedroom door and not let anyone in.'

'Very wise, Alf.' Florence leaned forward to pat his arm. 'Why don't you sit quietly for another few moments before telling me more. What you could do with right now is a good strong cup of tea with lots of sugar; I'll just step out and ask Mrs McDonald to make you one.'

'Thanks, Florence. I won't say no.'

She paused in the doorway to turn her head. 'Have you spoken to George?'

'No, I didn't want to risk rousing him out of his bed; besides, I thought it one of them times when t'would be best to get the woman's point of view. You're better than us men at understanding how each other's thinking is like to go when up against it.'

Florence agreed with this in general, but not always in particular. 'I think it would still be helpful to have him here, Alf, seeing the three of you have been friends for so long. Do you mind if I telephone him?'

''Course I don't, if it won't make things awkward for you.'

'Absolutely not. His Lordship and Mrs Tressler have made it clear that he is always more than welcome at Mullings. Now, you try and rest your mind as much as you can. I'll be back in a few minutes.'

She went into the kitchen. Annie was at the sink, but Mrs McDonald dispatched her to the scullery, telling her to clean the one in there before giving Florence a searching look.

'Something going on with Mr Thatcher?'

'Yes, and his wife, involving what I couldn't tell you last night about Bogmire. You'll find out without my needing to do so before this day's out.'

'My word, I'd never have connected them with the Tennesons. Want me to get him a cup of tea and bring it in?' Mrs McDonald definitely had the ability to read other women's minds, especially Florence's.

'Put in lots of sugar – he takes it anyway, but this calls for extra. I'm going to use the telephone in the passageway to get hold of George and ask him to come round.'

'I'll do that, Florence; I've lots to tell you, but it won't take a tick! I just spoke to Jeannie, and the name of the girl Miss Matilda Tenneson treated so wicked was Betty Taylor. The Betty was shortened from Elizabetta. That's why Jeannie remembered, because she'd thought it so pretty.'

'Thank you, dear Mrs McDonald. I'm glad you didn't wait till later to tell me.'

Florence went into the passageway and rang George.

He picked up the telephone instantly. 'Any word?'

'Alf's here. He hasn't explained yet why they decided to do so, but he and Doris spent the night at Bogmire, and he's in a frantic state because he thinks an attempt was made to poison her with parsnip wine.'

George didn't say a word. She could feel his riveted attention.

'He's in the housekeeper's room. I told him to sit and try to still his nerves while I went to ask Mrs McDonald to get him a cup of tea. Also I wanted to phone you out of his hearing, although he was all for my doing so, because I haven't said anything about going round to their house last evening and being worried by what we learned. I didn't want to upset him any further.'

'I'll not mention it either. Maybe later, when we've heard all he has to say. I'll be there in just a few minutes, Florence.'

'When I can get you alone afterwards I've something else to tell you. Don't let me forget.'

'I won't, my dearest.'

Florence returned to the housekeeper's room to find Alf with a cup in his hand. He looked up at her. 'I appreciate this – Mrs McDonald makes as good a pot of tea as anyone I know.'

'Your color looks better.' She shifted her desk chair to face him and sat down. 'George is on his way, it'll take next to no time in the car. Would you like to wait for him before starting on what's been going on? You'll want to get back to Doris soon as you can.'

'That I do.'

The door opened and Mrs McDonald whisked, for want of a better word given her vast size, through the opening with a plate of toast and a napkin. 'There's nothing like hot buttered toast of an early morning, I always say. And this is one of the raw sort.'

She was gone in an instant, before Alf could get out a word of thanks, closing the door behind her. Encouraged by Florence, he set his cup down on the table by his chair and started in on a half slice. He'd soon finished the rest – obviously hungry, without perhaps realizing it. When he was in his own home, Doris would have made sure he had something inside him before setting off on his first deliveries. Florence was about to ask if he had much of his postal route to do when the door

opened and George came in, filling even more space than Mrs
McDonald had done. He was carrying a tray with a teapot,
milk jug, sugar basin and two more cups, which he set down
on a trolley reserved for this purpose, before going over and
squeezing Alf's shoulder. 'Problems, mate?'

'You can say that again, Birdie, and there's no one to blame
but myself.'

'Can't go that far, surely, mate,' said George. 'It wasn't you
who put whatever it was in the parsnip wine.'

'I should never've agreed to go there, but for once in her
life Doris was proper worked up, and she said if the two of
them felt free to walk into our house when we wasn't even
there, it'd serve 'em right if we landed on them for a week.
Besides that, on the bus back from Tuswall after seeing
Winnie – who couldn't've been nastier; Doris was snarling
that it was a relief to find out they wasn't related even by
marriage after all – Doris got talking about Kenneth
Tenneson. She felt bad it'd only just struck her that with
him being the Greens' born son he'd be of a nature to do
right by her. It was comforting for her to see that blood will
out. 'Course, she knows as well as I do that there are nice,
decent people with offspring rotten as they come. It goes
the other way too. But it was understandable right then that
Doris wanted to think on the bright side of a bad business.
She said she owed it to Kenneth's memory to find out what
sort of life he'd had. Proper ashamed of herself, she was,
for not seeing it that way sooner 'stead of wishing he'd've
minded his own business where she was concerned. What
I'm saying is, it wasn't surprising – her being primed for
action, so to speak – how she reacted when we got back
home and heard from Rupert what'd happened.' Alf paused
for breath.

His listeners gave him a moment to catch it. Having poured
him a fresh cup of tea, George asked Florence if she wanted
one and when she shook her head sat down in the easy chair
under the window. She was about to speak when Alf
continued.

'It's the two Miss Tennesons I'm talking about – the ones
he'd thought till close to the end was his sisters. The girl, not

that we've anything against her, didn't come. She's probably got some manners, seeing as he brought her up. It put young Rupert Trout in a right pickle, it did, when they showed up at the door demanding to be let in.'

'Of course it would,' replied Florence. 'You mentioned yesterday you were going to ask him to watch the little dog while you went to Tuswall. So what happened when they arrived: did they demand to see you and Doris?'

'Like they owned the place, is how Rupert put it. He said that when he told 'em we weren't home, they brushed right past him into the hall, the one named Matilda poking him with a walking stick. He got the names from them talking to each other. They told him they'd come by taxi and would ring for it to take them back when they was ready to leave. Obviously, it hadn't crossed their minds we mightn't be on the telephone. Think they grow out of walls, I expect.' Alf picked up the cup of what must now be lukewarm tea.

'How did Rupert describe them?' George asked.

'Painted a vivid picture, he did; it was like we'd bin there ourselves.'

'Some people, including children, have that knack,' said Florence, gently encouraging.

Alf nodded. 'Rupert said the Matilda one looked like one of the church gargoyles, and not one of the grinning ones neither, and was far the horrider of the two. She talked spitefully, and if looks could kill he'd've been dead at her feet. He said the one called Lettice looked and talked daft as they come. Tried to come off friendly. Kept on yammering about this and that and nothing. Went round picking things up and looking at them, like a little jug Doris keeps on a shelf in the kitchen with "A present from Southend" on it. She twittered at him that she thought it sweet and wondered where we'd got it.'

'She was in the kitchen?' George's graying eyebrows shot up his deep forehead. 'Did they ask Rupert's permission or did she just wander in on her own?'

Alf set down his cup. 'She followed him there a few minutes after he'd left her and her spiteful sister in the sitting room. He'd wanted to escape with little Rex, who didn't seem to like them either, for a chance to think. When they'd forced themselves into the house, claiming they'd every right because they was some sort of family to us, he'd considered fetching his dad, but decided we'd rather there wasn't a rumpus created. He worked out that there had to be something he didn't know about going on between us and them. A very bright lad is Rupert. Me and Doris have grown very fond of him and can tell he feels the same about us. We'd asked him before we left for Tuswall if he'd like to call us Auntie and Uncle and he was tickled pink.'

Florence smiled, despite the seriousness of the situation. Doris and Alf had married late in life so there was no telling whether they would have wanted a family or not. Either way, Rupert had brought something special into their lives. She glanced at George, who had no children of his own, but was devoted to his godson, James. And she, admittedly in a different way, had Ned.

'I think that's wonderful, Alf. I can see how Constable Trout showing up at your front door in his uniform and helmet, with or without Rupert, could have caused the sort of stir you'd have been anxious to avoid. It might be assumed by anyone who saw him that he'd come in his official capacity, which in a way he would have done. But do you think Rupert would have told his parents when he got home what had happened?'

'No, I don't, Florence. He's a loyal little chap – you only have to look at how he's kept coming round to find out how Rex is getting along after the accident – not the sort to carry tales about our business. But anyhow, we asked him not to, said it would all go round soon enough about Doris and me and them at Bogmire, but we'd like to bide our time a while before saying anything. 'Course, all that changed after I'd walked him home and come back to find Doris had our suitcases packed.'

'We want to hear about that, and,' George looked at Florence, who nodded, 'there's something we should tell you, but a couple of things first, please. How long had the Tenneson women been gone, Alf, when you returned from Tuswall?'

'About half an hour – by then they'd been there more than two hours. Rupert said Miss Matilda banged on the floor and screeched she was tired of being kept waiting. We came in around four.'

'How did they manage without a phone to ring for the taxi?' George asked. 'Did they decide to lump it and walk?'

Alf almost smiled. 'Not on your nelly! They'd sooner have set the place ablaze to fetch the fire brigade, is my guess. But who should show up right then but Major Wainwright, looking all stiff and starchy? I can see you're both amazed as me and Doris was.'

'Well, well!' George responded, thinking how he'd been hoping for a word with the man on Inspector LeCrane's behalf. 'It had to be about the will and the part he played in it, don't you think? He's always struck me as a good sort. He'd probably been worrying how Doris had taken the news.'

Alf nodded. 'He came knocking on the back door. Turned out he'd parked on the road behind the house, so it seems like he wanted to keep tongues from clacking the best he could.'

'That was certainly thoughtful.' Florence had always liked the major from his occasional visits to Mullings. 'Did he come inside?' She was picturing Rupert, confused as to what to do about the Misses Tenneson – whether to let on they were there and get help in dealing with them, or keep quiet about them in case that's what Doris and Alf would prefer.

'No. When Rupert said we weren't home he asked him to pass on a message, that he'd appreciate us kindly coming to see him at his house, next day if possible. He'd be sure to wait in. He was telling the lad not to forget when those two biddies sailed into the kitchen, the Matilda one shrilling she'd heard the major's voice through the open kitchen door and he could take them back to Bogmire that minute. Waved her stick at him, too, she did.'

'How did he react?' Florence and George said simultaneously.

Alf definitely looked a little more cheerful now. 'He stepped inside and stared at them like he couldn't believe his eyes, then at Rupert, asking what in the world was going on here? And when the lad explained how they'd just pushed their way in, the major said he'd take them off his hands right away. Rupert said he looked so furious it seemed like his moustache

would fly off his face. Miss Matilda was struck dumb, her
face all twisted up, but Miss Lettice squealed she'd always
known he was a sweet man. And off the three of them went.'

George looked at Florence and again she nodded. He told
Alf how they'd stopped at his and Doris's house on the way
back from Large Middlington and been told by a couple of
the neighbors about the first taxi and then the one they'd got
into with their suitcases.

'Oh, dear!' Alf's face fell. 'Never thought about that
happening. We felt sure you'd want to get straight back to
Mullings, Florence, but we shouldn't have taken it for granted.
We planned to phone you from Bogmire, Birdie. They couldn't
have stopped us from using it, leastways we didn't think so
at the time. Now I wouldn't put any trick past them. Anyway,
with what happened with the parsnip wine, I forgot all about
phoning you. I feel awful, and so will Doris. I know you both
had to be worried sick, wondering why we'd taken off like
that. I can't say sorry enough.'

'There's no point in saying we weren't concerned – we
wouldn't be any sort of friends otherwise,' said Florence gently,
'but it wasn't either of your faults. You were bound to think
George would drive me straight to Mullings. It just so happens
there was a reason,' here it was she who glanced at George
and he that nodded agreement, 'but we can get to that later.
Were you nervous in the taxi? And what sort of reaction did
you get on showing up at Bogmire?' George poured Alf another
cup of tea.

'Well,' Alf said, picking it up, 'I have to say my knees got
to knocking some, but not Doris. Bound and determined, she
was, to show them two women they'd mucked around with
the wrong person. Thought they could march into our home
without a by your leave, did they? Then they'd get her and
me for a fortnight or more, depending on how we liked the
place. The difference was, we'd the legal right, whilst we could
have them for trespassing. Said she'd never done anything
impetuous in her life – you know Doris – but there was a first
time for everything.'

'She's one of the most level-headed people I know,' replied
Florence.

Alf drank some tea. 'Takes a lot for her to turn a hair. The most worked up I've ever seen her in all our married life was over Ivy Waters and Rex. Maybe this was one thing too much.'

'That could be in there,' said George, 'though I'd say the behavior of those two women would be enough on its own to push anyone to the limit.'

'You're right; I'm not thinking as clearly as I should.'

'Who could be after all you're dealing with, especially after the parsnip wine?' Florence murmured soothingly. 'What happened when you got to the door?'

'It was opened by the housekeeper, who let out a gasp. I expect she'd been warned we might show up sometime. She recognized me, of course, from being the postman. Doris spoke to her all brisk. "Don't worry we've samples of brushes to sell in these cases. Please step aside so's we can come in and then go and tell your employers we're expecting a nice welcome." The poor creature went staggering off without a word down the hall, great gloomy place, leaving us to close the front door behind us. The inside of the house is every bit as nasty as the outside, and I always thought it looked just the sort where you'd expect a murder to be committed.'

Something, ironically, that would not have been said about Mullings. This thought slipped in and out of Florence's mind, to be followed by another. Were Alf and Doris beginning to feel uneasy over the manner of Kenneth Tenneson's death? They'd never suggested this, even though they'd said Mr Pritchard had warned them to be cautious in regard to contact with the sisters. And what had led to his saying this? Merely that they were likely to be exceedingly unpleasant?

'Was the housekeeper long before reappearing?' George asked.

'Seemed like it. We'd seen her go into a room halfway down the hall. She must've bin in such a dither she left the door open, so we heard the sounds of a right carry-on. "Good!" is what Doris said, and added she'd have been disappointed if they didn't go up in smoke. She felt sorry for that sad-looking creature, but not half as much as she was for Kenneth Tenneson. The grave had to feel cozy after spending his life in this chamber of horrors. Next it was poor Rex. A ginger cat came streaking out the open door. I had Rex on the lead, but he got away from me and dived behind a huge old chest. Then the young Tenneson girl came down the staircase; it's all shadowy from there being so little light above and below. Starts just a short way on the left from the front door, it does.'

'How did she behave towards you?' Florence asked.

'Looked from us to the suitcases set on the floor and back again. Said "hello" and that her name was Mercy Tenneson.'

'Did she look surprised?' Florence again.

'She said she wasn't, that we was bound to be furious with her Aunt Matilda and Aunt Lettice for invading our home while we was out and they deserved paying back in their own coin. But she was afraid we'd get a less-than-welcoming reception from them, and mightn't it be best to go home and get in touch with Mr Pritchard? The girl was talking sense, I saw that, but we hadn't come just 'cos of feeling shirty. We couldn't tell her, at least straight off, that it was Doris wanting to know more about Kenneth Tenneson. She could've realized that for herself, of course.'

'She's said to have been very close to Mr Tenneson,' George put in.

Alf nodded. 'That's how it came across from Mr Pritchard. We thanked her for the good-willed advice, but when Doris said we wasn't budging she offered to take us along to the drawing room. Rex stuck his nose round the chest and she encouraged him to come out, and when he did she crouched down to stroke him, still talking nice and quiet, before giving me back his lead.'

'She sounds a nice girl,' said Florence.

'It didn't seem put on, neither. As we reached the open door the housekeeper came out and Mercy Tenneson said to her: "You go and have a cup of tea. Put a splash of something extra in it, Miss Bone." Fitting name for her, seeing as she looked like a bag of bones. I felt sorry, and know Doris did, that she'd got it in the neck on account of us.'

'I imagine, Alf, that her lot is a sorry one at the best of times.' After what she'd heard about Matilda Tenneson from Mrs McDonald, Florence was aware that this was liable to be an understatement. 'What was the atmosphere when Mercy Tenneson took you into the drawing room?'

'Well, for starters it was even grimmer than the hall, and that's saying a lot. Great big, hideous furniture, nasty-looking pictures, dark hangings, all seeming to get repeated over and over in a ghostly sort of way from mirrors with much of their silvering gone. Again there wasn't enough lighting, and what there was came from lamps looking like they was hiding. It was like looking at those two women through a gray mist. But there couldn't be no confusing which was which after Rupert's description of them. Hit the nail right on the head, he had! Matilda sat hunched in her chair, face like a gargoyle, walking stick in her hands, glaring up at us. Lettice got up from hers, looking as loopy as he'd said, with her sticking out teeth and frizzy fringe, going off into what sounded like happy squeals. 'Course, people can't help their appearance. We're all as God made us; but I have to say I'm glad Doris is nothing like either of them.'

'I don't wonder!' said George.

'Nor do I,' Florence agreed. 'What happened then?'

'Doris said, calm as could be, "Well, hello, both of you. How about you have your say, then I'll have mine." This didn't go down well with Matilda. She reared to her feet and threw her stick at us – missing, thank goodness – then marched out of the room.'

'And?' George and Florence asked as one.

'Mercy Tenneson followed her out, saying she'd talk to her. Lettice looked at Rex, who was shaking like a leaf, and squealed, "Oh, the poor little doggie! A wonder he's not halfway up the clock!" And then she giggled, "Oh, how sweet, Doris! You're wearing the coat and hat I gave for the bazaar. How about a little drink by way of getting to know each other as sisters?"'

'Ah!' George was now leaning forward in his chair. 'Here it comes!'

Alf looked at the clock on the shelf behind Florence's desk. 'I've been jawing on, haven't I? And besides taking up your time, I should get on with finishing my route and getting back quick to Doris.'

'What you've been telling us is too important to have been rushed,' Florence reassured him, 'but of course you're anxious to be with Doris. What was her reply to Lettice Tenneson?'

'She said without batting an eye that she wouldn't mind a glass of parsnip wine. And Lettice gave one of her silly ever-so-pleased squeals, saying wasn't that interesting seeing as she was partial to parsnip wine herself, whilst Matilda couldn't stand it. I said I didn't want anything. She told us to sit down and fetched a bottle and two glasses from somewhere or other. She filled one for Doris, then hesitated, like, and said perhaps tonight she'd have a sherry. She came back with it and said, "Let's toast the future – the merry one we'll share together." As soon as Doris had taken a swallow, I could tell something was wrong, and when I asked what it was she said about it having a nasty bitter taste, and she was sorry but she couldn't finish it.'

'How did Lettice Tenneson react to that?' urged Florence.

'She went into a dither about how some gardener had once told her parsnips can become poisonous if grown in an old bed. And wasn't she fortunate to have such an excellent memory? She never forgot things and was just as good with faces. Then she started on a rigmarole about how she'd bin shown a photo of a man just last Monday and recognized him at once, though she'd only glimpsed him out the window donkey's years ago.'

Florence and George took this in without interrupting.

'And all the while Doris was looking queerer by the second. I had her on her feet when Mercy popped her head through the doorway and said she was going out for a walk. I asked her if she could first get us somewhere with a basin, 'cos the wife was about to be sick. She hurried over to take Doris by the arm I didn't have hold of, saying there was a powder room across the hall. Made it there in the nick of time, we did.'

'Did Lettice follow you?' George asked. Florence was still reflecting on the business of the photograph. Monday . . . the day she had taken the train from Large Middlington.

'No. She'd started in on a ramble about how she'd bin horribly squeamish ever since she'd had her finger lanced when she was ten, and had never liked blue since because that was the color of the dress she'd bin wearing. Once Doris said she felt a little better, or at least steadier on her feet, Mercy took us to a bedroom. Not what you'd call inviting, it wasn't, but a bed's a bed and Doris needed a lay down. Mercy disappeared for a few moments then came back with our cases and said did we want her to fetch a doctor? And when Doris told her she didn't think that was necessary 'cos she was feeling more herself already, she told us her room was just two doors down to our left if we needed her.'

'She definitely sounds a nice girl, Alf.' George looked at Florence, who nodded, knowing what he was about to add. 'That brings us,' he continued, 'to what we want to tell you. We spent much of yesterday afternoon in Large Middlington with Inspector LeCrane, the one that was brought in to handle what happened at Mullings. He's taken an unofficial interest in Kenneth Tenneson's death.'

'Has he?' Alf sat up sharply. 'Thinks there's something fishy?'

'Yes.'

'That's what Doris and me got to thinking last night, that maybe Matilda and Lettice somehow found about the new will, either that he was going to make one or had done already. But go on, Birdie.'

George explained, leaving out only the part about the woman in the headscarf – that could be gone into later, and he needed to be as brief as possible. He ended with the inspector having concerns for Alf and Doris's safety, though relieved by their decision to refuse any part of the inheritance. 'Meaning you would at least not be under the same roof as the Tenneson sisters.'

'And then you stopped at our house to find we'd gone to Bogmire! Must have properly given you the wind up. So sorry about that, and so'll be Doris when I tell her.'

'Don't be, either of you,' said Florence. 'We didn't actually know where you'd gone, and there's been something gained, even if unpleasantly so, to be passed on to Inspector LeCrane. I wonder what happened to the parsnip wine bottle.'

'I'll take a look in the drawing room, see if it's still there.'

'Be careful how you go about it. Did Lettice say how she came by it?'

Alf wrinkled his brow. 'I can remember she did blither on about that, too; how she'd been given it by someone or other who'd claimed it was likely especially good because it was from a batch made by Mrs Weedy. But I can't see her making a mistake about poisoned parsnips, her being the keen gardener she is.'

'Lettice may have made that up on the spur of the moment,' pursued Florence, 'to deflect suspicion from herself or her sister, that it had been intentionally given. Maybe she questioned whether Matilda had gone completely off the latch and tried to poison her.'

'It would be one way of shutting her up.'

'Do you think,' inserted George, 'that after what we've talked about Doris may agree to leave Bogmire?'

Alf shook his head. 'More likely it will make her even more determined to stay there a while. She'll see it as her duty to stay on in the hope of helping to find out who's responsible for Kenneth Tenneson's death.' He paused. 'I can't think it was Mercy, her being such a nice girl.'

'Or seeming to be, mate.'

'But why, after he'd brought her up? And she was said by Mr Pritchard to have been devoted to him.'

'She has to be taken into account,' replied Florence gently. 'Dismissing any possibility could be seriously unwise. What we have to do is provide you and Doris, especially her, with someone to be there – at least for part of the time – who has her interests at heart in preference to the Tennesons'. I've an idea as to who might agree to do it. May I go ahead, Alf?'

''Course. I'd be grateful for the help.'

'Then I'll come to Bogmire later this morning, and hopefully bringing that person along. All you need do is act like it was your idea.'

'That I will.' Alf got to his feet.

As did George, a moment ahead of Florence. 'How about you stop outside the Dog and Whistle when you're done with the post, so I can go back with you to show you and Doris have support from the outside?'

'Thanks. I'll do that, Birdie.'

As soon as Alf had left the room, Florence gave George the

name of the person she would go and see, after waiting an hour in order to show up at an acceptable time. She then filled him in concisely on her talk with Mrs Tressler about Ned's encounters with Mercy Tenneson, followed by what she'd learned from Mrs McDonald about Elizabetta Taylor, who might be, not counting chickens yet, the Betty Taylor identified by the neighbor as the woman who had died from being hit by the bus. She also shared her thoughts on the photo mentioned by Lettice Tenneson.

'Yes,' said George, 'that could be important.'

'Before coming to Bogmire I'll go to Laurel Cottage and try and get Mrs Weedy to talk to me. Not only have she and Mercy Tenneson established a bond, but she also took an interest in Elizabetta Taylor.'

'It does sound like that could turn up more about Mercy's parentage, which might make it hard to fit in the parsnip wine, if it was poisoned, not just gone off. And it would take us down a different road as to why Kenneth Tenneson was pushed down those stairs, keeping Matilda and Lettice Tenneson out of it, though leaving Mercy as a possibility.'

'There could be several things in the mix.'

'Right. I'll telephone Inspector LeCrane as soon as I get back to the Dog and Whistle. He may decide it's time for him to step forward officially. I'll see myself out, dear.'

Florence immediately afterward sought out Grumidge and told him that something had come up that required her to be gone for at least part of the day. And would he kindly inform Mrs Tressler and say it had something to do with what they had talked about last evening. If this proved agreeable with her, which she, Florence, was sure would be the case, she'd very much appreciate Molly kindly taking over again on her behalf until she got back to Mullings.

'I'd ask to speak with Mrs Tressler myself, Mr Grumidge, but I'm somewhat pressed for time.'

He assured her that he was glad to be of help and made no attempt to enquire after her reasons.

Florence then went into the kitchen and, finding Mrs McDonald alone, was able to be more explicit, without mentioning the parsnip wine, thinking that only fair under the circumstances.

'Well, I never!' said this good friend. 'Though after our talk last night of Mr Tenneson dying the way he did and the rest, I felt in my bones you'd be on the move about it. Especially after I was able to give you that name I got from Jeannie this morning. Then Mr Thatcher coming in looking so stricken, wanting to speak to you, followed on his heels by your Mr Bird. I'm not asking how that fits in, but you did say last night there'd be more to come out about Bogmire.'

'You've been a big help,' Florence told her.

'Well, I'm pleased. You get yourself ready to go out and I'll have a cup of tea waiting when you come down.'

Florence went upstairs and sat down on her bed to think out what she would say during the two calls she planned to make. She then smoothed her already tidy hair before putting on her old coat and hat, and gathered up her handbag. Having drunk the tea kindly provided by Mrs McDonald, she set off.

Some ten minutes later she arrived at the cottage that also doubled as the police station. When the door was opened by Mrs Trout, she asked if she might come in and have a word with her.

This was met with a surprised expression on the other woman's face, but she was invited in with an apology that it would have to be in the kitchen because of her being in the middle of turning out the front room. Florence told her that would be absolutely fine, and was led down the hall and asked to take a seat at the table. It was cleared, apart from an old tin of the sort soup or baked beans might come from. Beside it was a black button that could have come off a coat sleeve. Memory surged of Hattie recounting to her the plot of *The Body in the Buttery*, and how a missing button had proved the undoing of the villain. In that piece of fiction, however, the victim had not been a man of retiring nature, but a woman who never stopped talking.

SIXTEEN

Elsie Trout was wearing a floral apron, her sleeves rolled up to the elbows, indicating that she had indeed been doing housework. She stood with arms folded, suggesting a defensive attitude – and she was struggling not to sound ungracious. She knew she didn't ought to feel that way. It was silly to hold onto her grudge that, instead of it being her Len, it had been Mrs Norris that had been helpful to the police. But then she lived at Mullings; he didn't. As to what had brought her here this morning, Elsie couldn't begin to fathom.

'Can I get you a cup of tea, Mrs Norris?' At least she wasn't dressed up to the nines as though she thought herself better than everyone else – excepting, of course, Lord Stodmarsh and his grandmother.

'That would be very nice, Mrs Trout.'

Elsie set to putting on the kettle and getting out cups and saucers. It had continued to rankle over the past weeks that all Len seemed to be appreciated for, beyond the everyday stuff, was being sent up trees after cats that didn't take kindly to his attempts at rescue. And then still looking like he hadn't wasted His Majesty the King's time if he came down with a ball that had got stuck amongst the branches. At least they stayed still to be caught, he'd say. Rupert would grumble that one day his dad would drop dead from the exertion, not being in tiptop shape due to his weight. Elsie worried about this, but her tart reply to her son was always the same: 'Well, I hope that doesn't happen, but if he does, he'll keep hold and not let go of the ball he brought down.'

The kettle came to the boil. Elsie warmed the teapot, filled it and brought it over to the table, where she'd already placed the milk jug, sugar bowl and cups and saucers. 'We'll just give it a minute to brew,' she said, sitting down in the chair opposite Florence, who sensed she wasn't entirely welcome, and the reason. If she were the police constable's wife she'd probably feel the same; also, she would have appreciated a telephone call ahead of time instead of someone just showing up.

She apologized for this. 'But I didn't want to delay getting here by explaining what this is about.'

'Oh, that's all right,' returned Elsie, 'but I have to say I'm in a quandary as to what it can possibly be.'

'A job.'

Elsie stared at her. 'A what?'

'I want to offer you one.'

'Well, this does knock me back.' Elsie mindlessly poured milk and then the tea into the cups, one of which she shifted towards Florence, who avoided glancing at the button that remained on the table to her right along with the tin.

'I've heard you've been looking for daily work and haven't found anything. Last week I was away staying with a cousin in London and when I got back to Mullings last night, Mrs McDonald—'

'That's the cook.'

'Yes. And a good friend of mine. She told me one of the kitchen maids is leaving to get married in a fortnight. A replacement is needed and we both thought of you. It occurred to us that the reason you haven't found a place already is because of who you are – Constable Trout's wife. People can be very silly, especially, funnily enough, those with the least to hide, and they've probably got it into their heads that you might snoop around on your husband's behalf.'

Elsie, still in a daze, said she'd wondered about that.

'The reverse is true with Mrs McDonald and myself. We want those working at Mullings to be observant, and if a little extra of that quality, in addition to what you come by naturally, has rubbed off from being married to a policeman, all the better. I know kitchen maid sounds a lowly position. It's where I started out, but that was a long time ago and things have changed. Young girls aren't quite so interested in going into service these days, so that job is more highly valued these days.' Florence smiled. 'This is an excellent cup of tea.'

'Thank you,' Elsie murmured.

Florence continued: 'Also the family at Mullings has shrunk down to Lord Stodmarsh and his grandmother, making it more sensible to have someone come in daily. And Mrs McDonald would prefer a mature woman, one who'd be more companionable, and she thinks you'd be companionable for her. So the job's yours if you want it.'

'I do.' Elsie still didn't know if she was on her head or her heels. 'I'm ever so pleased and grateful, Mrs Norris. What sort of hours?'

'As many as you'd like to put in. They can be worked around to fit in with your home life, especially when it comes to your son. You'll find Mrs McDonald very accommodating, and you can tell his school to phone Mullings if you're needed when not here.'

'It sounds perfect.' Elsie felt guiltier by the second for having resented Mrs Norris. 'When would it suit for me to start?'

'At the start of next week, or maybe sooner.' Florence paused. 'There's something I've been hoping you'll agree to do in the meantime. You'd be the ideal person, including being Constable Trout's wife. It has to do with Bogmire.' She was not surprised by Elsie's instant response.

'And Mr Tenneson's death?'

'Yes.'

'I've felt in my bones there was something fishy about it, even after it was decided it had been accidental.' Elsie hoped it didn't show that she was feeling smug. 'Thought the same, have you?'

'More importantly, so has Inspector LeCrane, who was brought in on the case earlier this year.' Florence added quickly, 'He's had the advantage over your husband of being able to talk informally with sources having information about the Tenneson family. Being upper crust himself, he moves in those sorts of circles; he knows the chief constable personally.'

'I can see that,' responded a mollified Elsie.

'Not having enough to go on to enter the picture himself, he contacted George Bird and me for a little help; he asked us to try and pick up what we could by keeping our ears to the ground. In the meantime something startling happened. It came to light that Kenneth Tenneson had made a new will, leaving Bogmire to Doris Thatcher, along with a sizeable amount of money.'

'Well, I'm stunned.' Elsie looked it. 'Why on earth?'

'This will take a little time to explain, Mrs Trout.'

'I'm all ears, Mrs Norris.'

She heard Florence out without interruption. When Florence had finished, she exclaimed, 'Rupert never said a word to me or his dad, but then he wouldn't, knowing Doris and Alf wouldn't want it spread around. The only thing to be grateful for is that parsnip wine didn't kill Doris Thatcher. I can see why you think she needs someone she can trust to be there besides her husband. I take it as a compliment you thought of me and will be glad to do it. The only thing is, I'd need to run home for a short while in the afternoon to make sure Rupert's home from school and has something inside him.'

'That's perfectly all right. You wouldn't even need to return afterwards. I'll be sure to be there when you leave, and have Doris invite me to spend the night. Could you meet me in an hour at the end of the street from Bogmire? I'd like to go to Laurel Cottage first and see if Mrs Weedy will talk to me about Mercy Tenneson.'

'Of course.'

'There's one more thing before I go.'

'What is it, Mrs Norris?'

'That button.' Florence pointed at it. 'Is it from an item of clothing here?'

'No, and I've been puzzling about it. Before getting started on the front room, I was dusting the shelf in Rupert's wardrobe and knocked over that tin there. It was the one he'd taken around collecting for bonfire night, and that button spilled out on the floor along with the coins. It ended up that him and his pals didn't celebrate with fireworks on the fifth of November because the boy that was having them in his back garden got ill. They decided to save the money they'd got till next year. It was Rupert's tin, so he's kept hold of it.'

'Would you mind letting me take the button with me?'

'You think it could be important?'

'Perhaps. There was one missing from Mr Tenneson's coat sleeve. I'm not even sure of the color of the coat, but—'

Elsie broke in sharply. 'The last night Rupert went out with the tin was the one Mr Tenneson died. I remember, because

I was cross with him for coming in late.' She added a little despondently that she supposed Len should've noticed a button was off that coat.

'That wasn't his responsibility, Mrs Trout,' said Florence. 'His job was to stay with the body and prevent anyone coming near it until the doctor arrived. And with the older Misses Tenneson being as they are, that would have kept him fully occupied. Once the examination was begun he'd have been expected to stand aside to allow a clear field.'

'So he would. Take the button by all means.' Elsie sounded vastly relieved. She went with Florence to the door. 'Allow yourself all the time you need with Mrs Weedy, I'll be waiting.'

'Thank you so very much, Mrs Trout.'

Florence set off for Laurel Cottage with the button in her handbag. How enormously fortunate that Rupert's mother had knocked over that tin on his wardrobe shelf that very morning. Sometimes there was nothing like chance for giving a helping hand.

She knocked on Mrs Weedy's door, aware she could be viewed as a nosy parker and swiftly sent on her way. The gray-haired, sturdily built old lady did stare on seeing her standing on the step, but after greeting her by name and saying this was an interesting turn of events, she invited her inside.

'Come through to the sitting room, Mrs Norris, and tell me what this is about; although, mark you, I've a good guess. Mercy told me she'd spoken to Lord Stodmarsh when she met him out on a walk, and it stands to reason he's had a talk with you about her.'

They were now in a cozily shabby room off the small hall and Mrs Weedy pointed Florence to a chintz covered armchair to the side of a brisk fire burning in the grate and lowered herself into the one opposite. 'So what do you want to hear from me, Mrs Norris?'

'Frankly, all you can tell me about her. Actually, I haven't seen His Lordship. When I returned to Mullings last night after being away a week, he wasn't there. He'd been needed at Farn Deane and it turned out he didn't get back until the middle of the night and wasn't up when I left this morning. It was his grandmother, Mrs Tressler, who told me about his conversation with Miss Tenneson, knowing he would do so as soon as he saw me.'

'I've heard he's close to you. Understandable, seeing you've been there for him since he was little.'

Florence smiled, noticing that the old lady's face was surprisingly lacking in wrinkles for a woman of eighty, if not more. 'We do share a fondness. He told Mrs Tressler that he suspected, from a couple of comments made by Miss Tenneson, that she was scared for her safety. This had him worried and wishing there was something he could do to be of help.'

'I'd ask why he'd even be interested, if he weren't known to be a fine young man, heading for being as fine and beloved a patron of this village as his grandfather before him. It's a pity that's not the case with all male offspring of the gentry. I'm speaking, Mrs Norris, of that disreputable sprig Gideon Blake. As if she didn't already have enough to contend with, he's been pestering after Mercy.'

'So His Lordship gave his grandmother to understand. On a morning previous to the one when he talked with her, he'd seen Mr Blake approach her on the bridle path below the village street side of the green. And His Lordship could well imagine her being disturbed by that.'

'But the next time he saw her he realized there was more to her being unsettled than that?' Mrs Weedy eyed Florence approvingly. 'Did Mrs Tressler say he walked her here after she told him she was coming to see me, like she often does, and it was while doing so that he got it out of her that she's afraid sometimes she's being followed?'

'Yes. That's how Mrs Tressler explained it.'

'Mercy admitted to me she hadn't been very nice to Lord Stodmarsh, even though he didn't seem the least full of himself, had his dog with him and you could just tell they were devoted, and hadn't acted anything like the predatory way that Mr Blake did. And she was rather ashamed of herself. He'd even gone to the trouble of fetching an umbrella from the newsagent. She just couldn't understand why he'd been so nice to her.'

'She's obviously had a bad patch recently,' said Florence, 'and that can shatter a trust in life. And then with these fears of hers, it isn't too surprising if she'd become leery of anything out of the usual. Do you know what first caused them, Mrs Weedy?'

There was now an acuteness to the face looking back at her. 'I do, but we can come back to that. Is there more to you wanting to know than His Lordship's concern? Has something else happened to make you want answers?'

'Yes. If you don't object, I won't take time going into it, but it involves two close friends of mine and George Bird.'

'That'll be Doris and Alf Thatcher. There's very little I don't know about people's lives in this village.'

'And you're right: this does involve them. Through no fault of theirs, they've found themselves connected to the Tenneson family. Last night they felt compelled to go to Bogmire to stay for a few days. Uninvited, of course, but what they had discovered gave them every right to do so. Not surprisingly, things turned very unpleasant, except for Mercy – I hope you don't mind my referring to her that way – who was very considerate.'

Mrs Weedy sat silent for a moment. 'I knew she'd been keeping something back from me these past few days. I've been urging her for weeks to get out of that hellish house and come and stay here with me, but she wouldn't, though she plans on doing so some day; we get on that well together. I love her like she's my own. It didn't take her telling me she wasn't going to risk bringing danger my way for me to know that something was very wrong. And I'm even more worried now.'

'I don't see, however,' said Florence, 'a relationship between what's happened with Doris and Alf and this belief Mercy has that she is being followed.'

'And I said I'd explain that. It came from Mr Tenneson telling her shortly before he died that he hoped she was cautious of strangers when she was out on her walks. It doesn't sound very much, does it, Mrs Norris? But she said there was something about the way he said it.'

Florence thought this through. 'He'd told Doctor Chester about the giddy spells he'd been having. Perhaps he had got it into his mind he wasn't going to be around much longer to look out for her.'

'That's what Mercy thought when he died. But recently she

had this feeling of being watched and on occasion followed. She admits it could be her imagination, which is bound to be what Constable Trout would think, or any policeman for that matter – that the idea had been planted and she's in a distressed state of mind.'

'But you believe her?'

'I do, Mrs Norris.'

'And wonder if it has something to do with her parentage?'

'How did you guess that?'

'I've found out that there's a striking resemblance between her and a young woman named Elizabetta Taylor who worked as a maid at Bogmire nearly twenty years ago.'

'Did you now?' Mrs Weedy's eyes displayed what could have been taken for mild interest. 'Go on, if you please.'

'I'd previously found the story of how Mr Tenneson came to be the person to raise her somewhat confusing. There was a friend of his from the war who left him money in his will. Was he, I wondered, her father, and the inheritance was to be used for her care? Or was she the orphaned child of another schooldays friend of Mr Tenneson's? That's the version I'd heard. But these things lose so much in repeated retelling.'

'That's always the way of it.' Mrs Weedy folded her gnarled hands, the only true sign of her advanced age, in her lap.

'What seemed apparent,' continued Florence, 'was that her mother was no longer alive. Unless, that is, she hadn't wanted Mercy, or for some reason hadn't wished or been able to keep her. All this thinking about it was mere curiosity on my part, but it led to my wondering why she was always referred to as Mr Tenneson's ward, although going by his surname, which would have seemed more likely if he'd legally adopted her. As I've recently discovered he didn't. I also learned last night, Mrs Weedy, that you knew Elizabetta Taylor.'

'So I did. She'd got in the habit of stopping by to see me and I liked her. I'd noticed her a few times standing outside looking at the garden. One time I went out and spoke to her. She told me she loved flowers and I invited her in. That was the start. She wasn't from Dovecote Hatch, of course, or I'd have at least known of her before she went to Bogmire. She was from some other village on the road to Tuswall. I don't remember which one – she only mentioned it the once. She hadn't been happy at home; said her father was a brute. He knocked her mother about – she was from Poland, that's how the name Elizabetta came about – and he laid into the youngsters with his fists too. Elizabetta said she'd been glad to get away, that bad as Bogmire was, with that old tyrant Horatio Tenneson, and his daughter Matilda nasty as they come, she wasn't about to go back home.'

'Did she think about getting another job?'

Mrs Weedy sighed. 'She should have done. But there was a man – young but older than her, in his middle to late twenties, I'd say. She was only seventeen. He wasn't from around here either, and I knew as soon as I looked at him he was a bad lot. He came round here looking for her one day, because he'd been on the watch for her at the back of Bogmire and when she didn't come out around the time she usually did to meet up with him, he remembered her saying she'd come to see me sometimes. He wouldn't have liked that. She should've been spending every free minute with him, that'd be the thinking with his type. He was standing at the gate when I walked out with her. He said it was a good thing she hadn't kept him waiting for more than a couple of minutes or she'd be looking for someone new.'

'What did Elizabetta say in return, Mrs Weedy?'

'She fell all over herself apologizing and hurried off with him. It wouldn't have done any use my trying to talk sense into her. Always the way with girls that age. Blinded, they are. I wasn't surprised she didn't come again. At least, not until weeks later to tell me she was going away because she'd got herself into trouble. I always hate to hear it put that way. Like the girl did it on her own!'

'I couldn't agree more.' Florence, without giving the mantelpiece clock a peek, was aware of the passage of time, but Elsie Trout had promised to wait for her as long as it took. And she had to learn what she could from Mrs Weedy. 'Did Elizabetta say if the man was going to marry her?'

'That would've been a wonder, wouldn't it? No, he couldn't get shot of her fast enough! And there was no way she could go home. Her father would've killed her.'

'So where did she go?'

'That was the amazing thing, Mrs Norris. Kenneth Tenneson had agreed to help her. He said he'd provide a home for her and the child in a city – he suggested London – where the man wouldn't be as likely to find them, and would continue to support them financially for as long as was needed. He said it would be the one useful thing he could do in an otherwise unproductive life.'

'It's also rather wonderful.'

'His kindness to her went back to when he'd walked in on his sister Matilda raging at her, striking out and slamming her into a wall after finding out she'd been meeting the man in the abandoned farmhouse across the field from Bogmire. Mr Tenneson got Elizabetta into another room, then went back to tell his sister if she ever laid hands on her again, or anyone else, she'd pay a heavy price. He told Elizabetta this when he rejoined her, and said if she ever felt trouble coming again to let him know immediate. He asked if she needed the doctor and when she said she didn't, he gave her a glass of brandy, then urged her to go to her room and rest, and in an hour he would send up the other maid to see how she was doing and report back to him. Her meals for the rest of the day would be sent up to her. She told me that after that he took time to talk with her every day. And when she discovered the situation she was in, it seemed natural to go to him.'

'Did you see her again before she left?'

'No. She said she felt she had to tell me what she had done, because she didn't want me to worry about her, and knew she could do so safely because I'd never breathe it to a soul. Which I haven't, Mrs Norris, until today. She told me one last thing before leaving: that if the baby was a girl she would name her Mercy.'

SEVENTEEN

As she walked to Bogmire, Florence did not allow herself to delve too deeply into how much what Mrs Weedy had told her would prove the root cause of Kenneth Tenneson's death. She had learned long ago from Mrs Longbrow, her predecessor as housekeeper at Mullings, to focus on the task at hand rather than getting caught up in the maze of projecting all that must follow. She turned onto the road where Bogmire stood, set well back from its few neighbors and the field opposite. It certainly drew the eye – what might once have been an ordinarily ugly red-brick Victorian dwelling, which seemed to have taken leave of its senses and started sprouting turrets, onion domes, and bulgy-eyed windows.

She had just reached the entrance when Mrs Trout came towards her from the opposite corner, looking solidly of the sane world. 'I saw you coming from the end of the street, Mrs Norris.'

'I'm so sorry,' Florence apologized. 'I'd said we'd meet there, hadn't I? Did you have a chance to talk to someone at Rupert's school and let them know they could telephone you here if there was a need to get in touch with you?'

'I did, and I appreciate you thinking of it. He's been behaving better in class since he's taken an interest in the dog that the Thatchers took on, so I don't think it would be about him mucking about, but there can always be accidents in the playground.'

'And what about a word with your husband?'

'Len happened to come home for a cup of tea right after you left and I can't tell you how chuffed he was about me soon getting taken on at Mullings. You'd have thought I'd been chosen to be sent off to foreign parts to do my duty for crown and country. I explained about putting in a few days here first by saying there was a sudden need for someone extra, but I couldn't tell him any more because you'd told me in confidence, and he's perfectly all right about that. Len's always thought breaking that sort of promise should be a hanging offence. Did I do right, Mrs Norris?'

'I'm grateful, but I don't like having to put you in an awkward position.'

Elsie looked gratified. 'That's all right, Mrs Norris. What are you going to do about the button?'

'Try to find out where Kenneth Tenneson put his coat when it was not in use, whether in an upper hall cupboard or his bedroom wardrobe, seeing he was wearing it on the stairs, although he could have been intending to go back out again almost immediately. The person to bring the coat up with would be the housekeeper by way of getting her talking about him in general and weave it in.' Florence paused, looking into the eager face. 'Or maybe that would be better coming from you, Mrs Trout, if you wouldn't mind.'

''Course I will.' Elsie eyed the house. 'Looks kind of wicked, doesn't it? I've always thought so.'

'This is the first time I've seen it. I suppose if Doris and Alf Thatcher can bear it we should do our level best,' Florence leavened this with a smile, 'even if we do catch a glimpse of a headless specter headed our way.'

Elsie wasn't sure what this was, only that it would be something, with or without its head, you wouldn't want to chat with over the fence while hanging out the washing. 'Least we're going in together.' This could have been voiced by a participant in the Charge of the Light Brigade holding aloft the Union Jack. Florence's heart warmed; it was good to feel that Elsie Trout had put past resentment of her aside.

Alf must have been on the watch. He had the hideously carved door open before they reached it and, still hollow-eyed, stood aside for them to enter. 'Oh, good!' he said, closing it behind them. 'I knew you'd come through with the right person, Florence, and you couldn't have done better. Thanks, Mrs Trout. Doris will be relieved to have your support.'

'A pleasure, I'm sure, Mr Thatcher.'

'I wish you'd call me Alf, and the same with Doris – it's so much friendlier sounding. And that's what we need – the feeling of some goodwill coming our way.' The little dog had crept out of the shadows to crouch at his heels. 'Besides, we've grown so fond of your Rupert. We asked him yesterday if he'd like to call us Auntie Doris and Uncle Alf and he said he would; hope you and your husband don't mind.'

'Not a bit, I think it's nice. And you call me Elsie . . . Alf.'

'Did he say anything about the two Tenneson sisters,' he couldn't prevent the grimace, 'coming round our house yesterday when he was looking after Rex here?' He looked down at the dog cleaved to his leg.

'Not a dickybird. Whatever his failings – and I'm not saying they're worse than any normal boy his age – he's fiercely loyal to them he's fond of. But Mrs Norris here put me in the picture some about that. How've they've been treating you this morning?'

'Matilda, miserable toad, hasn't come down from her room. Told her sister to inform us she'd remain there till we leave, even if it means the death of her. And in that case she'll haunt us forever if we dare attend her funeral. Well, that didn't work out for her.'

'She has to be barmy to think it would,' scoffed Mrs Trout.

Alf managed a grin. ''Stead of bringing us to tears of remorse and out the door with our tails between our legs, it gave me and Doris our first reason to smile since getting here. The other one, Lettice, is a completely different kettle of fish, falling all over herself trying to seem friendly. If she'd only shut her gob for two minutes she'd be bearable. She's still at it in there.' He nodded towards the closed drawing-room door. 'I wouldn't be surprised to go back in and find Doris and Birdie plugging their ears.'

'I'm so glad he's here,' said Florence.

'It gave Doris her second smile of the day seeing him come in with me, it did. When we met up outside the Dog he said he'd had a think about Major Wainwright, and that we should go and see what had brought him round yesterday wanting to talk to Doris and me, only Rupert had to tell him we was out.'

'Yes, Alf,' agreed Florence, 'there mustn't be a delay waiting for the major to stop by the pub for a drink to have a word with him. Will Doris go with you?'

'No, just him and me. She said she'd rather stay behind, perhaps go for a little walk with you and catch her wind.'

'Good idea. Would you mind if Mrs Trout and I don't go at once with you into the drawing room? We'd like to take a little time seeing what information we can get out of the housekeeper.'

''Course. Pathetic-looking woman. I'll bet Matilda has laid into her something terrible for letting us into the house.'

Left to themselves in the hall, Florence and Elsie Trout were exchanging glances when they heard footsteps scurrying down the staircase and a moment later beheld a gray-haired figure emerge from its shadows. If this was Miss Bone the house-keeper, she was not about to greet them as would routinely suit her position in the household.

'Oh, the poor dear,' Elsie exclaimed as agitated cries reached them. 'It sounds like what Alf just said about her having to take a bibful from Matilda Tenneson could've hit the nail on the head.'

Her identity seemed confirmed by the words scattered their way. 'I can't take it a moment longer – I won't. I've always known she was capable of the worst wickedness, but now . . .' Whether she was talking to herself or to the two people standing near the foot of the stairs was unclear. Her eyes were unfocused; the rest of her trembling like a sapling about to be uprooted.

Florence reached out a hand to steady her, before introducing herself and Mrs Trout. 'We're friends of Doris and Alf Thatcher. Is there anything we can do to help you, Miss Bone? It is Miss Bone, isn't it?' She might as well have said they were the March Hare and the Mad Hatter. Nothing was going to penetrate the blank stare of the poor dear, as Elsie had rightly referred to her. She was still rambling on.

'Miss Lettice can say all she wants, it was that solicitor bringing the news of that new will that's put Miss Matilda in this mood. She's never been right in the head either, only not lunatic violent with it, just stupid and wouldn't know the truth if she met it. Because she's all about making life up as she goes, never stopping to hear a word anyone else says.'

'It must have been hard on you, dear, all these years,' soothed Elsie.

This brought a flicker of life behind the eyes. 'It wasn't the solicitor that started this; it was that woman showing up at the door quite early last Monday morning. Looked at me, she did, and said, "You don't remember me, do you, Miss Bone?" And then she gave a sad sort of laugh and said she wasn't surprised. She was wearing a headscarf and there was this great bruise down one side of her face and other changes, but it came to me who she was – Elizabetta. Can't forget a name like that. I was about to tell her not to be a fool, that Mr Kenneth Tenneson was dead so couldn't protect her this time if things turned nasty, but it was too late. Miss Lettice had come out of the drawing room and heard. She took Elizabetta right into the lion's den, and even with the door shut I could hear Miss Matilda raging, and later, after Elizabetta had gone, I went into the room and found a ripped-up photo on the hearth.' Florence was eagerly waiting for more when Miss Bone stopped her monotone flow. 'Who did you two ladies say you are?'

Before Florence or Elsie could reply, she broke into racking sobs and a voice spoke from the staircase. 'I'm here, Miss Bone. I'll take you to your room and help you pack. You won't spend a moment longer than necessary in this house.' A dark-haired young woman descended and put an arm round the shaking shoulders. 'You'll feel better after you've cried it out. I've no idea how you've stuck it out this long, and with Uncle Kenneth gone there's no reason for you to stay.'

'There's you, Miss Mercy. I haven't been able to bear the thought of leaving you having to deal with her – both of them, on your own.'

'Now you must. You'll go to your sister in Devon, just as we've talked about. And one day I'll find a way for us to be together again, if that's what you'd like.'

'You know I would.'

Mercy Tenneson looked over the bent gray head. 'Hello, Mrs Trout, and you,' meeting Florence's eyes, 'must be Mrs Norris. Mr Thatcher said when he returned from his delivery round with Mr Bird that you would be here soon, bringing someone with you as a companion for his wife. I'll see you and Mrs Trout later, I'm sure.' She turned away with Miss

Bone and they went down the hall to turn left at its far end, presumably making for the back stairs which would take them up to the housekeeper's bedroom. Or perhaps the layout of this house was different from Mullings – her sleeping quarters might be off the kitchen. Florence reminded herself it didn't do to make more assumptions than necessary. She still thought the likeliest place for Kenneth Tenneson to have kept his overcoat was on the floor above.

'What now, Mrs Norris?' asked Elsie, clearly ready for action.

Florence smiled at her. 'We got useful information on the situation here from Miss Bone, which we might not have done had she not been terribly upset, and I'm glad for her sake that Mercy Tenneson came down when she did. But it means we'll have to hunt for that coat on our own, hampered by not knowing which room is occupied by Matilda, making it risky to look for the one where Kenneth Tenneson slept. I'm hoping we'll be lucky with a hallway cupboard; but if not we'll have to risk bearding the lioness. Are you up for that, Mrs Trout?'

'What can she do worse than throw something at us?'

'Come after us with her stick, although I can't see her doing that when she has vowed to stay holed up until the siege is over.'

'That sounds right.'

The stairs creaked even though the two women crept up them as cautiously as possible. The first thing they noticed upon reaching the top was an open door facing them just a short way down to their right. On tiptoeing closer they saw that the interior was furnished as a music room with a piano and sheet music stands occupying much of the space, leaving only enough over for two small armchairs. On hearing from Inspector LeCrane that Lettice had spent part of the afternoon on the day Kenneth died with Mr Sprague, preparing for her solo in church on the coming Sunday, Florence had pictured the room where they had done so as being on the ground floor. And, of course, there might be another suited to the purpose there. It was, however, another reminder that it was easy to make unwarranted assumptions, some of which might not be insignificant.

Elsie pointed out the door in the side wall to their left. 'Shall we inch it open and take a peek, Mrs Norris? I can't think it leads to Matilda Tenneson's room, or this one's hall door wouldn't have been left open.'

'That's a point.'

Elsie went to it and at a nod from Florence turned the handle. They stood together looking through the gap into a fussily furnished bedroom, with a number of wraps and hats scattered around it. 'I'd think it's Miss Lettice's, wouldn't you?' Elsie said after closing the door.

'Or Mercy's,' replied Florence, mindful of her resolution, 'although it does seem better suited to the image I've formed of Lettice, which I would think is very close to yours, Mrs Trout.'

Elsie again looked gratified. Going back into the hallway, they caught a glimpse of a toad-like figure in a dark dressing gown scurrying out of a doorway halfway down and vanishing through another at the far end. 'Well, now we know where she is, Mrs Norris, at least for the moment, because that could be the bathroom she's gone into.'

'Let's take a look at the room she just left. If it's a bathroom we're in luck.'

This proved to be the case. But they were about to be even more fortunate. In turning from it Florence spotted a pair of hinged doors, each with its own handle, close to the top of the staircase. Opening them revealed the sought-after cupboard with a shelf for hats, gloves and scarves above a coat rail. There were several women's coats and a man's black one hanging from the rail. Her heartbeat quickening, Florence looked at both sleeves and found one cuff button missing – the threads visible. Her eyes met Elsie's before taking the one she had out of her coat pocket and holding it next to the one on the other sleeve. They were a match.

'Do you want me to give this back to you, Mrs Trout, so you can hand it over to your husband and explain its importance?'

'I don't know; maybe you should hold onto it and I'll speak to Rupert when he gets home from school, see what he has to say – if he has any ideas about how it got into his collecting tin.'

'Do you mind if I tell George of this discovery and he passes it on to Inspector LeCrane? I don't want to create difficulties between you and your husband.'

'I don't think it would, Mrs Norris; he'll know this has to go up the ladder and will be pleased at contributing his bit. Conscientious, that's Len. Not out for the glory, he isn't. I'm afraid it's been more me wanting him to make a bit of a splash, get himself noticed by the higher ups.'

'And why not? But can it be he gets all the satisfaction he needs keeping Dovecote Hatch sorted out on a daily basis? I think for most people knowing Constable Trout is always there keeping an eye on things gives a foundation to their lives that's very much needed should something rare and ugly crop up.'

'I don't know why I didn't see it that way.'

'You're a devoted wife.' Florence smiled at her. 'And you've also been an enormous help over this matter. No harm in digging in on your own account, is there?'

'I've never thought that way before. For me it's always been about Len and Rupert. Or so I told myself,' responded Elsie. 'What's next, Mrs Norris? I could go and have a word with whoever it is comes in to help Miss Bone with the house. See what I can get from her.'

'Good idea.' They had descended the stairs and Elsie was about to head for the kitchen when Mercy Tenneson came towards them from the far end of the hall and gave her directions. When they were alone the young woman scrutinized Florence.

'Has Lord Stodmarsh said anything to you about talking with me when we met out walking the other day, Mrs Norris?'

'I haven't seen him. When I arrived back at Mullings last evening after a week's visit to London he'd just left to go over to Farn Deane to assist with a sick horse. He didn't return until the middle of the night and hadn't come down when I left this morning.' Florence didn't think it advisable to mention her conversation with Mrs Tressler. Reading Miss Tenneson's mood as prickly, she merely smiled encouragingly.

'He's unusual in that, I suppose, his being so personally involved in what goes on at the home farm, I mean.' This was said casually, but the gray eyes were alert.

'He has a great affection for Tom and Gracie Norris who run Farn Deane, and it's a mutual regard. He is also a very caring person, Miss Tenneson.'

This brought a shrug. 'Of course, you would sing his praises seeing as you've been with him since he was little and he clearly dotes on you. And compared to someone like Gideon Blake he would strike people as decent.'

'Has that young man been an annoyance to you?'

'Oh, I can deal with him,' came the airy response. 'It's Aunt Lettice who makes it annoying, talking about what a marvelous thing it would be for me if he should go down on bended knee and beg for my hand in marriage. She is so utterly feather-brained. In a way, I prefer Aunt Matilda's view on the matter.' Miss Tenneson's lip curled. 'She screamed at me last week – it would have been the day that woman came, the one Miss Bone talked about – that she hoped young Blake would drag me off by my hair and have his way with me, because coming from the mother I did I was a slut and deserved to be treated like one. That if he killed me in the process she'd rejoice. She even suggested a fitting place for what she described as a rendezvous.'

'My dear,' said Florence, 'you need to get away from here. Don't wait. I know you have a friend in Mrs Weedy. Go to her.'

'I don't know, I have to think. But you can tell Lord Stodmarsh, when you see him, that I'm not mad . . . imagining things that aren't so. And sometimes it's better to face up to the inevitable than trying fruitlessly to escape it. That's why I planned to go out for a walk last night after stopping doing so recently, but then things got too difficult here for me to leave the house. Now I have to go and get some money so poor Boney can go to her sister without that worry. I'll take her to the train, and then perhaps I'll go for that walk.' Mercy turned at the foot of the stairs. 'I don't know why I felt the need to be rude to you. You seem every bit as nice as Lord Stodmarsh said you were.' With that she disappeared upstairs, leaving Florence greatly concerned about her taking that walk unprotected, but of course it didn't have to be that way.

A moment later the drawing-room door opened, George

came out and Florence crossed to meet him. 'How are things going in there?'

'Lettice Tenneson was just reminiscing about her days in the nursery and how enchanting everyone had thought her with her ringlets, and how hard it had been on Matilda being the plain one. Alf has Rex on his knee and Doris is bearing up exactly as you'd expect.'

'Tell me about your talk with Inspector LeCrane.'

'I gave him all the new information and he said to thank you profusely,' smiling, George tapped her cheek, 'for getting the name – Elizabetta Taylor – and I told him something I'd remembered that'd been rubbing at the back of my mind, that was at odds with . . . but that can wait. I can see you've more to tell me and we could be interrupted at any moment.'

'Are you sure you don't want to tell me now?'

'It may not be of much, if any, importance. And I can tell your news is. Out with it, my dear.'

Florence ran through the events of her morning, starting with Elsie Trout, moving on to Mrs Weedy and culminating with what had occurred since her arrival at Bogmire. 'Let us say the killer pulled that button off Kenneth Tenneson's coat cuff during a struggle on the stairs and left the house with it – how did it get into Rupert Trout's collecting tin? Was it picked up by someone else after being tossed on the ground and dropped in as a joke? Is it sound to make the leap that Mr Tenneson was attacked by an outsider who afterwards went on his or her own way? Or if it was someone from the inside, such as Matilda or Lettice, might they not have felt the need to get away from the house to clear their heads? So much that's unanswerable on its own, George.'

'Perhaps young Rupert will come through with something.'

'Possibly, but it's a shame he has to be dragged into any of this. His mother's going to talk to him when he gets home from school. She said he was planning to go and see Doris and Alf during his dinner break and he won't find them there. It's a shame, his wasting the time. He'll be disappointed.'

'They'll make it up to him.' George touched her cheek again. 'It wouldn't surprise me if when this is over they talk to his parents and see if they'll let him have Rex. Just a feeling. Now, back to business. I'll have to give Inspector LeCrane another telephone call from the Dog and Whistle. Alf and I have decided to go and pay a call on Major Wainwright. It seems right enough to do so after him going round to their house yesterday, and Alf and Doris want to talk with him. Things are moving too fast to wait for the major to stop by the pub one night.'

'Of course. But doesn't Doris want to go too?'

'She says she'd rather go with you to the cemetery.'

'Yes, I can understand that. The need to spend time at Kenneth Tenneson's graveside. Oh, George, one thing more.' She told him of Mercy's talk of taking a walk that evening. 'I think you should mention that along with everything else to the inspector and have him arrange for someone to keep watch in case she follows through with it. Maybe Constable Trout would be too conspicuous, which is a pity, because this is his turf.'

'I'll put that top of my list when I make that telephone call.'

The following fifteen minutes passed in a stir of activity. Florence went first in search of Elsie Trout, which entailed finding the kitchen, which was not as straightforward an undertaking as would have been supposed. It incurred exploring a number of dreary passages and taking a couple of wrong turns before she descended some stone steps ending with a green baize door. By which time she felt it would have been more to the point if she'd been blundering in search of an Egyptian tomb. She found Mrs Trout alone in a gloomy chamber whose artifacts looked as though they had come from a dig, and was informed that the household helper had made her departure stating that an armed guard couldn't keep her a moment more in this dreadful house now that poor Miss Bone was throwing in the towel.

'Couldn't so much as get her name out of her, Mrs Norris. But at least it means I can make myself useful getting stuck into the washing-up.' Elsie looked in the direction of the piled high sink and equally jam-packed draining board. 'A torch would help, seeing that light bulb hanging from the ceiling isn't equal to a candle. And then I can hunt up something for a meal. It won't do for Doris and Alf to starve to death before, well . . . we don't want to go down too dark a road, do we?'

Somehow Florence felt cheered by this. 'No, but it doesn't hurt to keep our wits about us.' She explained about Alf and George leaving for a while and that Doris wanted to go with her to the cemetery. 'Would you like to come up and have a chat with her before we set off? I know she'll want to tell you how relieved she is to have you here.'

'Why not wait for that till she's back, so's not to make for a delay?'

'I'm so glad I asked for your help.'

Florence made her way to the drawing room and, after tapping on the door, went in. It was every bit as grim as she had anticipated, with a great deal of monstrously oversized furniture of hideous design that might long ago have passed for opulence but was now a moldering reproof of folly. Mustiness pervaded, harbored most likely in the excess of draperies at the windows and in the heavily fringed velvet or damask coverings cast floor length over every available surface, even sofas and chairs.

Seated on one of the sofas wearing an untidy assortment of clothes was the woman who had to be Lettice Tenneson. George, Alf – holding Rex – and Doris all got out of their chairs to greet Florence. Lettice followed suit. Hands clasped, upper front teeth jutting, she exuded a horse-faced enthusiasm on surveying the newcomer.

'Mrs Norris! How sweet of you to come. Our dear little Doris has been pining, positively wilting away out of loneliness for you.'

'I wouldn't put it that way, glad as I am to see you, Florence,' Doris interposed.

Lettice giggled. An unfortunate trait, some might think, in a woman of sixty-odd years. 'Oh come, come!' A wagged finger. 'Family members don't need to hide their true feelings from each other. Now, what was it that was floating round in my head? Ah, yes! It was that I am unable, Mrs Norris, to offering the poor darling a glass of parsnip wine, to which as you will know she is highly partial, because of last night's unfortunate incident with the only bottle we had on hand. And would you believe it only occurred to me seconds ago that something nasty might have been put in it by a naughty somebody to give me a fright, because I'm the only one who usually drinks it.' She gave the frothy fringe a tweak. 'I do dislike casting aspersions, but my suspicions go first to Miss Bone. She has been behaving very oddly this past week, and if not her, I am forced to consider our dear Mercy. One regrets to say it, but it has been borne in upon my sister Matilda and me in recent days that the girl comes of highly questionable stock. Of course, we always had our suspicions, but Kenneth made some quite nasty threats which enforced our silence.' Lettice finally drew breath, then hurried on to remark on their all standing when they could be cozily seated.

To this Alf replied that he and George were taking off for a while with Rex, and Doris inserted that she and Mrs Norris were going out for a walk. She added that she had to go upstairs to fetch her coat and hat. At a nod, Florence went with her, leaving Lettice looking like a pouting child excluded from an outing to be filled with delights that she alone would fully appreciate.

'Though why she'd want to spend any more time with me than necessary I can't think,' said Doris as they mounted the stairs. 'Sometimes I catch a look in her eye that gives away how she resents and dislikes me every bit as much as her sister does. Not, like I said to Alf, that I can blame either of them for that. Any idea I had about blood being thicker than water has got knocked on the head. But what do you think, Florence, about that parsnip wine being meant for her?'

'That she might well be right.'

'Unless Mr Pritchard mentioned to her in passing that I'd said I liked it,' said Doris shrewdly, 'by way of letting her know that although raised apart we had something in common. It doesn't seem all that likely, but you never know.'

'Or she could have slipped something in it without your noticing.'

They had entered the bedroom where the Thatchers had spent the night – undoubtedly an unpleasant experience given Doris's fastidiousness, it having the look of not having been dusted in months, leaving one wondering how long it had been since the bedclothes had been given an airing. Doris retrieved her red coat from the back of a chair and donned it along with the black astrakhan hat that matched the collar. On the way downstairs she explained how she had bought it at the bazaar, only to discover on the previous evening that it had been donated by Lettice.

'I won't be caught dead in it after I leave here.'

Florence agreed that this was understandable. Before setting off outdoors, Doris said she absolutely had to thank Elsie Trout for agreeing to come to Bogmire, and when Florence told her of the departure of Miss Bone and the household helper she said she felt doubly beholden.

'I'm that touched you'd think of it, Florence. Just knowing there's somebody around that's in Alf's and my corner is no end of a comfort. We can't expect you to stay gone from Mullings too long, and George has to get back to the Dog and Whistle.'

'Don't worry about that; he can find time to pitch in if necessary and there's no rush for me to get back. Molly proved while I was away how capable she is of managing without me there.'

They found Elsie in the kitchen as Florence had anticipated. It still presented a depressing appearance, but was no longer in the slovenly state it had been before she set to washing up and clearing away. She had a broom in her hands, indicating that further improvement was underway, and mentioned a macaroni cheese with grilled tomatoes on top by way of a midday meal that would keep nicely until wanted.

'I just don't know how to thank you enough.' Tears glistened in the usually undemonstrative Doris's eyes.

'Well, I'd say you and I have known each other long enough to be there for each other when push comes to shove. So off you two go and I'll be here when you get back if it's before I have to leave to see Rupert home safe and sound from school.'

The temperature had dropped since Florence had entered Bogmire, but there was no wind and the sky was colorless with no hint of rain. After leaving by the kitchen door, the approach to the churchyard was a straightforward crossing of the rear grounds. Although unkempt, there was a path wending its way beyond the lawn that remained reasonably clear even as it entered a stretch of woodland. She and Doris came out onto the pavement near the house with the tree in which Rupert had spotted the ginger cat proclaiming its need to be rescued, which he had shortly thereafter learned from Mr Sprague belonged to Matilda Tenneson.

Florence and Doris looked towards the iron gates in the brick wall, beyond which rose St Peter's Church, remarkably unchanged throughout the centuries, its insignificance having proved an asset during the Reformation and Cromwell's time as not worth despoiling. As it happened, it possessed, in addition to its gargoyles, some very fine stained glass windows. The Reverend Pimcrisp took no pride in these, nor did the villagers. But Ned's grandfather, the late Lord Stodmarsh, had taken pleasure in them and had advised Florence that they were worthy of study. She remembered this now, but only fleetingly, because her thoughts were centered on Doris and how she must be feeling as they made their way between the tombstones towards the Tenneson family plot.

They reached it shortly and looked down at the inscriptions. Above that of Horatio Tenneson, the name Bagmure had been carved several times.

Before Florence could say anything, Doris explained, 'I said to Lettice last night, just to pass the time, that it was strange the house being called Bogmire when there isn't a bog anywhere near, and she said it came from her . . . our mother's maiden name being Bagmure and people slipping into calling it the other.' Her voice petered out as her eyes settled on Kenneth Tenneson's newly etched name. Florence, thinking it the moment to slip away, touched her arm and said she would take a walk around.

She was in the process of doing so when she saw Miss Hatmaker, primly garbed and kind-faced, coming towards her from the direction of the church. They met midway down a path and expressed pleasure in meeting. Indeed, there was an eagerness to Miss Hatmaker's expression.

'I do hope you won't think me impertinent, Mrs Norris, but I wonder if you have the answer to something that has me puzzled. I went to Bogmire early this morning as previously

arranged to do some sewing for Miss Matilda Tenneson and
was told by the housekeeper, looking quite ill, I must say, that
it would be best for me to come another day because Miss
Tenneson was seriously indisposed and all at sixes and sevens,
because Mr and Mrs Thatcher had descended on the premises
last night and it all had something to do with Mr Kenneth
Tenneson's will. Can this indeed be true, Mrs Norris?'

Florence assured her that it was, adding that she was not
in a position to say more without revealing what she had been
told in confidence.

'Oh, indeed not,' avowed Miss Hatmaker. 'I will not mention
to anyone that I have spoken to you. Such a very odd family,
if you will not think me wicked to say so, Mrs Norris, and
just as I'm taking flowers to the church for the altar – the
sisters, I mean, not Mr Tenneson – such a good, kind man.'

'So I've heard.' Florence was wondering how to bring up
the button when Miss Hatmaker continued.

'Miss Lettice said something to me after he died that quite
bothered me, Mrs Norris. She wanted to know if I checked
his coat for loose buttons the day before he died, because one
had been found missing from a cuff. I was there, you see,
doing work for Miss Matilda, and I always took it as a privilege to take a look at his clothing when having the opportunity,
just to make sure there was nothing that needed doing.'

'And was there a loose button?'

'Oh, indeed no. Had there been, I would have taken the
time to deal with it.'

'Exactly what I would have thought.'

'Even though I had been asked to return the next day to do
more work for Miss Matilda, I would have taken care of it
then and there. There was something odd about the way Miss
Lettice asked me about it. I shouldn't speculate . . .' Miss
Hatmaker's voice trailed off and a moment later she said
goodbye and headed off.

Had she wondered, thought Florence, if Lettice feared that
her sister, or Mercy, had argued with Mr Tenneson on the
stairs and the button had come off in the process, or had she
been trying to cover herself by having seemed perplexed should
it become an issue? A sharp cry startled Florence out of this

reverie. It came from the direction of where she had left Doris and she hurriedly retraced her steps to find her friend leaning forward and clutching her back just below her left shoulder.

'What happened?' she exclaimed.

'Something hit me! It hurt, but I'm all right.' Doris straightened up as Florence reached her. 'At least it wasn't my head.'

'Thank goodness for that! If it was a rock or a stone . . . Why, you're trembling! Lean on me.'

Doris did so. 'I think it's more from fright than anything else,' she managed.

'You need to sit down.'

Florence looked around for a bench, but none was in sight. Her eyes lit instead on a tree stump and she led Doris over to it; her face was worrisomely pale and Florence urged her to put her head down between her knees. She sat like this for several minutes, then straightened up, saying she was feeling better. Florence waited a while longer, then went to hunt around for whatever had been thrown. She soon returned with an India rubber ball in her hand, hard enough to have made contact like a stone if pitched with force.

'Oh, well,' Doris attempted a laugh, 'that's a child for you – better me, I suppose, than somebody's window.'

'Not,' said Florence, 'if someone aimed directly at you.'

'Oh, but surely . . .'

'I don't think there's much we can be sure of. Still hurting?'

'No. Fine as can be,' came the stout reply.

Florence didn't believe her, but understood the wish to minimize what had happened. She'd be thinking about Alf, not wanting him to be worried, though of course he would be. Neither he nor George had returned when they got back to Bogmire. They went in the way they had left through the kitchen door to find Elsie setting a sizzling macaroni cheese topped with the promised grilled tomatoes on the newly scrubbed deal table. When told what had happened, she ushered Doris into a side room with an easy chair, which had presumably been for Miss Bone's use and was reasonably presentable. Elsie quickly returned with a cup of tea, which Doris was glad to drink down as instructed. Afterwards Elsie served up the tasty meal, accompanied by slices of bread and butter, with

Florence and herself partaking as well. They had just finished when George and Alf came in. Elsie made herself scarce, saying she would see if the others wished to eat. Suggesting that Alf and Doris might like a talk on their own, Florence beckoned George back into the hall to tell him what had happened in the cemetery. She admitted that there was no way of telling whether the ball had been thrown at Doris intentionally, although it did seem suggestive of spite.

'How about your outing with Alf, George? Did you call upon Major Wainwright?'

'Yes, we did. He let us in himself, as his housekeeper was off to Large Middlington doing the big weekly shop. He was very pleasant, though lacking his usual bluff, hearty sort of manner. He was bent on apologizing to Alf for being party to Doris finding out about her background, and explained that was the reason for his showing up yesterday. He knew it had to have come as an enormous shock, but at the same time he couldn't think ill of Kenneth Tenneson for wanting to do what he thought was right, and said that he was just that sort of chap, stuck with that confounded nuisance – a conscience.' George smiled in repeating this. 'When Alf and I asked him if he'd thought Mr Tenneson had seemed worried about anything else apart from the will on the afternoon of his death, he said without hesitation that Tenneson had mentioned being troubled by receiving several letters from someone from his past threatening to make difficulties if he did not agree to a meeting.' George looked down his great height at her. 'It sounds to me like that fellow that Elizabetta Taylor was mixed up with when she worked here had figured out that Tenneson had stepped in to care for her child, and was out to reveal himself as the father if he wasn't paid to keep quiet.'

'And now,' answered Florence slowly, 'he may have decided to see what he can get out of the girl herself, knowing her to be an heiress with every reason to keep her origins hidden. He may be keeping an eye on her comings and goings in the hope of getting hold of her to pressurize her, or those close to her, to pay up before she comes to serious harm. George,' she pressed his arm, 'Inspector LeCrane needs to know about this and take some action.'

'I just spoke to him again on the telephone after we'd left Major Wainwright and he was on his way to meet with the chief constable, confident he now has enough to move on. He told me to tell you he will be here within the next few hours to begin questioning the sisters and Mercy. He'll also need to know where to contact Miss Bone, and the name of that woman who came in to assist her. And there'll be others. But it's his presence here, on the spot, that counts.'

'Yes, of course it is,' said Florence. 'I feel better already. Mercy is a headstrong girl, but from what she told me she's aware of being in danger, and on second thoughts I can't see her leaving the house to prove the point that she can do as she chooses. I also think she's far too fond of Mrs Weedy to cause her worry. I have to say I can see why Ned took to her. She has courage and spirit.'

'Speaking of His Lordship,' George gave her arm an encouraging squeeze, 'he came round to the pub looking for me. He sent you his love and said he wasn't at all surprised to hear from his grandmother that you'd gone to Bogmire to keep an eye on Miss Tenneson. I explained there was more to it, and he just grinned and said of course there would be. And if you needed anything from him to get in touch, but otherwise to stay where you was needed.'

'Yes.' Florence smiled mistily. 'Did he say how the horse fared at Farn Deane?'

'He said you were bound to ask that. Recovered, apparently.'

'Oh, I'm so glad.'

'His final words were to be sure to take care of yourself; that there's only one of you. And, my dearest Florence,' George added soberly, 'he's not the only one feels that way.' He put his arms around her and kissed her slowly.

The afternoon progressed. Alf talked Doris into going to the bedroom they'd been given for a lie down. She must have been sufficiently unsettled by the experience in the cemetery that she agreed to do so, and very sensibly he stayed with her. George returned to the pub in case the inspector should telephone. Needing something to occupy her, Florence asked Elsie for some rags for dusting, and while that lady continued her work in the kitchen she set to in the drawing room. Anyone else might have found it a hopeless task, but she applied herself to one piece of furniture at a time, as she had been taught long ago upon first entering service, focusing only on results, never getting overwhelmed by the broad picture. She was slightly hampered by Lettice, who shortly drifted into the room to wander about and talk incessantly, skipping at random from one subject to another. She had been her father's favorite; although Matilda remained convinced that she had been the one preferred. People had been so wrong in thinking dearest Daddy a crosspatch for no reason; their mother had been such a sad trial to him, never bestirring herself to be gay. As for Kenneth, he had been equally dreary, though perhaps he was too recently dead for her to speak ill of him. But it really had been wounding that he had never admired her voice, whereas a man as knowledgeable as Neville Sprague thought it much too fine to be wasted singing in a village church.

At last she left the drawing room, saying that Mrs – she couldn't remember her name – would understand she had no more time to talk with her as more pressing matters awaited; then Elsie Trout came in like a breath of fresh air. She said she'd had quite a nice chat with Mercy Tenneson, who'd given a hand turning out the larder. And she had also taken up a plate of macaroni cheese to Miss Matilda and returned with it after being told it would be thrown back if handed to her.

'Sweet soul, isn't she, Mrs Norris?'

'Earning her crown in heaven, I'd say.'

They both stood and laughed. Florence saw this as the cementing of a new friendship and had the feeling Elsie felt something similar.

'Is it all right if I leave now so's to be home in time for Rupert getting in from school?' Elsie asked.

'Of course. You've been a gem.'

'Well, if that isn't nice to hear!' Elsie's face turned rosy. 'Of course I'll speak to him about the button and come back fast as I can to let you know what he has to say about it, Mrs Norris.'

Florence experienced a hollow feeling when Elsie had left. With dusk pressing up against the windows, the room seemed more than ever a monument to decay. Reminding herself that

George would also return in the shortest time possible, she sat down on a sofa she had cleared of an overabundance of pillows and cast-off garments, leaned back and closed her eyes. She thought of Hattie's neighbors, the Carters, and their decision to help their unmarried daughter bring up her child, and of Doris and Mercy, whose fates had taken a different turn. Was there ever a safe choice in such a situation? Not expecting to fully relax, Florence almost instantly dozed off. The brief conversation in the hall between Mercy and Lettice did not rouse her, nor did the opening and closing of the front door. There was, however, nothing she could have done had she been awake other than utter a protest that would have been ignored.

The young Miss Tenneson walked purposefully down the drive, not feeling quite as brave as she looked, although determined not to have second thoughts. Having turned left on reaching the street, she made for the field with the abandoned farmhouse about a third of the way down. Shivering, despite her warm coat, she heard footsteps behind her, felt a hand grasp her arm and caught her breath in terror when a male voice within an inch of her ear told her not to scream.

'Or what will you do?' she managed defiantly.

'Try me and find out,' came the cold reply.

EIGHTEEN

Florence came groggily awake at a touch on her shoulder and opened her eyes to find George seated beside her on the sofa. 'What is it, what's happened?' she asked, knowing from his face that something had and that it was worrying. She struggled to sit up. A couple of lamps had been lit in the Bogmire drawing room, emphasizing rather than reducing its shadows. It was darker outside than when she had fallen asleep.

George reached for her hand. 'Matters seem to be coming to the boil; LeCrane just rang from the police station after explaining the situation to Constable Trout. He'll be here very soon; meanwhile he's sent his sergeant out searching for—'

He was interrupted by Lettice hovering in a shamble of scarves and shawls a few feet away. 'Dear Papa, so very set in his ways, would not have approved of entertaining police inspectors at Bogmire, any more than he would have countenanced the two of you being granted the status of guests. But I have never seen any sense in railing against the inevitable. Oh, dear! Forgive me if that sounds rude. I'm the tiniest bit tired.' She moved a couple of steps and continued, 'I've spent the greater part of the day trying to persuade Matilda to that point of view, but she is enjoying her tantrum too much to give way. And now this with Mercy! So inconsiderate of her taking herself off like that! I'm not sure how long she's been gone; I'm never good at keeping track of time. She was in a most peculiar mood, spouting some nonsense at me about having a strong idea as to where the person who'd threatened Kenneth might be holed up and she was determined on a confrontation.'

'And you're fearful for her safety.' Florence spoke over a thudding heart and the need to assemble her thoughts.

'Oh, no! Nothing like that. Though Doris and Alfred refused to be reassured and have gone to see if she is with Mrs Weedy.

They took the dog with them, but it's hardly a bloodhound.'
Lettice poked at her fringe and in doing so dislodged a scarf.
'Not that it matters. The whole thing is in the girl's mind.
Kenneth didn't have any worries. Unlike Matilda, I didn't
dislike him, but it must be owned he was rather a stolid man;
one might even say stupidly incapable of imagining anyone
behaving as he would not. A characteristic, I now realize, of
his peasant stock. At least it was of the respectable sort, the
outcome of marriage, which cannot be said of Mercy's
parentage.' That this was said with a lightness that could have
accompanied a remark on the weather made it all the more
unpleasant. 'My dilemma is the bread and milk.'

'Maybe my own low background is showing through, but
I don't follow you, Miss Tenneson.' George squeezed Florence's
hand before getting to his feet.

'Matilda is demanding that a bowl of it be brought up to
her. Miss Bone and that helper of hers having abandoned ship,
Mercy should be here to see to it. Although now that you have
woken, Mrs Norris, perhaps I may impose on you to . . .' She
was stayed by a tap on the drawing-room door, then it was
pushed open to reveal a frazzled-looking Elsie Trout standing
windblown, her coat unbuttoned.

'Excuse me barging in, Miss Tenneson, but it's about my
boy, Rupert.' Florence immediately understood that Elsie was
talking to her through Lettice, not wanting to appear to be
overstepping. 'I got home to find him all upset; he'd been
crying. And then I brought up something I'd found out that
made things worse. He hasn't shown up here, has he, wanting
to talk to Doris and Alf?' Elsie obviously read the answer in
the eyes looking back at her, for she went on with barely a
pause. 'Just a hope. I couldn't stay put waiting any longer.
He's been gone near on an hour. Normally I wouldn't get
worked up, but the state he was in after I talked to him about
a discovery I happened upon this morning,' her gaze went to
Florence, 'makes all the difference. He must have slipped out
while his dad was in the front room with the inspector who'd
come round to discuss things, and me in the kitchen clearing
away after the tea Rupert didn't eat. Len's gone looking for
him.'

'And the inspector?' queried George.

'He'd left a few minutes before. It was right after that I realized Rupert wasn't in the house.'

'What an evening this has been for people running off,' Lettice was saying over Florence and George's exclamations of concern, just as the peal of the front door bell jarred through the house. 'Will someone please see who that is?' she asked, before dropping into a chair like a heap of tossed garments.

'Let it be Rupert!' Elsie whispered.

Florence steered her out into the hall in the wake of George, who was opening the door to admit Inspector LeCrane, who then turned to beckon in two others – Rupert and Neville Sprague, the boy pale and uncertain, the man's arm around his shoulders. Elsie hurried over to her son, eager to have hold of him, but it was clear, at least to Florence, that he wasn't ready to be pulled away from the church organist.

'Don't go fussing, Mum; I'm all right.' His brown eyes squinted up at her through noticeably damp lashes. 'I needed to talk with Mr Sprague to straighten some things out in my mind, that's all. He offered to walk me over here so I could see Auntie Doris and Uncle Alf. Why don't you go home,' this was suggested with pathetically false cheer, 'and have a nice time to yourself, knitting or ironing or something.'

'A tempting sounding invitation, Mrs Trout,' Inspector LeCrane cast his charming smile upon Elsie, 'but I think it best that you take him home.'

'I'm not going,' protested Rupert defiantly.

'I think you should,' said Neville Sprague with a meaningful look.

'Are you sure?'

'Yes.'

Dispiritedly, Rupert left with his mother, whereupon the inspector addressed Sprague. 'My name is LeCrane. I am a policeman, come here at the request of the chief constable in light of new developments to take a second look into the death of Kenneth Tenneson. Am I correct in assuming you to be Neville Sprague, the church organist?'

'Yes.'

'Good. You have saved me the necessity of fetching you

here. Having been in this house on the afternoon of Mr Tenneson's fall down the stairs, it is possible you will recall something, however trivial, that supports our growing belief that there is more to this business than was concluded at the inquest.'

'Indeed, yes. I have no need to hurry home. I arranged for a neighbor to stay with my father while I'm gone.'

Florence wondered at Mr Sprague's flat voice and the apathy in his eyes, and what Rupert had talked to him about, but overriding all else was her anxiety over Mercy Tenneson's absence. It had been the height of folly for her to leave the house intent on seeking out the person she feared. Were she older, wiser . . . Florence drew in a sharp breath as she reevaluated this thought. Wasn't it a human impulse, at any age, to take one's life or death into one's own hands rather than waiting for it to pounce from behind? The image came of the woman in the headscarf, Elizabetta Taylor, poised in apparent readiness to throw herself on the railway line as the train drew into Large Middlington. Her resolution had failed her at that moment, but she had regained it at a London bus stop. Or had she? A possibility stirred; one Florence had not previously considered because her mind had been set on what she had seen and from that assumed an outcome. She had been looking as though through a telescope focused only on a moment in time. An overhead thumping rocked her back to the present.

'And that will be?' enquired Inspector LeCrane.

'My sister, Matilda Tenneson, demanding sustenance,' responded a voice from the drawing-room doorway. 'She is of a somewhat imperious nature. And you are?'

He told her. 'Your name, madam?'

'How very brusque! And yet you look the gentleman. I'm Lettice Tenneson, several years my sister's junior.' This was accompanied by a toss of shawls and scarves and a coy smile which appeared to leave Inspector LeCrane unmoved.

Indeed, he eyed her coldly. 'This is a necessary visit, so I make no apologies for invading your home. That said, I will endeavor not to detain anyone longer than necessary. With this end in mind, perhaps you will convey to your sister my request that after partaking of something to eat, which she will not dally over, I require she present herself for questioning.'

'She will decline. Very likely throwing something in the process.'

'In that case I will have no option but to conduct my enquiry in her apartment, bringing with me all other interested parties.'

'Oh, dear! Matilda was never one for romantic novels, so is unlikely to find your masterful manner stimulating, Inspector.' Lettice fixed her gaze past him. 'Does your knowledge of my sister not support this contention, Mr Sprague? How I wish unpleasantness could be avoided and you could listen to me practicing a song that has captured my fancy, and I believe you would be enchanted.' He looked through her, either unhearing or uncaring, and her smile tightened to a girlish pout as she moved away to mount the stairs without haste.

Inspector LeCrane looked at his watch then made his way into the living room, with Mr Sprague following at his heels.

Florence turned to George, her voice low. 'Perhaps you should stay and talk to the inspector, and provide Mr Sprague with some bolstering, while I go along to the kitchen to make that bread and milk. It'll be a chance to keep my hands busy while we wait for word of Mercy and for Alf and Doris to get back. I wonder what can be keeping them.'

'Perhaps they're still talking to Mrs Weedy. If Mercy isn't there and hasn't been, they won't want to alarm the old lady by letting on that's why they came, so they'll make an excuse to sit and chat.'

'Yes.'

'Something else on your mind?' He could read her so well. It was such a comfort.

'Maybe it's foolishness, but I think I should mention it to Inspector LeCrane, although he may well have thought of it himself. Come with him to the kitchen if you get the chance. It would mean leaving Mr Sprague in the sole company of Lettice if she comes back down, and I sense that is not something he'll relish, especially if she decides to seize the moment and burst into song.'

George smiled gently before kissing her cheek.

On reaching the depressing kitchen Florence set an ancient

kettle of water on the stovetop to boil. On its doing so she poured it over some bread she had found in the pantry, cubed and put in a bowl. Having let this sit before draining, she added some milk she'd heated in an equally battered saucepan and sprinkled on a layer of sugar. She had just set this on a tin tray with a spoon alongside when George and Inspector LeCrane walked in. The officer's elegance put the kitchen's dreariness further to shame and, as always, he was in complete command of his environment. The look she gave him was sharply enquiring.

'Any news of Mercy?'

'Safe and sound! Lord Stodmarsh just telephoned. She had been about to cross the field down the road from the front of the house when he came upon her and, given that she went into a panic that it might have been someone other than he, took her back to Mullings to be soothed by his grandmother. Time slipped away in the process.'

'That's understandable.' Florence sagged with relief.

'His Lordship met Miss Tenneson purely by chance. He had been on his way here to see you, Mrs Norris.'

'Is he bringing her back here?'

'He offered to do so. But Bailey, my sergeant, had moments earlier shown up here to let me know his search for her had been unsuccessful. I have sent him to fetch her back. It seemed the better course, should Miss Tenneson put up any resistance to returning. A point of view which, despite my having as yet been here only briefly, has my utmost sympathy. By the way, the Thatchers have returned with assurances that they said nothing to alarm Mrs Weedy. Their delay was due to her interest in their lives being turned upside down and their feeling it would be unkind not to answer her questions. Also, they met young Rupert and his mother on the road and asked if they would be willing to take the dog home with them, at least for the night, as he hasn't taken at all well to this house, in particular the presence of the elder Miss Tenneson's cat.'

'Oh, I am glad for Rupert!' Florence exclaimed. 'He was clearly so much in need of cheering up.' She looked down at the bowl of bread and milk. 'This needs to go up to Matilda

Tenneson. You must be eager to get started on your questioning, Inspector.'

'I'll take it to Lettice,' said George. 'Her sister told her to come back downstairs and wait for it. You can fill me in when I come back about what's on your mind.'

'Which is, Mrs Norris?' Inspector LeCrane enquired when it was just the two of them.

She told him.

'It's certainly a consideration,' was his response.

'But one that can't be delved into until you're finished here this evening.'

This produced a sardonic smile. 'I advise against troubling yourself on that account, Mrs Norris. Why not make yourself a restorative cup of tea and take fifteen minutes or so to relax before coming to the drawing room, which has been put at my disposal.'

'By Lettice?'

'Incurring the already enraged Matilda's wrath against herself? That was unnecessary, although I suspect the younger Miss Tenneson derives entertainment from such turmoil and presenting herself as the more engaging of the two. It was Mrs Thatcher, who has more rights here than either of them, who encouraged me to take over any room I chose. A very pleasant couple, she and her husband.' Inspector LeCrane paused at the door to the hall. 'I admire your choice of friends, Mrs Norris. Indeed, you have my highest esteem in all aspects of your character.'

He went, but Florence was not left alone in the kitchen with her thoughts for more than a few minutes. George returned, made the tea and produced a boiled egg for each of them, along with slices of buttered toast. Her concern that Doris and Alf would not have eaten in several hours was assuaged by his telling her that Mrs Weedy had supplied them with sand-wiches, biscuits and cake.

Time to head for the drawing room. Whatever else could be said against it, there could be no complaint about lack of seating. Florence's gaze immediately lighted on Mercy Tenneson, who must have arrived while she and George were in the kitchen. There was no sign of Sergeant Bailey, so

Florence assumed he had been dispatched on some other business by Inspector LeCrane. She took in the assembled company:
Doris and Alf occupied a sofa; Matilda, Lettice and Mercy sat
in armchairs at some distance from each other; and Neville
was perched on a wooden chair set even further apart, thus
forming an uneven semi-circle. Inspector LeCrane stood in its
midst, his back to the fireplace; its meager blaze giving out
more smoke than heat. He was speaking when Florence and
George entered, broke off while they settled themselves, then
continued in a conversational tone.

'Forgive the brief delay, but I am expecting, any moment
now, some additions to our group. There will be no need for
anyone to admit them as I set the front door on the latch.'

'Such impertinence!' Matilda, huddled low in her chair,
glowered up at him. 'Could I but lay my hands on my father's
whip I would drive you from this house.'

'I don't doubt it,' answered Inspector LeCrane indifferently.
'You have acted violently on other occasions, have you not?
There was the instance when you brutally attacked a maid by
the name of Elizabetta Taylor—'

'That was well deserved! She was a slut of the most
disgusting order, and had I known my supposed brother would
one day foist her spawn upon us, I would have finished the
job and relished in her every expiring breath.'

Mercy reared up in her chair, hands clenched, before
subsiding with a shudder.

'Oh, do take care, Matilda,' crooned Lettice. 'I know you are
only prattling, but the inspector cannot be expected to realize
that and may take it into his head that you pushed Kenneth
down the stairs in a fit of similar exasperation. For that is what
he is intent upon,' her eyes flickered to LeCrane, 'finding a
culprit, because accidental deaths must seem a little dull in
comparison to . . .' Her voice petered out at the sound of footsteps in the hall. All eyes went to the drawing room doorway.

'Ah, here comes my sergeant,' said the inspector. 'Satisfactory
results, Bailey?'

'Well, sir, that depends on the point of view,' replied the
incomer, his voice wooden despite the gleam in his eyes.
'Constable Trout has some considerable bruising from being

attacked, but he's not complaining. What he's fixed on is that his son hasn't come to any harm. Like I told you, sir, when I telephoned, Trout had gone looking for the lad on finding he wasn't in the house. It seems that earlier this year he'd gone with some pals to play around in an abandoned farmhouse. He'd been told never to go back there because the upper flooring was unsafe, but the constable thought it worth trying there. Turns out that was a futile exercise.'

'So I understand.' The inspector waited encouragingly.

'But on going inside he heard movement and was set upon from behind by a man it turns out had been hiding there for some days. Fortunately, I was searching the area for the missing young lady,' the sergeant's eyes caught Mercy's stare, 'saw the farmhouse and arrived there in time to prevent the constable coming to greater harm. He and I got the man down to the police station, which is where I phoned you from, and tried to get him to answer questions, but pretty much all we were able to get is that his name is Stanley Hodge.'

'That, as it happens,' the inspector smiled thinly, 'is more than enough to get started upon. I presume he is presently in the hall in the company of someone capable of preventing a precipitate departure?'

'Yes, sir. Constable Trout.'

'No surprise there. Never underestimate the stalwart village bobby, Bailey. Fetch them in.'

How pleased Elsie would be to hear him speak of her husband in such terms, thought Florence. Then she was looking at a burly man with curly salt-and-pepper hair, wearing a seaman's jacket, who came into the room with Constable Trout and Sergeant Bailey. Her curiosity shifted to recognition. He was the one who had nearly collided with her at the railway station in London. George experienced a similar sensation. He recognized the man as the stranger who had shown up at the Dog and Whistle.

Doris and Alf sat expectantly. Matilda rustled angrily, Lettice shifted in her seat for a better view, and Neville Sprague evinced no expression. The man stared belligerently around the sea of faces.

'What is this,' he jeered, 'a rich people's tea party?'

'Hardly that at this hour of the day,' replied Inspector LeCrane laconically. 'Indulge me by taking a seat, Mr Hodge; otherwise the sergeant will insert you into one. I have no doubt the constable would perform this task, but I believe he has experienced sufficient physical exertion for today, thanks to your efforts.' He looked to Constable Trout. 'Good work. Now go home to your family and get some well-deserved cosseting. I'll be along to see you tomorrow morning.'

Trout's face flushed with repressed pleasure. 'If you're sure, Inspector.' At a nod of reassurance he took his departure. Stanley Hodge snarled his way over to a chair.

'I done nothing more than stay in an old wreck of a house. You've got no right to keep me here. I got nothing to do with whatever's going on here.'

'No? Then let's say it's for the pleasure of your company. Now, where was I before you joined us?' Inspector LeCrane watched Sergeant Bailey position himself against the wall behind Hodge's chair. 'Ah, yes! I was on the point of bringing up the possibility that someone to whom it mattered had discovered about Kenneth Tenneson's new will. The impact of this most drastically affected the two women who had believed him to be their brother, but the possibility cannot be ignored that his ward, even though faring well under both testaments,' Inspector LeCrane swiveled towards Mercy, 'may have anticipated being the chief beneficiary and then have found that this was not to be the case, and that instead the beneficiary was to be a woman whom she was aware of, if at all, only as the postman's wife.'

'Well now,' Doris spoke up, 'I'd as soon you left me out of it. "The poor young thing!" I said to Alf this afternoon. "She strikes me as a nice girl."'

'So you did, love,' agreed her spouse.

The inspector countered with the statement that regrettably appearances were often deceiving. Florence and George, though sensing what he was about, cast worried glances at Mercy, whose hands were pressed to her face.

'Stop this!' Neville Sprague burst forth. 'I'm the one responsible for Tenneson's death, Inspector. I came here to admit it – it's what I told young Rupert Trout I was going to do. He wanted to stay with me; be at my side. That's one very decent boy. I was glad that you sent him home. But then every time I attempted to speak to you—'

'I had my reasons for thinking he should not have to endure listening to your admission. My belief that he needed to be with both his parents was why I also sent his father home.'

'How astonishing!' Lettice burst out. 'I had no idea you disliked my brother, Mr Sprague!'

He turned to her, his level voice at variance with the hatred in his eyes. 'I didn't. I barely knew him. It was your fault, you stupid woman, with your hideous singing voice and your incessant talking about everything and nothing. I told you that afternoon that I was short of time when I had already stayed beyond the time I had agreed to accompany you while you practiced for your church solo. I explained that it was my father's birthday, I needed to get home to him, that I had to pick up a cake on the way, but there was no getting through to you. I should have been more forceful, but I have never been good at asserting myself. For that I despise myself, but that does not bring me to forgive you.'

'You're mad,' Lettice tittered, before casting an appealing glance around the room. The only response came from Matilda, by way of a thrown cushion.

'On my rush from the music room I collided with Mr Tenneson, who was coming up the stairs, apparently just having arrived home since he was wearing his coat. He was halfway up when I missed my footing, slipped and in reaching to drag myself up clutched at his sleeve and tore off the button. He was still standing when I apologized, but I didn't take much of a look at him. I raced out onto the drive and couldn't have closed the door properly behind me because on reaching the road I heard a thud and saw it hanging open. I knew I should go back, but I didn't. I told myself I'd worked myself into such a state I was imagining things, that the sound could have been anything. Halfway down the road I came upon Rupert, collecting for the fireworks celebrations. Knowing him and feeling the need to act normally, I reached into my pocket for change and dropped it into his collecting tin, not realizing until later that I must also have let go of the button.'

A hush followed, broken by Inspector LeCrane. 'An accident. No intent on your part to harm Mr Tenneson, but your failure to return and offer aid, useless though it might have been, after hearing a sound indicative of trouble is a matter of blame. Rather than fully face that truth, I suggest, you chose to exact punishment on Miss Lettice Tenneson by making her life to some degree as troubled as your own. One way, Mr Sprague, was to put the bitter aloes you had purchased in an attempt to stop your father chewing on his thumbs into a bottle of parsnip wine in a cupboard here. Not a full bottle, because you wanted her to be aware of the nasty taste and worry that she had been poisoned, possibly by her ill-tempered sister.'

'I wish I had thought of it,' Matilda flared back.

'Oh, dear! You are naughty!' Lettice returned, but in a very subdued voice.

Stanley Hodge, who had been looking increasingly relaxed, emitted a rough laugh. 'Says a lot for the upper classes, don't it?'

Inspector LeCrane held up a restraining hand, his eyes not wavering from Neville Sprague. 'Because of Lettice Tenneson, you were too late to pick up your father's birthday cake. The shop was closed. I think that may have mattered more to you, Mr Sprague, than Kenneth Tenneson's death. Early this afternoon you saw a woman in a red coat with a black astrakhan collar and believed her to be Lettice Tenneson. Both items had been hers, but she had given them to the local bazaar where they had been bought by Mrs Thatcher. So when you threw a ball with the intent to startle, it hit the wrong woman.'

Sprague looked at Lettice, then away. 'You're too lenient, Inspector. I hoped to cause pain. It was tough, hard rubber. The impact could have been that of a stone and I was aiming for her head. Let me explain, if I may. My house is around the corner from the cemetery. I noticed a cat stuck high in a tree and climbed up to fetch it down. It was a ginger cat and I knew it belonged to Miss Matilda Tenneson, but that could not allow me to ignore its plight. Rupert had seen me bring it down from the same tree yesterday. I took the chance to mention having seen him collecting for fireworks, to see if he would say anything about the button. He didn't, but said the money was still in the tin, on his wardrobe shelf, because his firework night had been cancelled. I thought about attempting to get the button back, under some ruse, but the idea was distasteful. Rupert respects me; it comes from earlier in the year when he went into the river and got into difficulties. I happened to be walking past and went in after him. It was nothing. I'm a strong swimmer, but I suppose he made me into a hero. Disappointing him bothers me more than anything else, even more than the question of what will happen to my father if I go to prison.'

'I don't think it will come to that – a dressing down and a rap over the knuckles by a magistrate is more likely. Let us get back to the events of this afternoon.'

'Oh, yes! It was when I was about to reach for the cat that I came upon the ball, and at the same moment looked round and saw the woman, whom I took to be Lettice, in the cemetery. I took aim at her, heard the resultant sharp cry and saw Rupert standing a short way off, staring up at me. It was obvious he had seen. He got back on his bike and turned the corner, and I knew I'd have to face him. I was planning on going to his home this evening, when he showed up instead, torn between bewilderment and horror at what he called my attack on Mrs Thatcher. He's very fond of her and her husband.' This was said as if neither was in the room. 'There was more. His mother had come upon the button while he was at school and then learned where it had come from. She asked what he knew about it. He wouldn't tell her. He didn't want to believe it had come from me, but the pieces all fitted together: my being so close to Bogmire that evening, the last evening that he went collecting; my asking yesterday about the money he'd collected and what he'd done with it when it wasn't used. He came out of hope, that if what he thought was so, I would do the right thing. He held my hand all the way here. It was so much more than I deserve.'

'He's a dear boy, all right,' said Doris, 'and I understand, Mr Sprague, why you have trouble looking at me. You're too ashamed. It comes from being a decent man that's gone off track. Too much worry from looking after your old dad, who doesn't think he needs it, is my guess. That's the sort of thing can make anyone turn queer; but I don't doubt you'll come about if you make up your mind to it and are given a little kindness.'

Neville Sprague stared at her wordlessly, but with something close to hope and gratitude stirring behind his eyes.

'Some might think you overly generous, Mrs Thatcher.' Inspector LeCrane gave her a smile he reserved only for people he liked. He then turned a somber expression on the man sitting forward awaiting an announcement as to his fate. 'Very well, Mr Sprague, you have told us nothing that does not support the facts as we know them, but the insight into your motivations is enlightening. Tomorrow Constable Trout, if he is feeling up to it, will come to your address to take your written statement; otherwise Sergeant Bailey will do so. As for now, you may go home and free your neighbor who has been staying with your father to return to his.'

'I don't understand . . . I was sure . . .'

'Bailey,' said the inspector, 'assist Mr Sprague out of that chair, to which he appears to have taken root, and escort him out onto the drive. Unfortunately I can't spare you to walk home with him as there are still a few matters needing to be wrapped up here.'

'To do with me, I suppose,' ground out Stanley Hodge on the departure of the sergeant and Mr Sprague, followed immediately by that of Matilda and Lettice Tenneson, both presumably having heard enough to reflect upon if they so chose. Mercy had not looked at Hodge once yet and did not do so when he continued, 'I know why you had me dragged over here. It wasn't about me spending a few days in an abandoned house, Mr Policeman, or even helping myself to a chicken and a few seed potatoes from Mullings – if you've heard about that.'

'I hadn't, but thank you for being open about it.'

Hodge rose up in his chair. 'You'd made up your mind it was me who pushed Tenneson down them stairs. But seeing as you now know you was barking up the wrong tree, I'm off and there's nothing you can do to stop me.'

'Must you be so hasty? Ah, but such is one of your regrettable characteristics, is it not? If you had laid low after Tenneson's death instead of deciding to frighten Miss Mercy

Tenneson into paying up what you hadn't been able to get out of him, matters might have gone better for you.' Inspector LeCrane reached into his jacket pocket for his cigarette case, and after enquiring if anyone objected to his smoking and receiving no objection, lit up. 'Oblige me by sitting back down, Mr Hodge. I have been looking forward to talking with you about another death – that of Elizabetta Taylor. How to begin? Ah, yes, let me put it to you in the form of a story.'

'You can put it any way you bloody well like!'

'How very accommodating of you! I will endeavor to take that into account and refrain from addressing you in a badgering manner. The first chapter in what is in many ways a tale of woe has you in an amorous relationship with the young Elizabetta, then a maid in this house. From your point of view, things must have seemed entirely rosy. A beautiful girl sufficiently besotted not to resent being kept under your thumb. Was she not the daughter of a bullying father and a mother too cowed to stand up for her? As such might she not have accepted any rough treatment you dished out as the natural way of things between a man and a woman?'

'And why not?' Hodge's face contorted. 'If she'd done right by me, not gone up against what I told her I expected, I wouldn't never have needed to lay a hand on her. Then what does she do but come telling me she's in the family way, thinking I'll take her word it's mine? Like I'm some kind of chump. If she'd be that easy with me, why not any other Tom, Dick or Harry? So, I told her to get on with it and maybe her face didn't look so pretty when I was done, but what I didn't do was give her permission to take off and make decisions along with Tenneson about what to do with the child.' He looked over at Mercy. 'It was five years before I got their whereabouts out of Elizabetta's mother, one time when I was back on shore. Gone to sea, I had.'

'Commendable.' LeCrane lit another cigarette. 'Why don't you give me the next paragraph or two of the story.'

'The old bitch spilled the beans that I'd been round. When I showed up on Elizabetta's doorstep the child had gone. Adopted by a couple in Australia, was the lie I got told. I made my feelings plain about that.'

'I imagine you did.'

Hodge now appeared to enjoy opening up. 'After that it was on and off again between Elizabetta and me, depending on if I had other fish to fry. She'd come to realize there was no point in trying to lose me again, that I'd find her sooner or later. It was one of those times when I hadn't seen her for a while, a few weeks ago it was, when I met someone from round here I used to talk to at the pub who mentioned Kenneth Tenneson and the young woman he'd brought up. Described her, this bloke did, and he could've been talking about Elizabetta when I first knew her.'

'It didn't take you long, I suppose, to see the possibilities of the situation?' LeCrane's lips twitched as if in amused admiration. 'That there was money for you to be had in return for your not revealing to the world, in particular those who knew her, that Mercy Tenneson was not as had been accepted the daughter of a deceased friend of Kenneth Tenneson, but the illegitimate daughter of a former maid in this house. Where, if I may say so, you went wrong in this regard was in taunting Elizabetta with your plan instead of keeping it under your hat. But of course you counted on her fear of you preventing her from acting. Unfortunately you underestimated a mother's feelings.'

'I've had enough—'

'Surely not, when the story is about to reach its climax! Mrs Norris and Mr Bird appear riveted.' LeCrane smiled faintly at Florence and George. 'The night before Elizabetta's death, Mr Hodge, she stood up to you, despite the blows with which you vented your rage.' LeCrane eyed the scraped knuckles of the hands on the arms of the chair. 'Did you miss her face and hit a wall or a door instead when she told you she would let Tenneson know you were intent on blackmail? No wonder you were annoyed. He could send Mercy to some undisclosed place, making your revelations about her illegitimate birth worthless. Did you feel confident on leaving Elizabetta that night that you had persuaded her against this course? And then have second thoughts the next morning – following her to the railway station, but not getting through the barrier in time to catch the train she took to Large Middlington so she could make her way here? She wasn't to know Tenneson was dead. It wasn't a matter of sufficient interest to be picked up by the national newspapers. And she hadn't remained in touch with anyone in the area.'

'I didn't go anywhere near her that day!' Hodge's face darkened. He shifted in his chair, his hands curling tighter around the arms.

'Oh, but I suggest you did. According to a boy,' LeCrane took another look at Florence, 'with red hair, one of a number of children taken up to London that day on an outing by a vicar and his sister. He'd kept quiet about what he'd seen for fear of being accused of making up stories and not being included in the next outing. Elizabetta didn't throw herself in front of that bus, tempted though she might have been to do so as the only means of escaping more of your brutality after defying you once too often. She was pushed. By a man closely fitting your description. That's murder, Mr Hodge, meaning you're likely to get more than a rap on the knuckles and a recommendation that you mend your ways in future.'

EPILOGUE

I t was the week before Christmas and Dovecote was readied to embrace the traditions of the season. Mrs Hewett was kept busy from morning till evening coping with the customers streaming in for treats such as dates, crystallized ginger and Chinese figs. The vicar, Mr Pimcrisp, did not approve these secular indulgences, but few had ever paid much attention to his views in this regard, and this year even more deaf ears were turned, because he was due to retire from the parish in January, and it was rumored that his replacement was youngish, good looking and only reasonably high church. As it was also known that he was unmarried, several young ladies were considering additions to their wardrobes.

This flutter of excitement did not entirely banish the talk about Doris Thatcher turning out to be a Tenneson and her brief stay, along with husband Alf, at Bogmire. But only so much could be said about that when little was known about the details, and neither of them was willing to discuss it. Neville Sprague's involvement in the death of Kenneth Tenneson did not leak out. The chief constable accepted Inspector LeCrane's suggestion that a blind eye should be turned in order that no criticism should be leveled against the verdict brought in at the inquest. It had not been possible to prevent knowledge seeping out that the man who had pushed a woman under a bus in London was the father of Mercy Tenneson. That information, however, was swamped by the revelation that Lord Stodmarsh and his grandmother had invited her to accompany them for the Christmas season to a house they had in Scotland, taking with them Mrs Norris's cousin, a Miss Hattie Fly. The idea was that she would provide companionship for Mercy, who would continue her stay for a month after His Lordship and Mrs Tressler had returned to Mullings. Mrs Hewett was able to report this with utmost confidence because she'd had it from Old Mrs Weedy, with whom Mercy planned to live after this holiday, intending to give her a cheer-up. Hope was floated of a romance between the girl and Lord Stodmarsh, but Miss Milligan dashed this on coming into the shop for a pound of Mrs Hewett's best sliced boiled ham, by announcing that Miss Tenneson had been highly indignant on hearing this tale had been going round.

'She told me she'd been tempted to refuse the invitation to Scotland because she'd known people would jump to ridiculous conclusions. She said His Lordship is perfectly pleasant but they are forever arguing, besides which, she has mapped out her life without a view to marriage.'

'Fancy that!' Mrs Hewett had said encouragingly.

'Her ambition,' Miss Milligan continued in the barking voice worthy of one of her boxers, 'is to one day work at an orphanage with children who are not as fortunate as she in being given a home by a wonderful person, who made not having parents unimportant.'

'Well, what I think,' Mrs Hewett informed Elsie Trout, after Miss Milligan left, 'is that those two young people are headed to the altar. Always a good sign when they start off not getting along. 'Course, His Lordship could do a lot better, but I call it romantic, a proper Cinderella story.'

'I couldn't say,' replied Elsie.

''Course you couldn't,' agreed Mrs Hewett, 'not with you working up at Mullings. Going well, is it?'

'I'm settling in nice.' Elsie resisted the temptation to say that she and Mrs McDonald got on a treat. She asked for half a pound of dog biscuits.

'I'll put in a few extra. Glad your Rupert ended up with the little fellow. Is Constable Trout happy about it? Looks cheerful whenever I see him. Has something nice happened for him? Been offered a promotion?'

'Well, it so happens he was. But he turned it down. He knows he's needed here, and never one to shirk his duty, he isn't.'

'And it's nice he'll be here for the wedding.' Mrs Hewett took the lid off the jar of dog biscuits. 'I'm talking about Mrs Norris and Mr Bird. People are always asking me if I know

when it'll be. But I don't and I know you can't say. Still, it's
something to look forward to after the year this has been, with
the murder at Mullings. Spring would be nice . . .'

'So it would,' said Elsie, pleasantly, and rather smugly, in
the know.